98% Grey

A Novel in 3 Colours

- Wendy -
Thanks for coming!

[signature]

GRAEME COTTERING

infinity
press

æ
infinity
press

This book is set in Caslon.

Cover design and illustrations: Graeme Lottering
Photo portrait: © Bernard Ramos 2010
Lime Glory Caps font from www.houseoflime.com

ISBN 1-453-80168-5 (pbk.)
EAN-13 9781453801680   2010

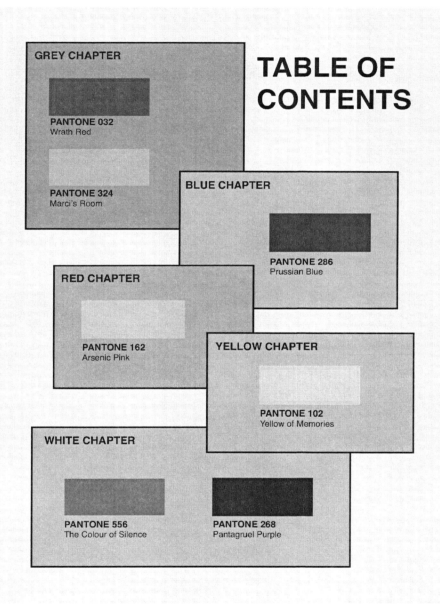

TABLE OF CONTENTS

This book is dedicated to Oupa Lottering, who told me stories in my youth, and to my father, the survivor

Prologue

Pretoria, South Afrika, 1978

My father, William Lottering, a natural athlete, was 22 years old when he broke his neck. He was completely paralyzed from the neck down because of an illegal move: a suplex. It happened in the finals to make South Afrika's National team, the Springboks. The opponent, Gerhard Duplessis, was a newly recruited policeman. He fought recklessly and with pure strength. What he lacked in technical skill, he hulked over opponents in muscle. Now, my dad was really fit as well (185 pounds of toned muscle), but he wrestled technically. He was a scientific wrestler. His father was the coach of Ridgeway Amateur Wrestling club, a renowned team which included two champion wrestlers who were blind.

When Gerhard slammed my father down on the mat, it was immediately clear something was wrong. My grandfather called the illegal move as soon as he saw the brute crush my dad under his weight.

(Who knows what really happened. The details are lost

i

in the mix of pandemonium and intense emotions that followed. Maybe the opponent tripped and fell. Maybe he just didn't know that he had to drop onto one knee to take down an opponent who has both feet of the ground. That was the rule.)

My grandfather, who was himself a wrestling champion, blew the whistle and told them not to move my dad. They let him lay there and didn't touch him. My grandmother cried and watched along with everyone else in the Athletic Hall, while some people unscrewed a door to slide underneath my collapsed father. I picture him watching the *tick-tocking* clock in the hall. The only sounds: the echoing ticking and his mother's hysterical voice, talking to him nonsensically in the background. My grandfather, however, instantly understood the gravity of the situation.

They successfully got him to the HF Verwoerd Hospitaal in Pretoria, where he lay immobile while doctors told his parents he had broken the 4th and 5th cervical vertebrates of his neck. The doctors told them my father would never walk again.

When my grandmother heard this, she didn't stop crying the whole night. She wept and wept, and by the next morning, she had gone completely grey. Her hair, which had been a ruddy blonde, was silver grey when my dad finally understood what was going on.

Apparently, the doctor gave the bad news to his parents while my dad was in the room. He has very little recollection of the whole experience. Even more than thirty years later, he doesn't like talking about it. My father, the artful dodger of conversation.

I firmly believe that in every tale there is a strange twist of fate, just waiting to pop out *deus ex machina*. In my father's case, it was that a leading expert in neurological surgery happened to be in South Afrika at the time. My family thinks that he was German or Swiss, but no one lays claim to any proof. He might as well have been an angel fallen from Heaven for all they cared. He was their slim, last hope of salvation.

The hospital physician, who had met our mysterious

expert at a conference in tropical Durban the day before, called him, and our man swore to be on the first flight over to Johannesburg.

He operated on the broken vertabrae. The surgeon transplanted a piece of my dad's pelvic girdle (a spiralling curl of the iliac crest) into his neck. Today, he still has the scars and when his Canadian students ask about the one on his neck, he claims to have been bitten by a crocodile or another exotic animal in Afrika during the dusty days of his youth.

In reality, however, things weren't quite so sunny. The surgeon, skilled as he was, confessed that the probability of my father's recovery was very low. He told my grandparents, "With incredible luck, the chance of his recovery is still less than 2%." He added, "But it is always worth the smallest chance."

Meanwhile, my dad was having fevered dreams. Nightmares in his mind, while his paralyzed body was unable to cry out, communicate, or voluntarily manipulate a single muscle. He was completely cut off from the world, and of the days after the accident, he can recall nothing except for a single memory that stands out: the first moment of sober consciousness, or what a Freudian might call 'a coming to terms'.

What he does remember is his grandfather coming in to talk to him. Oupa Lottering was a farmer, a Boer in Rhodesia. This man was legendary. He was an enormous human being, and a lover of animals, a tamer of horses. He was known around the neighbouring farm towns as the man who once caught a runaway bull, which he was training to pull a plough. You see, my great-grandfather was skeptical of technology. "I'll wait to see if the tractor catches on before I buy one," he would say. Anyway, the young Afrikaner bull with its wide horns remained obstinate, disobeying his commands.

"*Kom!*" Oupa would call. "*Kom hier!*" The bull would not come to be reigned in. And when Oupa Lottering stepped forward to whip it, the bull charged. He caught it by the horns and used the bull's own momentum to throw it to the red, African earth. The bull fell on its side and Oupa Lottering punched it in the snout. After that, the bull stood up and joined the team of oxen hauling the plough.

Oupa Lottering drove four hours to Pretoria when he heard what had happened. He asked to see my dad alone. When he came into the room, he was disturbed to see my dad lying on the hospital bed, floppy like a straw scarecrow. My dad smiled when he came in, but could muster no other response. In a heavy Dutch accent of Afrikaans, the giant of a man said this:

"Willi, glo dat jy gesond sal word. Jy moet glo dat jy eendag weer sal loop en die Here sal dit vir jou gee. Glo net en jy sal heel word!"

He was encouraging my dad. I believe that these words became almost religious to him in the following year. Basically he said: "Believe that you'll heal. You must believe that one day you'll walk again and God will let it happen. Just believe and you'll become healed." (The word *'heel'* in Afrikaans can mean 'to heal' as well as 'complete'. And when I heard the story from my grandpa at a young age, I thought my great grandfather's message was "your body will become whole". It will heal and join together with your spirit, your conscious soul once again.) It was a powerful message to hear from such a great man.

The next day, my dad awoke fully from his fevered dreams. He tried moving his finger. He must have spent hours doing it. My grandmother saw it first. She was so happy she screamed at her husband.

"Come look!" she shouted. "Willi's moving his finger!"

My father was the first person in Afrika to walk out of the hospital after that kind of injury. But it took time, operations, and patience from his friends, family and his future wife, who read stories to him while he was in the machine that rotated his outstretched body. His face would go red with blood seeping in when he was upside down, hanging parallel to the floor from the giant wheel, but he would listen to her reading something to him—sometimes the newspaper, other times a book. My father was spun ever so slowly and tilted. He was Leonardo's Vitruvian

Man on a gyroscope—neither Leonardo's proportional human, nor he could move.

His body had been shut off.

I imagine that he knew it was there outside of his vision, he just had to let his thoughts access to it. Connect the wires, you know. However, he would not let this stop him. With belief and voice of utter determination, he told his parents: "I *will* walk out of here."

One day, his parents came to visit, and a nurse, whose name no one can remember, said: "Mr. and Mrs. Lottering, I have a surprise for you." She told them to wait outside my dad's room. They waited and the door opened from inside. My dad, frail as a dormouse, was leaning against the wall on the inside of the room. He was walking—standing or shuffling, rather—on his own. That day, he sat down on the chairs in the lobby with my grandparents, his parents, and chatted as if nothing was wrong. My grandmother cried. She cried a lot. After a few minutes he said that he was tired and they helped him stand up and lean against the wall. He shuffled back into his room and onto the bed.

Exercise and massage also helped. My grandfather, the wrestling coach, almost never left his bedside. He massaged my dad's muscles whenever he could. And for months afterward, he would help my dad train his body using small weights at first, until he could do a pushup by himself.

Recovering from this accident is a true miracle. My dad fought to get through it. Perhaps it was the purest force of will—consciousness impressing itself on matter. Otherwise, you might want to call it co-incidence, fate, or even the poetic sense of fortune in a universe of ever-increasing variables. I believe that even cut off from the world in the purest, timeless, placeless, liminal space, he found that with the electrical storm of firing neurons he could still affect matter. One positive thought brought him a thousand paces closer to his ultimate recovery. Steadfastly, he believed that he would heal—ever determined to walk out of the hospital.

And three months and one operation later, he did walk unsurely out of the hospital, where his parents were waiting to pick him up in a sunburst yellow Mercedes to take him home.

I have often wondered what it was like for him. What kind of thoughts drifted through his mind in the moments after losing his body? This story is, in a sense, his story. The story of people who step towards annihilation. Some recover, bringing with them wireframe images of the hereafter. Such messengers were often held in the highest regard in ancient cultures. Some became soothsayers, or hermitic druids; in Egypt others were mummified along with cats and hawks and crocodiles; they were believed to act as the guides of the dead.

Then there is the vast majority of others, the remaining 98%, who enter the void and, I hope, peacefully discover the beauty and harmony of life as they cross from this world.

98% Grey

We find our girl standing in an elevator that smells of something…you can't really put your finger on it, but it's not nice. Not terribly foul, but unsettling and odd in the same way you might feel if you were invited into an ethnic family's pantry. Marci was reading the "in case of emergency" sign above the buttons. It was an old elevator and Marci Wood was inclined to expect the worst. If I were a psychologist, I would describe her as conscientiously introverted, suspicious, and slightly neurotic. If I were an artist, I would say she was stylized. Something out of *anime*, rather than an Ingres or Jacques-Louis David. And it's true, her face, although cute, was not really beautiful in any sense. She looked like she would make a beautiful cartoon if she had a thick outline. Were I a hairdresser, I would shout "Highlights! C'mon girl, make an appointment already!" And then I would ask if her dirty-blond hair is naturally curly or straight. It's nearly impossible to tell. It seems like it has a will of its own, alternating at random between frizzy and perfectly straight.

"Does it depend on how you sleep?" I'd like to ask her.

"Nope. I can't control it. It channels a force far greater than me," she would almost certainly respond. She was a naturally self-critical person and regardless of the state of her hair, whether that day straight and shiny like a catwalk model, or wavy like Botticelli's beauties, she would preen until eventually giving up to the untamable nature of it.

Her gestures are often graceful, sometimes childlike, usually fascinating in a way you can't describe. You might find yourself staring at her if you saw her waiting in a bus station. She's somewhat sassy, and if you had to sum her up in one word, you could call her a 'gal'. A funny gal.

To describe Marci, I could talk about gardening, French Existentialists, type-setting, photo chemicals, lazy cats, "Le Petit Prince," lips, as well as ancient manuscripts.

Which brings me to why she was standing in this elevator: her dream job.

The bell dinged, and the door opened. She walked out into a beautiful office on the 13th floor of the University Library. Softly lit by lamps hidden behind the mahogany counter, the room had the ambience of a CEO's reception area. The woman behind the counter was about 30 years older than her: grey hair, grey suit, thick glasses, slightly tubby, with an asexual feel to her as if she reproduced like an amoeba. Marci noticed her little mouth: tight-lipped, dry, top lip angular, bottom lip nonexistent.

"Hello. May I help you, miss?" She asked in an unintoned tenor.

"Uh, yes. I hope so." Poor Marci always fumbles for words whenever she introduces herself. It's funny, because once you get to know her, she always has a catchy phrase or saying even for the everyday things. Like she'll bring up inflation when you try to buy those 5 cent candies at the 7/11. Or she'll make some sound-effect when you say something stupid and say, "Lottering, I'll send you back to Afrika." Ok, ok, bad examples, I know. But you get my drift.

She goes for damage control: "I mean, I am here for the archives position. This is a really nice office, you know. I thought it'd be more drab or something. Not that...uhh, nevermind." The receptionist just stared at her blankly.

2

"I'll call Dr. Brown. One moment." The walls were decorated with two Miro-esque prints and a strangely art deco Soviet propaganda poster. Outside, the sun had already fallen behind the cityscape moonlighting as the horizon. And in the reflection on the large window, Marci could see herself. Wow!

A petite girl, hair obviously forced into submission under the butterfly pin, black suit, orange shirt that screams "I am a creative force!," shoes she hasn't worn since a cocktail party five years ago. Her body, hidden beneath the black suit, although small, seems athletic. Ok, perhaps not athletic, but acrobatic—flexible, at least. The kind which might be very attractive if it were 10% bigger. Under the layer of clothes (and invisible to the receptionist) is a body as white as snow, toting some blue, non-descript underwear. She is checking herself out in the reflection on the window. We all do it. She eyes the suit and thinks: *Man, formal wear can be sexy. Love the orange.* In order to avoid the hair, which she knows will only lead to a self-conscious fit in the nearest washroom, she scans downwards: orange shirt, boobs ¾ view, jacket tight around the waist, hips fading into the outside world below the office.

"Ms. Woods?" She spun around and came eye to eye with a dark-haired woman in a grey suit. The woman, in her late 40s, had a powerful Catherine Deneuve presence and she was looking at Marci in a somewhat displeased way.

"Actually, it's 'Wood', not 'Woods'. No plural."

"Like a branch, not the forest, eh?"

"Like the material that floats on water." They shook hands (firmly) and exchanged some courtesies, followed by brief small talk, then on to business.

"Right this way. Have you ever worked with rare books before, Ms. Wood?" The woman spoke with an English accent, the grammar school type of posh that would have put her in a different social bracket a few decades ago.

"No, but I'm very excited. This is kind of my dream job, you know. I mean, it feels as if I have been trained for this day. Everything from my background to my interests, to the day

I was born…"

"Sorry to interrupt, but I believe you are rambling, Ms. Wood. You already have the job. I am well aware of your certifications, there is no need for the sales pitch. Please take a breath and listen, for what I am about to tell you is important."

Marci was silenced. Shocked. The woman didn't seem so forceful during the interview and now all of a sudden she seems displeased.

"Yes, ma'am." Catherine Deneuve led her into a small room. Looks like a storage closet, but with enough space for two or three people.

"Take off your suit." The fluorescent light buzzed in b-flat, filling some awkward void left after the word 'suit', which echoed in Marci's mind. This was a moment quickly growing into a minute, and before Marci could stutter her response, the manager jumped in: "I know it sounds bizarre, but I just expected as an expert colour corrector, you would have thought about the colours you chose to wear to work the first day."

The movement of Marci's eyes: right, left, (a slight frown), and slowly down to her orange blouse. She *did* think about the colours too.

"Yes, Ms. Wood. We are in the business of colour preservation, so please wear this uniform." The woman opened a locker and pulled out a grey suit on a hanger. She passed it to Marci nonchalantly, lips flexing and relaxing in a tiny, almost invisible way. "I expect this is close to your size. Please be sure to return it next week after you wash it." As Marci recovered from this scene, which she thought seemed to happen like a *film noir* slow-mo clip, she looked up to see the door click closed. Catherine Deneuve had disappeared leaving an empty room for her to change in. When she finished, she seemed to vanish into the grey cement. And for the first time she noticed that almost everything in the room was the same colour. Or at least the same hue. *The colour of a rainstorm*, she thought and stepped outside, leaving her orange and black garb hanging like a highlight on the hanger inside the locker inside the grey room.

"Excellent. Now let us continue," the dark haired woman said, startling Marci. Was she waiting outside the whole time? *She's like a robot*, Marci thought.

"I'm unaware whether you know this or not, Ms. Wood, but the technology used for colour preservation requires a 98% grey environment in order to produce accurate colour capture."

"Oh yeah…That's right." She did read that in a textbook once at school, but had completely forgotten it. Actually, she thought it was just another technical rule which could be bent, and promptly forgot it once she started using chemicals and Photoshop. Ahh, Photoshop! The alpha and omega of colour correction.

"So I am sorry if I surprised you just now, but I suppose I had expected that you would arrive in a grey suit. In the future please make sure to wear nothing far outside this range of grey."

"Of course," she nodded. You see, Marci is a relentlessly self-critical person. So after this first slip up, she immediately scolded herself internally for forgetting something like this. Of course, the reason was her own artistic nature. She is a lover of colour and therefore enjoyed the beautiful balance of the black and orange, and the simultaneous contrast of the orange blouse and blue underwear. Now, if she pictured her body under the suit, it felt as if the blue itself became grey, the blue camouflaging chameleon-like, spreading to the skin. She became grey in her imagination. Like a plastic cast of a Marci doll. A figurine.

Well, this is my dream job, she thought. And truly a few months ago she had prayed for an interview. She would have offered, without a single doubt, her pinky toe if it could have secured her the job in the rare books department. The little toe is a small thing, but life is not the same without it, trust me.

Anyway, they moved along through the library's collections. Rubber footsteps *squeek-squeeking* a little against the polished cement as they walked past the stacks. The rare books were kept in a temperature controlled dark room. Imagine one of those high security rooms in any generic heist movie. Yeah, you know the one I'm talking about. With the precious artifacts kept in glass cases, surrounded by more glass, with machines that measure vibration, ambient air temperature, etc. inside a cement room with no windows. Then imagine a single, soft spotlight falling onto each case. The rare books were displayed like that. The even rarer ones were kept in morgue-like drawers in a lock-up (also environmentally controlled by all sorts of high-tech gadgets).

Now, the Catherine Deneuve clone was, in fact, the curator of the Rare Collection. She was the straight, no-nonsense type and you could tell this from the perfume she wore. It was clean, a clinical non-fragrance fragrance. The smell of a cold winter night on the icy parking lot of a dentist's office. She was taller than Marci, more muscular (though probably more fragile), and had an angular sculpted face you would see everywhere in a Modigliani museum. The behaviour of her lips intrigued Marci as they walked side-by-side down the vast emptiness of the library.

"It seems pretty quiet around here." Marci was obviously trying to make conversation.

"Well, it is a library." *Squeek-squeek*. "But this floor is limited to the employees and the faculty. In fact, once we arrive at the operations room, I will give you your access card."

"Thank you," she said, wondering why the manager's lips are so squirmy. They have the tendency to leap up at the edges very briefly. *A facial twitch?* she wondered. You see, Marci has this way of being able to draw out personality traits from analyzing a person's lips. Plump ones, thin ones, round ones, wet ones, dry ones, grim ones, red ones, juicy ones, 'kiss me' ones: the orifice leaves you wondering, doesn't it? Marci loved staring at them. Like little facial vaginas, they are your secret sexual fingerprint. She often wondered why palm reading was invented but lip reading was only for the deaf.

They stopped.

"Alright. Here we are." (*Finally!* she thought). The door said '**Archival Office**' in Helvetica 74 point type in golden

6

letters. It was a beautiful door. And in they went, crossing the boundary that would forever change Marci Wood's life.

"This," said the manager, "is where you will spend your days." The room was immaculately clean, and housed some of the latest computers. Shiny steel tables with dark matte surfaces, a huge assortment of mostly unused lights, wires and other devices hanging from the ceiling. It was a 98% grey technological paradise, all centred around an old illuminated manuscript lying closed on the table. The screens showed shots of one of the pages, zoomed with incredibly lifelike—perhaps perfect!—detail of an illustrated letter 'J' in blue, red, and gold gothic letter form. Behind it, the heavenly sphere with stars and comets hung frozen in time.

"Well, *allons-y!*" she said and stepped into the room. Marci took a deep breath and followed. The air was a little cooler inside and she had the funny feeling of disappearing into the room. It seemed like the only real thing inside the room was the thick leatherbound book, everything else was just an outline in a fog of greyness. Marci's own hands felt detached, floating around independently in grand swaying motions of hyperbole. They mesmerized her.

"Wowwww." The word escaped her when she exhaled the deep lungful of anticipation she had inhaled a moment before.

"Quite something, isn't it?" said the manager referring to the book. "Dioscorides, *De Materia Medica.* Circa twelve-hundred AD." In fact, Marci hadn't even looked at the book. She was so enchanted by the way her hands floated on the grey that her attention never settled on the enormous book of parchment laying on the table. But now that she mentioned it, her eyes were drawn to the tome. Beautiful, aged, heavy as if it contained some secret of life that would take one person ten years to read, and another ten just to understand.

But here was her chance! She knew *De Materia Medica,* had studied it in school, and might even be able to find the exact page he lists *sylphium,* the most magical of plants. When she applied for the job, knowledge of the books was something she lacked. She got the job based on her exceptional skill as a colour corrector. In fact, she could give you the Pantone™ number for any colour you pointed at. The perfect pitch of the colour world. The library decided to hire her despite any previous experience with books because, as the director put it, "she had a certain charm". Catherine Deneuve was the deciding vote and although she didn't like the idea of Marci cruising by based on her charm (and idiot savant-like talent), she supported her for three reasons:

a. the library was severely short-handed.
b. politically, if she voted against the director it would ruin her career.
c. deep-down inside her, Marci made her feel alive; she stirred some fleeting feeling of erotic attraction.

Anyway, when Marci saw the book, she felt recharged. *What a wonderful chance, what glorious providence,* she thought. Although she knew every manuscript was different, she also knew that she would be able to find her way to the mystical plant with a quick flick of the pages. It was all charted terrain, you know. So she turned to the book, placed her hand on the hard leather (it felt cool and tough. *Like dinosaur skin,* she thought) and then she lifted the cover.

"Hands off! Ms. Wood!" The voice echoed in the room with præternatural energy. Shocked, Marci dropped the cover with a padded *thwimp!* and turned around. Blood flowed upwards into her face and head. There was a quiet pounding behind her left temple.

"We *never* touch the books," the manager said. "Sorry to startle you, but you see, Ms. Wood, the books we work with are extremely old. Some are antiques beyond antiques, travelling centuries to get our present. They are like trees growing through the 4th dimension, if you will. And, unfortunately, they are almost more natural material than reading material at this point. They are just about as close to a heap of minerals as you can get without disintegrating." (*She's lecturing me,* Marci thought).

8

"Therefore, we must preserve them in the most accurate state possible."

"I see," was all Marci could muster. She wanted to punch herself. Of course they were old. She thought about that, but she was going to handle it with care. But didn't they let her touch the copy when she did her report on Dioscorides in university? She was allowed to flip though it without an old owl hunched over her shoulder then. *What's the difference*, she asked herself. *Why can't I touch the books*, she asked the universe.

"The proper procedure is as follows: the book you are to scan will arrive in the morning from the collections. You are not to open it under any circumstances. Alexander will show you how to scan them. At the end of the day, please cover the book with the plastic lid you see here." She pointed to something that looked like a large, inverted industrial sink.

"It looks heavy."

"It's not light, but you should be able to manage." The dark-haired woman then crossed the room and pressed a button on the wall.

"Alexander," she spoke into the intercom, "would you please come to the Archival Office. You are needed here." *So now what?* Marci thought. (An awful, awkward silence.)

"Well, Ms. Wood, I trust I can leave you here alone. Alexander will be up here in a few minutes. You can look around, but remember, please don't touch the book under any circumstance." *What if there's a fire?* The image of a fire in that grey room made her pause for a second. It was like some logical paradox: what could possibly catch fire in a grey room?

"Ok. I'll just wait here then," she managed to mutter. The manager left, peering back over her shoulder as the door was closing. Finally, she was alone with the book. She stared at it. It stared back. Then suddenly her eyes zoomed, microscope-like, onto the surface of the book. Tiny stitches around the border, well-worn creases where it has been folded by generation upon generation of hands, tiny pores on the leather surface exposed under faded pigment. It seemed heavy. She just wanted to touch the leather skin. She didn't want to open it, just feel the friction on her fingertips. It was beautiful. The feeling Marci was experiencing at that moment was akin to the sensual anticipation of making contact with your lover's skin for the first time. Electrons fired in her brain, tingling all the way down her spine.

The door opened.

"Hello, hello." Marci spun around. The man standing in front of her, melted into the grey. His head, a smiling face topped with a monstrous black afro, seemed very out of place amidst the grey. He was kind of tall, definitely lanky and the afro lent a presence of a circus clown. I think he was Greek, or at least of the hairier Mediterranean pedigree. He had the look of someone who always distracted the class in elementary school without meaning to. The inadvertent 'bad kid' who just followed his nature. Something like this bred in him a sense of rebelliousness, and confidence that stirred at nothing. He definitely wasn't handsome. Alex was a little too tall and lanky, speaking with a slight slurring of consonants, glasses, and a particular geeky coolness that you might find in alternative rock bands. *What instrument does he play? The bass? Or the keyboard? Too skinny to be a drummer.*

Marci noticed the enormous head, and then turned her eyes immediately to the mouth. He had almost no lips. And what lips he had were all in the top one protruding over the bottom. They were well maintained and gave her a sense that this guy really only cared about himself. But for some reason unknown to Marci, she had an instant affinity for him. It might have been how he said hello twice; it might have been his harmless marionette-like demeanor, who knows. My personal theory is that:

a. She was not threatened by Alex like she was with the others at the library, and thus he became her retreat from the formality; and

b. They had met in a previous life, where they were travel companions on one of the few transatlantic dirigibles.

10

"Hi! I'm Alex Propoupolis-Oloupos. You can call me Alex…or Ace, if you like."

"Hello," she paused, "Marci Wood. Nice to meet you, Alex." (Marci always says names three times upon meeting someone in order not to forget it. So here comes the storm!)

"So Alex, that's some hairstyle you got there."

"Thank you. So Marci, may I call you Marci?"

"Sure, go ahead Alex." (Yes! Number three!)

"You didn't touch the book, did you?"

"No, I was just looking."

"Your nose was pretty close just now…You must like the smell of history."

"Well, it's uh…very fine…uh…So why can't we touch the books?"

"They're old. Some we can touch, but those ones aren't a priority for the archives." His giant head floated into the room and looked down at the computer screen. "You see, we start with the oldest ones and move to the most recent."

"Yeah, but how do we scan them without touching them?" It was a question that finally surfaced through the subconscious and popped out like a buoyant object that has been tugged deep under water.

"The million dollar question!" he exclaimed and spun around to face her, excited to put on the show he has been waiting for since Catherine Deneuve called him on the intercom.

"Well," his tone took on that of a petty street performer or an amateur stage magician, "we might as well get this show on the road! This is what we have come here to do, after all." Marci prepared herself for whatever was to come next. She was leaning against the cool cement wall, perhaps in an attempt to take herself away from the action.

"It's OK," he said, "You won't get in the way over here." Alex had a problem with subtlety—he had no idea how it was done. He grabbed some tools from the desk next to the computer. They were a strange set of cables, and handles, and one looked like a white, fiber-optic cat o' nine tails. "You're not afraid of a little fun, are you?" he said.

"Ok. What should I do?" she asked, finally determined to get in on the action.

"Do you like dusting?" He was waving the fiber-optic cat o' nine tails in the air.

"Um, not really."

"Oh come on!" he said. "Loosen up a bit."

"What is that thing? I've never seen anything like it before."

"This," he smiled, "is our bread 'n butter." She took it from him to see. It was an extremely thin plastic blade, with fiber-optic cables coming out of it. Marci imagined what that kind of thing could be used for, but she couldn't come to any conclusions. It looked alien to her. Foreign in a way technology shouldn't look to someone her age. *Am I getting old already?* she thought.

"I half don't want to show you, because you look so amazed by this thing."

"Well, as I said, I never saw one before." She knew he was just delaying this moment because it was part of his show. She could hear it all in his voice and see it on his used-car-salesman smile. "But how do you use it?" And this was the line he was waiting for.

"Let me demonstrate!" He hit a power switch and the fibers sprung to life, lit up like some sort of high-tech angel wings. It might have been just the fact that it altered the balance of colour in the grey room, but Marci was entranced by its beauty. *Such a brilliant white*, she thought. He was talking, but she didn't pay any attention. Everything seemed surreal in that room. He took it back from her and waved the wand around, mesmerizing her. To him this was nothing new, but having her there made it interesting again. He carefully slid the edge of the plastic blade into the book. Then he dragged the fibers between the pages. This all seemed to happen in silence, but really Alex was giving a pretty impressive play-by-play of the action. His voice was becoming a slurring echo in her mind as she watched and absorbed the method, the speed he was dragging it, the gentle resistance of the pages when he cut the negative space between them. Marci had an incredible memory. In fact, this was the best explanation for her virtuoso-esque power with colour. She memorized every colour she saw and could recall it perfectly.

Behind him the beige of the manuscript was appearing on the screen. Slowly, just as he finessed the fibers, it was collecting data. Some green plant sprigs, drawn by medieval hand and catalogued by methods long lost to modern science, revealed themselves.

"Lemon balm," she whispered as Alex finished his scan. He was still talking to himself, but once the fibers slipped out of the book, illuminating the room again, he turned around to witness his work.

"Not bad, if I *do* say so myself. And I do say so myself!" he said. Marci was stunned by the whole process. It was like magic. If this was what he tried to do, he succeeded; yet, somehow he was surprised at her reaction.

"You OK?" he asked with a serious tone this time.

"Yeah, just fascinated by this method of scanning."

"It is pretty BOSS!" he laughed—chuckled is more like it. "Wanna try it?"

"Sure." Things were settling back into reality, but Marci thought about how much this entire experience seems like alchemy. They were like ghosts in a grey room wielding wands of angel hair, collecting information through osmoses. *This is magic*, she thought as she grabbed the brush from him.

"We mark the pages with this orange tag. It attaches to the last scanned page, so you should put your wand in beneath that." *Oh my god, it's even called a 'wand'!*

"Got it," she confirmed, finally getting excited about her new job. Alex was already excited. He leaned in over her shoulder easily as he was about a foot taller than her. Instructions followed, but Marci watched well enough from before and she had it down.

Thus passed her first day.

13

ONE YEAR LATER

"Yo Marci, what's up?"

"It's a beautiful day outside. The sun is shining, trees are blooming, lovers are loving. And we are rotting away inside here."

"Eeeaasy there, Tiger."

"What, now I'm not allowed to be blue? I mean, I know it was a 98% grey policy, but this is too much, man!"

"Oh, come on Mars, what's wrong? Bad date last night?"

See, this is exactly the kind of thing that would get young Alexander in trouble when he was in elementary school. It seems like an unfailing ability to make people feel worse instead of better. Kind of like reverse empathy, he knew he had to say something, but it was always the exact wrong thing.

"Alex," she sighed, "what the hell, man?!" She busied herself with the screens, trying to get to work.

"What? Did I say something bad? I'm just trying to pay a little attention to your...er, love life, you know. Who else does?"

"Ok, man, let's just get to work. No more talk about my love life. I just wanna get this done and get out of here."

"Fine, but Marci if you don't talk about it, you'll never get it off your chest." She stopped fiddling with the screens and looked directly at him in the way he had come to know as the 'you-little-fucker!' look. Then she addressed him in the same way a teacher might address a bad pupil. First there is the frown. Then, she licked her lips. Finally, she dropped her tone of voice and spoke slowly, annunciating each syllable in a slow, purposeful way.

"Alex," she might as well have said 'Alexander Cyril Propoupolis-Oloupos in the best parental voice, "You. Are. An. Ass."

"Alright alright alright." They continued in silence until a few minutes later when he was called by intercom to the basement.

Actually it was a sad state of affairs. Marci Wood had found her dream job, but she was yet to touch a rare book. It takes about 3 months to scan an entire librum, and when they finished with it, they cover it just like they do every other night. Then in the morning the book is replaced with an equally valuable treasure she was not allowed to touch. Marci smells the books, though. Yessir, she does! She used to arrive early just so she could sneak in, put her nose 5 millimeters away from the leather and inhale. She did this for about 3 weeks straight after she started. In fact, she still does it every now-and-then after they exchange the books or when she gets a moment alone during a slow day.

During a particularly heavy snowstorm she was stuck in the Library for 30 hours. She slept in the stacks amongst the books, enveloped in a warm emergency blanket, huddled near the radiator in the gothic part of the building. It was on that day that she discovered the cameras. They were everywhere: between the aisles, peering down hallways, on the mezzanine, watching the water fountains, guarding the rare books, and even in the Archival Office. Somewhere behind a glass screen, a man in a security suit was watching her every move. I see him standing there in his navy uniform, arms crossed, watching her floating hands in the sea of grey. Would he be able to make out her body in the grey suit? Was she human? I bet he was enchanted by the human puppetry the first time he looked in the grey room. Unable to take his eyes off her, he found himself imagining her as a doll. You know those paper dolls on which you clip the cut-outs of clothing? That's exactly what he thought. She was like a blank canvas for his imagination. And although he couldn't see her body, he imagined her in a tuxedo, a swimsuit, a Sunday dress, a nurses uniform, generic blue jeans and a hooded sweater, as well as every other genre, style and conception of clothing possible to the human imagination.

Marci knew this.

She met the security guard during that blizzard. He was noticeably surprised when they met. The kind of surprise you get when you meet a movie star and see their wrinkles close up. Marci, as was her habit, stared at his mouth and gleaned every piece of information she could from it. His mouth was big, bottom lip sagging a little, top lip protruding. It was the mouth of control and frustration, of desires and imagination, of taboo and sensation. Marci was smart and she put the clues together, but most of all, his mouth told her that he had been watching her. She didn't need to enquire further.

Why are there so many cameras? she had wanted to ask, but it never came up in conversation. In fact, their conversation was strained and awkward at most. The woman Marci Wood could not live up to his idea of the doll in the grey room. And so he left her alone.

The incident was a small realization amidst a grand show of nature's power. The city was frozen in white and inside the library, twelve people slept along the wall lined with radiators. I assume that their ferret instinct—in other words, the instinct to sleep in a pile of gathering body heat—was suppressed by some social taboo of sleeping next to a stranger. After all, the radiators weren't nearly as comfortable as a human body.

Sleeping there, next to the wall, she thought about being captured by the lens of a closed circuit camera wherever she was in the Library. She wondered how much she got away with, how much they *let* her get away with. Her sloppiness had a lot to do with how she felt at work. She was still new at the job and thus didn't want to break the rules, but it was becoming clear to her that she soon would. The encounter with the security guard made her realize that if she did, in fact, touch a book, not only would it probably crumble into 600 year old parchment dust, but also there could be a youtube video swimming around virally in cyberspace within minutes. Soon she fell asleep dreaming of Ruby, the cat of her youth, who was always still alive in her dreams.

The thing was, Marci needs a lot of stimulation. She is the kind of mineral that oxidizes if it isn't exposed to all kinds of stimulus. The job was good. It paid well, but everyday she became more and more depressed. Perhaps the novelty had worn off. Otherwise, it could have been the grey environment. Or maybe she was ready to move on. It could have been any number of factors, but the truth behind Marci's big dilemma was that she had reached the apex of her dreams.

What would her mom say if she were alive? Marci wondered what advice her mother would give her. Irene Wood was a free spirit. She never went to university but had a certain wisdom and thirst for knowledge like, a village sage. *Mom would would tell me to move on*, she thought. Marci could see her mother, standing in the early morning light in their little kitchen. They never used the kitchen. Irene always brought meals home from the restaurants she worked at. The fare changed frequently, progressing from Italian and French, to breakfast only, to the ethnic palette of Chinese, Indian, and finally to the establishment of 'World-Fusion' cuisine.

Irene never stayed at any job long enough to form an attachment. She was deeply against attachments. If people asked why they hardly owned any furniture, she would quote a sanskrit verse about 'true action' and 'true belief' and 'non-attachment'. Marci, however, sly little girl that she was, knew better from a young age. Her mother, the artist, the protestor, had a secret life. It was contained in the other little room in their bare loft.

There were 2 rooms and the kitchen. Marci and her mother usually slept together. Sometimes Marci would fall asleep on the floor of the second room, but mostly they slept together. They did this until Marci moved out to go to university. The first person in her family, as far as she knew from her mother's side. The man who donated his X-chromosome might have come from a long line of cosmonauts and philosophers for all she knew.

Marci always recalled her mother in the bleached out, warm tones of a photograph taken in the '70s. The sun was falling through the hanging plants and warbled glass onto her mother, who was dressed in a black tanktop and an apron she used for painting. She spent her mornings, painting lavish colours onto wooden planks—her style was a wonderfully feminine mix of Keith Herring meets Jackson Pollock. As a little girl, Marci would sit in the studio, cross-legged on the floor and watch her mom throw buckets of paint at old planks of wood. Often while reading a book, Marci would wonder, "Where does she collect those wonderful pieces of wood?" These moments were her happiest ones.

Memories of the kitchen were always more serious. It was in the kitchen that the emotional conversations happened. Scoldings and chidings, confessions and breakdowns, as well as counsel and advice. The kitchen was the mental place Marci went to ask her own subconscious for advice.

"Mom," she'd say, "am I doing the right thing?"

"What's the right thing, Marci?" Irene Wood had the manerisms of a hardy country girl. She had a swash of sky-blue paint on her face. Perhaps where she brushed her wavy, blonde hair off her cheekbone.

"I found the job I've worked for my entire life. The one drive and desire I've had ever since I could pick up one of your art books. Mom, you know how much I've wanted to work with books and colour."

"So what's the problem then, honey?" Today, her mother was especially warm. When she was alive there were definitely darker periods as well, but today, as always in Marci's daydreams, Irene put her arm around her grown up girl and kissed her on the temple.

"I hate my job."

"Ohhhh, Marciiiii," she cooed. "Don't worry. You're free to do whatever you wish. Just do what comes naturally."

Marci's mother generally took a non-interventionist approach. And always gave the same advice: "Just do what comes naturally." Even in her doting daydreams, Irene always told dear Marci to do what comes naturally. This non-advice could sometimes seem extremely sage; on the other hand, it usually came off as non-committal and overwhelmingly useless.

So every night, lying alone in her bed, surrounded by posters of Klimt, Rothko, and Matisse, she thought about quitting. She wanted to talk about this with her boyfriend, but they were temporarily on non-speaking terms. She thought about him, her job, the future. Then she thought about where she would go next. The back-and-forth,

back-and-forth,

back-and-forth

never stopped and never led anywhere. Because the job of scanning rare books was something she had dreamed about since she had reached intellectual maturity, she wasn't able to imagine anything beyond that. Where could she go? What does it mean that she spent her entire post-secondary life preparing for a job she unknowingly bet the wrong chips on? What do you do after you taste your dream and it is bland like three-day old mashed potatoes?

You keep eating and hope that one day they serve you gravy. So Marci steeled herself and endured the day-to-day dullness in hopes of a future promotion.

Here are some bits and pieces of the following 3 months:

EPISODE I

PANTONE 429
Suicide Grey

It was a rainy February day. Cold as sin. The winter was passing gas, it seemed. And the sky was dull. When Marci looked up, she noticed that the sky itself was an opaque grey. Not quite 98% but a Pantone™ 429 or perhaps a 'cool gray 7'. In other words, a wintery, blue grey. Pantone™ 429, by the way, was in Marci's opinion suicide grey.

Of course, she was wearing her grey suit—now one of many she owned. Her self-expression at work was limited completely to the hair accessories she chose to wear and the pair of shoes she ran out of the house with. Today was 'gun smoke' leather shoes, and a very oldskool barrette. Technically, they were brown shoes, but the hue was so close to grey that she could get away with it. Besides, shoes weren't really important since the light always fell on them last.

She was a little late, but could still make it on time. Her phone vibrated in her pocket. She ignored it and ran to the subway stop. She got a little wet in the rain, and as she got close to the subway entrance, she heard a squeeking sound.

It all happened so fast. From her peripheral vision her distracted eyes saw an object approaching. It was elliptical, blue and black and was heading for her legs. Next, she heard a bell.

Ding-ding-ding!

She turned her head just in time to see the bicycle. It struck her on the shin and swept her off her feet. The cyclist had slipped in the rain, and along with his contorted bike, he slid under her. She fell on top of it. The pedal thrust into her side and her head hit the pavement with a hollow *thud*.

She may have been unconscious for a few seconds. Or was it minutes? Either way, while some pedestrians were picking her up off the bicycle, her phone vibrated a second time. She regained consciousness quickly, brushed off some sand from her coat and descended the stairs into the underground. She was now officially late. On the train, she checked her phone. There was a missed call and a text message.

The text said: DEAR M, I WANTED 2 TELL U IN PERSON BUT NO ANSWR. IM LEAVING THE COUNRTY SO PLZ DONT CALL ANYMOR. SRRY. I STILL LOVE U. FAREWELL, SEAN.

Her head was still reverberating a little and the message didn't sink in. Sean was her boyfriend—or her ex-boyfriend now. They had had some long talks recently. Once, he took her to a nice restaurant, and while they were munching on appetizers (grilled lotus roots wrapped in bacon with a pesto-tomato sauce), he asked her if she wanted to have a threesome with his co-worker Sunny. They argued and argued, she slapped him, walked out, he followed, and soon they were naked in her apartment surrounded by Klimt, Rothko, and Matisse, a trio of a very different kind.

She had met Sean about 6 months before. It was spring and tulips were just protruding their wrapped-up colour bundles out of the earth. The sun had started shining. Toronto was warming up and Marci was at her best that day.

The only factor standing against her was the wind. It was tremendously blustery, so as soon as she entered a building, she had to quickly tame her fuzzy hair. This process made her vulnerable to strangers approaching her. And apparently, the windswept look is what attracted Sean to her. He was on his way out of the bank and passed by her.

"Whoa. I mean this in the coolest possible way, but your hair is magnificent!"

Of course, this kind of comment was surprising—

shocking even! She didn't know what to say.

"Well, I…" …*want to strangle it for not co-operating* "…just. Wait! Are you kidding?"

"Ok you got me," he admitted. "I guess I'm trying to hide what I truly meant to say, which is that you are very cute."

"Like a teddybear? …Or hello kitty? That kind of cute?" She had finally managed to contain the frizz of her hair.

"Like…" He struggled for a brief second, but you could tell that the man had charm just by how he rested his thumb on his top lip. Anyone that can do that move and not look like a complete joke, certainly has charm. "What's your name?" he asked.

"Marci."

"I mean like Ms. Marci McCute cute," he said, setting the foundation to a 5½-month long dating period, followed by a rough patch after she got the job.

They spent one glorious summer together in the city, picnicing, sitting on patios, and sleeping together in Marci's new house. Sean loved how she would have redecorating fits periodically, channelling all her issues with life into the painting of a wall.

What Marci loved most about him was that he took care of her so well. He was protective and caring in a way she had hardly ever experienced in a relationship. He would help fix the house, carry things for her and give her space to redecorate. They seemed to fit so well, which is why the news of him fleeing the country hit her so hard.

Two weeks ago they argued over Marci's job. Sean thought that she had given up, that she had no goals left in her life. He told her that achieving her dream made her a more boring person. The damage was instantly visible on her face and when she physically threw him out he didn't resist in the slightest.

She called him names too. And said things that were not deserved by a man who generally spent most of his energy shielding her from the outside world.

This is what she remembered while she was crying in the women's washroom of the library. She remembered this and felt the sadness of someone leaving her life again. Her mother's death left a significant psychological scar which easily could have turned into an obsessive fear of the outside world. Fortunately, this was not the case, but the void in her life filled by Sean was once again empty. It was a gaping hunger, a sullen solitude, that bubbled in her chest when she thought of being alone again.

Needless to say, the rest of the day was a disaster, and Marci spent the first 40 minutes redoing her hair and makeup. Then she walked up to Dr. Brown, and politely told her that someone close to her had died and that she needed to go home. Of course, this was a lie, but perhaps she meant it metaphorically.

On the way back, she managed to control the anger and the sadness. She sat in the subway car, looking outwardly glum. She wondered: *Why did I say he had died?*

Am I getting a neurosis? I really don't want to be sick in the head. Aww...come on!

The whole train ride was a philosophical rollercoaster. *Why is life taking away everyone around me?!* She became disturbed and desperate in a way that dangerously careless people usually are. *What did I do wrong?*

A good question in most break ups, right? 'What did I do wrong?' A loaded questions in most cases, so I won't go into it.

In this case, however, the fight a week before could have easily been resolved with a simple apology. And Sean's overreaction was quite out in left field. There was no possible way she could have expected it. And on top of all of that, it was done through texting. *The most impersonal of all the modern communication methods*, she thought.

That bastard. That fucking bastard!

EPISODE II

"I think we need to redo these scans."

"Why?!" The tone was a duellist challenge—a sweaty glove-slap to the cheek.

"Uh…" (*What just happened?*) "Because the hues are tinted, and the lines are a little fuzzy."

"Alright. Good luck, Captain!" Then Alex walked out, emotionally slamming the door on her.

Suddenly, the grey had become a burnt grey, the colour of oil. She wasn't sure what happened, but something was off today. Did she do something? No, it couldn't have been her. A motherly instinct kicked in and she wanted to help Alex, wanted to cool him off, to ask him what was wrong. On the other hand, there was such aggression in his voice and it seemed focused on her.

The question kept popping up: did I do something?

When he returned, she had been stewing in her own misguided thoughts and fragile emotions. She was a raw mix of chemicals set on boil.

Do you know how easy it is to fuck someone's day right up? All it takes is one sidelong remark, one snappy comment or rude word and you start an avalanche of negativity. I once witnessed the beginning of such a depressing exponential curve.

I stood in a convenience store, wondering if I wanted orange or apple juice. A man came in and paid for eggs, and the clerk must have given him the wrong change.

"What? Are you a fucking moron?"

"Sorry?"

"It says $3.65 change. You gave me $2.65."

"Er…oh. Here you are, sir." Thus it began. A few minutes later a man came in and asked for cigarettes. The clerk, still shocked from the previous experience, handed him a pack.

"I said 'King size'!"

"Oh, I'm sorry." The clerk gave him a different pack and caught a look in the man's eyes saying "You speak English, don't you? Fuckin' Paki". Of course it was a look the Indian man knew very well and it hurt every time because his English was really quite good. This was the beginning of a bad downward spiral that would culminate in the man getting off at the wrong bus stop, being mugged, stabbed, and left for dead.

Similarly, Marci was left with her thoughts far too long. Her motherly instinct turned sour and instead she felt injured and vulnerable, victimized into a passive-aggressive state.

Alex said nothing. But in her head they fought. Her imagination fanned the flames of her feelings and she visualized herself shooting lasers from her eyes at him whenever she looked in his direction. Imagination, pixelated in comic book style, Roy-Lichtenstein-dreams tinted in *wrath red* (Pantone™ Red 32).

They worked in silence. An awful silence, filled with the b-flat *buzzzzz* of flourescent lights. But the moment came when communication was essential, and Marci heard her voice crack pubescently as she spoke. Blood rushed to her head. She clenched her teeth.

Alex grunted a response. It was the absolute minimal of communication, and aside from a few technical terms, an early *homo errectus* might have had a similar conversation over 15,000 years ago. The absence of communication made the problem worse and it drew invisible territorial lines across the room. They reverted to animal instincts—survival instincts. The work was sloppy. *We'll have to redo all of this tomorrow,* she thought. *What was the point in continuing? Why do I have to stay here in this oil-grey room with this man who is casting deep, dark shadows onto my zone?*
Why? Why why why? There's no point…
So she walked out.

EPISODE III:

"Ms. Wood." That voice seemed so robotic. Marci paused, her shoes clicking to a halt on the hard floor. Today was (semi) high-heels, regulation style, with a red banana clip tying back her hair in a pony tail.

"Yes, Dr. Brown?" They never got onto first name terms, she and the manager. The woman seemed too formal and Marci had trouble looking her in the eye.

"There will be some very important visitors arriving today. I asked Alexander, but he seems to think you are better for the task. So, Ms. Wood, I am placing you in charge of guiding our visitors around the Library. You are to act as our ambassador. Give them anything they need. Understand?"

"Yes, sir."

"Sorry?" the manager said, eyebrows twisted upwards. Marci was herself surprised at the remark.

"Sorry," she said quickly, "I'll start the preparations immediately." And at that, she walked away *klik-klaking* down the hallway. The manager let it go. In fact, she turned around with a beaming smile. See, secretly the 45 year-old liked being called 'sir'. It gave her a sense of power—of dominance. On top of the obviously latent S&M issues, she honestly liked the sound of it. Images of 1950's naval officers popped into her mind: uniforms, the wind, metallic hulks, men lining up on deck in perfect order, and scandalous man-on-man rendezvous below the deck.

Anyways, let's get back to Marci.

Marci entered the Archives scanning left and right for Alex. He was nowhere to be found *en route* and therefore must be in the basement lock-ups. However, even the intercom yielded no results. So she turned on all the computers and equipment and

26

started the daily routine. This had become all too familiar, and her floating hands felt like automata, powered up by entering the grey. Inside her head, she was a little lonely. *Where was Alex?* she wondered. His bobbing head and hands were missing from the morning start-up process. But inside her mind the conversation was raging. His usual morning comments were fairly predictable. ("Yo, *Mars*! What's up?", "How'z it hanging?", "Last night was dope-*tacular*, man! You gotta check this out.")

Suddenly, the door burst open. The voice was the same but the tone entirely different: "And this is where the magic happens! Our archival equipment has some of the best pieces of technological gadgetry money can buy. Designed by computers that build computers to design space-age machines." Alexander stepped into the room in his grey suit, followed by two men in black. They were both bigger than him, which meant that Marci was dwarfed in the room. It might have been more obvious if she didn't fade right into the background.

The interruption had thrown off her morning routine.

"And this lovely room decoration is also our chief colour corrector, Ms. Marci Wood." She was still a little stunned, but the generic 'how-do-you-do' handshakes, along with names she instantly forgot, were passed, and Alex continued on his sales pitch.

She wondered exactly who these VIPs were. The data was being categorized in her mind: apparently Ministry representatives, black suits, big men, expensive shoes, one mid-fifties, the other younger. The one man winked at her as they left.

She continued her work. After a few minutes she felt out of place. Wasn't it her job to guide those men around? Why had Alex told the manager she would be better if he was going to do it himself? Things somehow went slower without Alex there, even though one person just as easily did the scanning.

Exactly 23 minutes had passed when the intercom sparked to life: "Marci, would you mind heading down to the lock-up for a few minutes? The gentlemen requested an explanation of colour preservation."

"I'll be right down," she said, happy that she could leave the room.

The elevator door opened to the three of them hovering over an opened drawer containing some of the untouchable books.

"Hello again, gentlemen," she said, interrupting Alex's running commentary. Marci was trying to reclaim her responsibility from Alex—besides, they did ask for *her* in particular. And this was her area of expertise.

"Ms. Wood, you look even better outside of that room!" the younger of the men said in a deep voice. Every syllable pronounced by his lips echoed visually inside her head. The sounds were silent, but she drew his personality from the lips: abusive, egotistical, power-hungry. This was the norm for most men in politics, and some in business.

"Marci, we were hoping you could guide us through the ups and downs of colour preservation," Alex said.

"I'd love to." She straightened her back and stepped into what would have been a spotlight position, had this been a play. *Where do I even start?* she wondered.

"Ok. Well, I suppose I should start at the beginning. The basis for what we do here is pigment. Now, just for the sake of detail, pigment is an insoluble powder mixed with a matrix, any kind of liquid in order to bind it and turn it into paint. The powder itself can be made from earth, mineral, or biological matter and must be solid at ambient temperatures." *Not a bad beginning!* Unfortunately, a strand of hair had come loose from the red banana clip and she flung it back with a quick, spastic spasm of the right hand.

"The two main qualities a good pigment should have are: permanence and stability. This means they must not fade over time, with exposure to light or air, or —as some do—blacken over time." Again a flick of the head redirects the falling lock of hair to the back.

"Unstable pigments are called 'fugitive' colours." She said and paused for a breath. The damn hair, it made her lose her train of thought. She took the time to tuck it behind her ear—out of the way for now. During the brief repose she made eye contact with the younger of the two and she realized it was the same man who winked at her in the Archives Office. Why was he staring at her like that? *At* her? …More like *through* her.

"Let's jump back about 400,000 years. Humans, barely more than animal at this point, were using grinding equipment to mash pigments in order to decorate their bodies and the walls of the caves. The first signs of aesthetics, developed simultaneously with religion, art, and cultural memory. If we stood in one of those caves we might sympathize with those monkey men. Some feelings are universal, after all." She was rambling. *Dammit, Marci!* she thought. Eye contact again. This man was staring into her soul.

"But I digress." Alex nodded in the background. "During the prehistoric times, mainly ochres and oxides were used. And until the Industrial Revolution the technical range of colours was severely limited. That's why scanning these pigments is such a meticulous job. Most of the books we work with were made before William Henry Perkins synthesized *mauveine* blue in 1856 and spurred on a century of modern synthetics."

"Sorry, you mean there were synthetics before the 1800s?" the older man was asking.

"Well, yes. Good question!" she smiled, genuinely happy that someone was taking an interest in her spiel. "In fact, prior to the 19th Century, there were two synthetic pigments in existence. One was lead white, which was being used widely by the renaissance for underpainting in oil painting. It's still used today, despite being a toxin due to its structural properties." She could see on their faces there was a question coming so she preempted it.

"Although it is harder for artists to find, it is still available in small tubes, but no longer in large quantities required for underpainting. For the most part, lead white has been supplanted by 'titanium white', a mineral so benign that you will even find it in toothpaste. Lead white, however, is still used by militaries around the world, as well as by industry. The most common example of which is lines on the road."

"Really?"

"Yes. It is valued for its resistance to water and its durability. The funny thing is that other poisonous colours are readily available, but lead white has become a rarity these days."

"What about the other one?"

"Pardon?" The question had thrown her off. She could have gone on about white for a long time, but the other synthetic had a longer history and was by far more…er, colourful, so to speak.

"I mean, what about the other synthetic? You said there were two." Again, the older man. You see, he had been a history major in university many years ago. This mini-lecture somehow made him feel in touch with the days when he could abuse drink and womanize freely. He was returned to an era when youth and brilliance shone brightly and he was convinced that anything was possible. It was the beginning of a new age of promised wealth and technology, and people all over North America were opening up to the sexual revolution. It was his heyday. And here he was, time-travelling back vicariously through Marci's presentation.

Whether the others were genuinely interested I cannot say. Alex had never heard this before and despite his urge to interrupt with comments, was enjoying Marci's act. The younger man was staring at her with a hunger.

"Ah, yes! Egyptian blue!" The prospect of talking about these colours was creating physical changes in her body. Chemicals in her brain fired off, her heartbeat increased and her pupils dilated.

"Egyptian blue was the very first synthesized colour. Its first occurrence was in the 4th Dynasty on limestone sculptures and cylinder seals. Egyptian blue is a marvelous colour. It was likely produced in order to imitate *lapis lazuli* or turquoise, which were both cherished stones at the time. Using the stones to create

30

a pigment was impractical and the Egyptians had to figure out another way to create a blue paint.

"You see blue was important in Egypt because it was used to paint the eye of Ra. In fact, the word 'blue' also meant 'the human eye', and thus 'the eye of Ra'.

"What word was that?" Alex asked. You could tell he had been waiting for a while now to get a word in. This question was not really out of interest as much as trying to put her in a bind. He thought she might just wing it and make it up; likely a word with no vowels, he thought.

"The word is '*wadjet*'," she said calmly and continued. "*Wadjet* is the name for a local deity. She was a snake goddess and a protector of the land over sea."

"Probably because of the annual flooding," the older man added.

"Probably." She nodded, paused and noticed that lock of hair had come loose again. She let it free and it hung like a perfectly placed lock, covering the edge of her left eye and rested against her chin.

"Anyway, Egyptian blue is amazing because the production method is so intricate. I guess a bunch of factors contributed to allow them to make it: One, Egyptian society had settled and had a large class of clerics who didn't have to do physical labour. Two, they had entered the Bronze Age so were aware of the blue-green bronze oxide. Also bronze was readily available. Three, they needed pigments to decorate the huge building projects the pharaohs were sponsoring.

"As I said, the process is intricate and required many ingredients." She looked to the ceiling, avoiding eye contact this time and continued, "I won't bore you with the details, but basically the pigment was a luminous sky blue captured in a glass matrix. It was incredibly versatile and durable and spread to the limits of the Roman Empire. The manufacture of this colour lead to a vast industry that would eventually become the art of glass craft. Egyptian blue, or *blue frit* as some call it today, was used until the end of the Roman Period; then suddenly its process was lost to history."

"Around AD. 400, right?" It's remarkable how once you get post-middle-age men talking about history, they feel it is their duty to impart their knowledge to the younger generation. History is the catnip of older men.

"So," she realized that she had to bring this discussion back to her work at the library, "these colours are all categorized according to their physical spectrum. And it is our job to make sure that they remain accurate."

"And how do you guarantee they are accurate when you archive these ancient books?" This time it was the younger man, surely sensing that Marci's talk was wrapping up and seeing a gap to steer the lecture back down to earth.

"It actually has a lot to do with physics, but I am no expert there." In the background, Alex was pulling a funny face. The two men were all business, but he still somehow wanted a piece of the spotlight, even if it meant trying to make Marci smile. And she did.

"I can, however, say that since pigments selectively absorb and reflect light, perception of colour is intimately connected to the colour of the source light. Sunlight has a high colour temperature and uniform spectrum, so it is classified as standard white light. If the light source changes, so does the colour. This means the ideal laboratory uses a light source close to sunlight. In our lab, we use 'Daylight 6500K' which is equal to bright sunlight. Also, as you probably noticed the lab is 98% grey. This is necessary to reduce ambient colour reflection."

"Good job, Marci," Alex chimed in. "I suppose that about covers it, eh?"

"It certainly does," she said, "Any questions, gentlemen?"

"No, not at all. Well done, Ms. Wood," the older man said, "Excellent presentation!" Really he wished it kept going, but he was getting tired standing around.

The younger man, however, smiled a classic fake smile (lips tight and corners tucked deep into the face), raised one eyebrow and clapped his hands. It was clear to Marci what was going on in Alex's mind: *What a fuckin' douchebag, this guy is! I hope he gets beaned in the junk by a flying wrench.* She telegraphed a secret agreement by means of a brief flash of mutually intelligible eye contact.

"Well, gentlemen, this concludes this portion of the tour. May I ask if there is anything pre-Guttenberg that you would like to have a look at? Ehrenberg, Vitruvius, Shakespeare, da Vinci, the Bible? Anything that strikes your fancy?" Alex was clearly baiting them; he knew they didn't have any da Vinci. *Da Vinci?* Marci thought.

"Da Vinci!" the young guy says.

"Oh, I'm sorry, that one is being processed right now. How about some Dum-*ass* instead?" Marci smiled. Even though he purposefully mispronounced it 'dum-*ass*', Alex maintained his composure. It was a lame joke, but kind of unexpected. There was a brief millisecond of silence and then the older man gave a sudden, explosive laugh. Just one, as if he suddenly got the joke.

"Was that French?" he was seriously thinking about it. Then, quickly, "I suppose we should move on, shouldn't we, Mr. Olopolous…uh, Oulopolis-Propos." It was the younger man.

"Propoupolis-Oloupos, that is."

"Right," he never looked at Alex, the whole time he was staring at Marci, unblinking.

"Um, if you'd excuse me gentlemen, I must get back to work." Marci turned around and walked to the elevator. Behind her, she heard their voices and the metallic friction of the humidity-controlled drawer closing. She breathed, relieved to leave the situation. She pressed the elevator button. Then suddenly:

"Ms. Wood, one moment please." She closed her eyes. It was the young guy. She realized that she didn't even know his name. *Shit*, she thought to herself.

She turned around.

"I was wondering if you could show me to the washroom?" he said.

"Certainly." She smiled. "Right this way." The elevator

doors slid open and she watched Alex debating with the other man as the doors drew in like operatic curtains.

Inside the elevator was quiet. No muzak even. Just the sounds of distant mechanics and breathing; two humans contained in a space the size of a walk-in closet. He stood close to her.

"Ms. Wood, you're not an academic, are you?"

"I…no, I'm not. I used to be a colour corrector for a film company about—"

"I'm gonna be honest with you. Women approach me five or six times a day, but I'm very particular about what I like. And you look faaaaaar too sexy to be an academic. So I'm giving you an opportunity here…" The elevator stopped and the doors slid open.

"Right this way, Mr…"

"Haywood," he said, "Aaron Haywood."

"Well, Mr. Haywood, the men's room is just down this corridor on the left."

"Ms. Wood, what colour is your underwear? I think the colour of a person's underwear tells a lot about their personality."

"Excuse me?! I could be wearing stained grandma undies, but I don't see how that's *any* of your business!"

"It will be soon enough. You see, I am irresistible. A real catch. And I hope this reaction is just timidness. Next time we meet, don't wear the grey, we'll go for some haut-cuisine and let the romance begin." (He pronounced the 't' in haut)

What the hell is this? Who is this guy? she thought.

"I hope you enjoy the rest of your tour, Mr. Haywood." She walked away, half expecting him to continue this ridiculously egotistical mating dance, but there was nothing. When she looked over her shoulder just before entering the Archives, he had disappeared—into the toilet most likely.

The rest of the day proceeded as normal. Alex soon returned and continued his work scanning a copy of Blake's *Book of Thel*. They talked and laughed about the day. Marci explained

34

how the young guy just kept getting stranger and stranger. She exaggerated his expressions and almost danced him into caricature when she acted out the scene during the elevator ride.

"What a doofus, man." Alex said.

"Yeah, I've never been hit on like *that* before. I should record that in my diary." Alex laughed, messing up a scan of the plate when Thel talks with the Clot of Clay. "Dear dairy," she went on, "today I met a man who hurled words like turds at me in an attempt to flirt. His name was Douché Dumb-*ass*." The rest of the day flew by, partially because they wasted about an hour or more chatting to the suits, and partially because they enjoyed talking smack about the weirdo pick-up artist.

"You should have said 'Moby *Dick*!'" she laughed.

Alex always changed his clothes after work. Without exception. From grey to silk-screened shirts, tight jeans (he is European and could get away with it!), and brightly coloured sneakers. He looked like an artifact from the wax museum, lavishly decorated in a mock-70s style. He changed in the storage room, which served as a locker room as well, despite the fact that anyone could walk in on you at any time. Alex didn't care, though. In fact, he fantasized about someone walking in on him almost every time. He'd select a voyeur-victim—a female librarian usually—and craft an elaborate situation in his mind about how she would be scavenging the library for a bucket, and as a last resort she'd wander into the Rare Collections floor, and open the grey door to find Alex in his underwear (red boxers with a tiny superman crest on the leg and a marquee saying 'MAN OF STEEL'), while flexing his abs. He always flexed his abs when he was changing, even if no one was around. He'd been doing it so long that it became a reflex.

On the other hand, Marci remained in her grey suit until she got home. Actually, she had accumulated over 5 grey suits, some with pants for wintertime and other with skirts for fun. But today, Marci wouldn't make it home in a clean suit.

"See ya, Marci! I'm off to the races!"

"Bye bye," she said, fumbling in her purse. The lights were being turned off systematically. And somewhere in a little room, a security guard was watching them on 32 different monotone screens.

The night was a cool, early October evening and the wind blew a perverted chill into her shirt. She pulled her suit jacket tight and proceeded to walk around the building to the parking lot. Her stomach was empty and her hands a little weak. There was a *grrrrrrrrrrrrrrrrrrrrrrowlllll* from inside her, which seemed to echo as soon as she stepped onto the asphalt of the parking lot and, as if on cue, Aaron Haywood stepped into the light halfway between her and the parking lot.

There was something very theatrical about his sudden appearance, something posed about his stance, and his eyes seemed to reflect like a cat's in the headlights. His tie had been removed and his shirt was unbuttoned to the chest. *How long had he been waiting?* she thought. She then intuitively counted the cars in the parking lot: two. Only two left. The manager and the security guard's. *Maybe he is watching on the CCTV cameras. In a few seconds he will run down here. He leaves around the same time as us, doesn't he? Oh my god. Ohmygod, omigod!* There was no hope of the security guard coming down. The thought of her being alone in the parking lot without help started to settle in her mind. Alex had already left, and the parking lot was shielded behind the buildings. In a flash, all the possible scenarios ran through her head, most of them bad. At that thought she immediately freaked out inside. Thoughts ran like rail-lines through her brain, crisscrossing with those yellow and black barriers chiming "DANGER! DANGER!" to nearby traffic.

As I mentioned before, Marci was a tad paranoid and expected the worst in this situation. The only thing to do was run. NOW! Before he could close the distance.

So she did.

She ran around the library, through the alley and onto the road. As she exited the alley, she turned her head and noticed his shape in profile cross the boundary of the parking lot.

"Why are you playing games?!" His voice echoed between the brick buildings of the alley. Motion became a blur as chemicals flooded Marci Wood's brain and body. The ancient reactions of threatened animals returned through time to enter her as she jumped the curb and sprinted, leg muscles tight, towards the nearest intersection. The street was dark and sounds bounced of the pavement: the staccato of her clicking high-heels, the swishing of clothes behind her, footsteps beating a rhythm, him closing in on her.

"I'm single!" he yelled. And Marci hopped over a parked car. "Don't play hard to get!" She now felt her heart, pumping, pumping in her chest. In her throat. Her legs. In her head. A bass beat.

Duff-duff. duff-duff. duff-duff.

When her feet hit the asphalt she was suddenly illuminated by the streetlight, features were exaggerated in ciaruscuro shadows, and there was a bitter taste in her mouth. She ran in the middle of the street—in and out, in and out, of the lights. He was gaining behind her.

"There's nothing wrong with me, you know!" His voice was close. Too close. *I've gotta get out of the street*, she thought. Her jaw clenched. She heard someone else yell something, but it was just background noise to her.

"Do you have a mental problem?!" He sounded truly irritated, and she could hear his breath on her. The opposite curb was approaching and she leapt, lingering in the air like a lithe deer. The landing was superb, but something went wrong. Something was caught. The sewer grate! The physics at play tossed her body onto the sidewalk in a tight arc, tethered to the metal covering by her heel. It snapped off as soon as she hit the ground and she rolled a few feet into the narrow alley between the old courthouse and the Pottery Barn.

She quickly rolled on her back to kick him as he approached. A moment passed and luckily she was not raped yet, nor harassed, or propositioned by this lunatic. In fact, she couldn't even hear his raving voice anymore. There was only silence. *Am I going crazy?* She picked herself up and stepped to the dark edge of the alley—one foot high, one foot low. Peeking out from there, she witnessed a figure stumble from behind a parked van. *It's him!* But there was someone else there too. The other shadow threw a punch that looked professional and knocked the dazed Aaron Haywood down. Kay-OH!

At this point Marci turned and ran out of the alley down the street towards the lights. And when she looked back over her shoulder, they were both gone.

THE HOUSE

A violent act leaves deep tracks, like knuckle-prints on a sandbag. Above her closet, she wrote "This too shall pass..." She repainted her room in a pastel green, a pale jade. Pantone™ 324. She then employed a gold marker once used in a homegrown bookbinding operation to scrawl enormous French curves and daffodils along the edges of the green field. The room changed to a meadow, to an Art Nouveau *altier en plein air*. And above the door "**This too shall pass**" in her own variation of a hand drawn Garamond.

She had owned the house for about 2 years now. It was actually sold through a police auction. The basement area, where Marci has domesticated, was once the crime-den of an ecstasy production ring. It was the laboratory—what the chemists-*cum*-gangsters called 'the Pit'. It was an old house in the Annex area of the city, in a neighbourhood of beautiful gardens and ancient, wooden Victorian houses. There was no way one would assume a pharma-criminal ring was producing MDMA in a basement next to old widows and city-council members. Marci's old associate first discovered the massive auction. It included all kinds of science apparatus, furniture (in particular a mahogany desk circa 1816 which he had his eyes on), as well as holdings all over the city. Marci acquired the house on Euclid Street mainly because the inheritance from her mother allowed her a large wager. It was a difficult time for her and, I suppose, she needed something concrete to pour her feelings of loss into. The house had been her saviour.

     A week after she bought it, she moved in with a weapon-rack of brushes, rollers, paints, and palet-knives. The building was a chemically altered, deteriorating zombie, and Marci had to operate. She started at the heart, the lab in the basement, and worked her way up. Initially, she painted what would be her future room, a deep red. It was crimson, a velour close to Pantone™ 202 or 222. She then decided it was not deep enough. It needed more. A profundity which matched her sadness: a deep, pure blue.

She found the muffle-furnace on her second day of living in the house. It was hidden behind a stack of drywall sheets. Marci saw this as a sign. She would build the blue from scratch. It became her process, her catharsis.

She decided to make ultramarine, the deepest and most permanent of the blues, and easy enough to make from scratch. (Ingredients needed: Clay,
                         Fine, soft white sand
                         Charcoal,
                         Sulphur.)

The baking started on the 6th evening. She watched the white clay heat, turn green, then red. It was an alchemical process that burned inside the oven and inside her heart. She watched it shift, transform and magically settle on a pure blue. The colour of the sky and water, of all things natural and emotional combined, heated into a brick the size of a deck of cards.

On the 7th day, everything was silent. The oven had finished and when Marci, in a spotless white apron complete with long gloves and a doctor's mask, tried to look inside it, she could not see through the window. There was an opaque blue blocking her view. When she opened the furnace, a fine blue mist escaped and filled the room. Momentarily, Marci was enveloped in the blue of her mother's death. Staring through the cloud of mourning was like looking into the evening sky, beyond which she could barely make out the fuzzy outline of the muffle-furnace with its own deep cavity on the other side.

And when the dust settled, she was covered in a blue film and she found the ultramarine sitting in a blue-coloured vault, where malign chemicals were once baked into designer drugs.

She removed it with a pair of tongs, careful beyond necessity, as if she was birthing it, the blue, her twin from the feeling of loss itself. After placing it onto the table, she crushed a corner of the brick and spontaneously started weeping, as if she had committed some crime against this brick she had just given life. You see, Marci had grown incredibly attached to the clay during the making of this colour. It had transformed inside the oven and grown inside her mind overnight, becoming a living essence. And the moment she broke the corner of the small, powdery rectangle, she felt she had hurt it, caused it to suffer. Immediately, manically even, she mixed the powdered blue with oil and dripping tears, made it transparent: a thin blue glaze. She rubbed this nurtured blue all over her crimson wall, daubing it with tissues, covering the red in the depth of the heavens. It deepened, opened up space and felt somehow alive. She had breathed life into the walls, made it a womb. When it dried, she knew this would be her bedroom. The terminus of her emotional system, where she could sleep, live, heal.

Since then, she had single-handedly renovated the house, turned it into a triplex, repainted the walls over 38 times in a spectrum of colours that could give the crayola 48-set a run for its money, and officially become a landlady, though she detested that term.

The ground floor was her own kitchen and bathroom, as well as the apartment she rented to an old man, Mr. Killarney. He was a gardener and she allowed him to make the best of the small front plot she had. He was a genius in his own right and the front plot, little more than a 2 meter square, became the back corner of the Garden of Eden itself, filled with an array of flowers, a variety of leaves big and small, and a vine climbing up the old oak tree shielding the house from the sun.

The top floor was an apartment she once rented to Avram Israel. He was a well educated, middle-aged man. Marci believed he lived a pious life of solitude and poverty. He was an orthodox Jew, who had to climb up to his flat using the fire escape in the back. It was a small apartment with everything he could possibly have needed: a bathroom; a balcony; a huge kitchen (relatively speaking); and a room with an enormous, curtainless window, which let the sun in early in the morning.

Avram's space was beautifully decorated, colour-coded by Marci according to his personality. At first, he was angry, fuming when he saw that she had painted his room puce. Do you know what I mean by 'puce'?

According to the comedy-sized Oxford Dictionary I use mainly as a free-weight, puce is *"flea colour, a reddish- to purplish-brown."* It looks like a homeless pink.

Over time, however, Avram noticed that the flea colour calmed him. Maybe that paranoid, eccentric Marci was right after all? During the time he stayed there, he knew Marci only as his landlady; they rarely talked about personal things.

There was one occasion, however, that would return to him much later. It was after Marci started wearing only grey, when his toilet had broken and Marci entered his house with a portly Portugese man in order to do some maintenance. While the contractor worked, fishing old pieces of plastic out of the pipes with a long wire hook, Marci sat down at Avram's table to drink a cup of tea. She had noticed a painting of Jacob wrestling an angel, hanging in hallway and asked about it.

This simple act opened the door to the only profound conversation she and Avram Isreal would have. He told her about his name.

"Do you know vat 'Israel' means?" he asked her with his subtle accent.

"I'm not sure," she replied blowing onto her hot tea.

"Well...This painting is of Jacob Israel. He is the fadder of the 12 tribes of the Jews."

"He has your last name!"

"Indeed," he continued. "Jacob is popular these days for his son and the 'technicolour dream coat', but he is also the same Jacob who dreamt of a ladder to Heaven and wrestled with an angel."

"Hmmm..."

"The name 'Israel' means 'he who wrestles with the

Divine Angel'. But some Jews believe he actually struggled with God himself."

"I forgot about that story from the Bible," she admitted.

"Yes, Ms. Vood, dat story is much *much* more important for us than for you Christians. You see, Jacob is my relative. He is the patriarch of Jewish people everywhere. He is related to all Jews, perhaps."

"So do you feel like you wrestle with angels sometimes?"

"Ach, ve all fight with the divine from time to time," he said then looked at her over the frames of his glasses. He seemed to be inspecting her, judging her character. "And how about yourself? I sense you wrestle with angels more than me, Ms. Vood."

Marci considered this suggestion deeply, swallowing a mouthful of hot tea.

"I'm not sure," she said. "I haven't really thought about it. But I can say that I don't believe in God."

"Vhy not?" The man asked in the polite tone of a parent, or a wiseman tactfully avoiding offence to his host.

"Well, to be honest," she inhaled deeply, "I don't think God would let innocent people die in horrible ways. I also think that a divine being would have some sense of purpose for every person."

"Good questions. Dhey are all relevant," he said, furrowing his brow. "But all life has to come to an end some time. Ve all have our time, and death, unfortunately, is unavoidable. In fact, I think death is the one thing that makes life worth something." He said then continued, "but I feel like you have a specific quarrel with *Shaddai*."

"I do." In the background she could hear the contractor swearing at the process of dredging the sewage pipes.

"I am always listening," he said as he fetched some cookies from the cupboard.

"You may not know this, Mr. Israel, but my mother died a few years ago. Her death was a stupid accident that left my life empty."

43

"Ahh, so you think her death was unnecessary? You think that God vould not take her from you?"

"Yes. I cannot believe that a good God would leave my life so empty. If God existed, He would not take my only parent so soon. I mean, she was still young. She could have lived another 40 years at least!"

"I understand your pain." He looked down at his hands. "But don't forget dat God is good, too. Despite all the suffering in the world and in your life. I am sure he has a plan for you, too."

"The universe is senseless," she said biting her bottom lip and furrowing her brow. "I feel stuck in my job. A job I would have given my right arm for a few years ago. You know, I always thought that this job would be my destiny. But it hurts my heart to wake up every day and dress in this grey suit. And what a cosmic joke it is for me to get my dream job and hate it so much.

"Vhy do you hate it so much?"

"Ugh," she sighed. "Well, to start, my manager is an anal book-Nazi—excuse the expression. I can't actually touch the books I work with. They are treasures of history and literature, but I can't actually touch them!"

"That is a good start. It sounds like you are hafing power struggles with the people above you. How are your coworkers?"

"Oh, they are fine. I spend most of my time with this Greek guy, who ranges from outright annoying to hysterically funny."

"I see. So, if you hate the job so much, vhy not quit?" Avram Israel had, in that moment, asked the one question that could have changed Marci's entire destiny. Of course, it was a question Marci had asked herself many times before, but to hear it from another person, someone who had that caring parental aura she needed in her life, made her consider the posssiblity in a realistic sense. It also made her angry. She didn't realize it at first, but after a few moments the ire boiled up beneath her scalp and drained into her body in the form of a downwards flushing of blood.

She stayed quiet, staring at her half-empty tea cup. *Why*

not quit? she thought. *I don't have to sit here and listen to this old man give me advice,* she thought. It was an irrational process inside her. And perhaps because she had no idea how to address her

anger, she simply said with the lump of emotion in her throat: "My mother's accident was senseless and if I believed in God, I would not be able to forgive Him for her death."

"Perhaps you just need someone to talk to," he said staring at her with his amber eyes. "You know, Ms. Vood, you can talk to me anytime. My own daughters live far away, and it is nice to share a cup of tea with a young voman every once in a while."

"Well, I suppose I will just continue to wrestle with my angel until I come to terms with her pointless death and the irony of my perfect job."

"Amen." Avram knew he could never convince Marci of the error in either of these beliefs. He just wanted her to feel happy, to heal the pain of her mother's tragic end. He was a clever man and diverted the conversation to a lighter subject: the house.

This is where he discovered her deep love of the house. He knew that she had made it, that she had given it a second chance. And everything inside was masterfully finished because of her.

His one deep conversation with Marci left him with the impression that she was a seed. She had the potential to be truly happy, but that she was encased in the longing for love. She needed a parental figure who could support her and guide her to fruitful pastures. Unfortunely, she—perhaps subconsciously—avoided any further personal conversations with him, the one man who might have stepped in to be her father figure.

Avram was a kind man who loved her for who she was. He knew Marci was wrestling with an important existential question. A question that every prophet and pope must have considered at some point. He sensed that she was locked in the grips of a force far greater than her—a divine angel she would have to confront alone, without the help of anyone else.

Anyways, let's continue with the story…

ALEX

"Hey *Mars*-icans, you look a li'l blue? What' up?"

"Nah, I'm OK. Just bored stiff these days. It's like I have no life anymore."

"That so?" He smiled a broad open-toothed smile. The kind you see in children's cartoons. "You know, you *could* go out with me every once in a while."

Marci was scanning a book, *Arte Subtilissima*, a beautiful book about letterforms. One of the first typography manuals, and written by a Basque painter and mathmetician in the 1500s. In fact, this book was not as old as most of the others they had been scanning. She inserted the wand and scoffed, "What is that supposed to mean? Like you want a date?"

"*Non, non, non, mon chou-chou*, I mean, you and me in tight jumpsuits, running about with beats in our heads, *alcool* in our blood, and animal-like desire in our souls. Naw what I mean?"

"You want to rob a bank?"

"Well, yes, but I meant you could join me on my bi-weekly night time adventure."

"I—"

"No charge the first time!" This made her laugh and Alex felt satisfied. They laughed together like bobbing heads in the sea of grey. Then he pushed the capture button and when the screen cleared the image of a page with four scripted letters: t, v, u, and an x with a crossbar. On the top of the page is smaller, but equally beautiful script was written "*de libros*", and on the bottom, "*domini*" in what could have been a very modern uncial at that time.

"Hey, do you know what *Arte Subtilissima* means anyway?" Alex seemed genuinely curious. He hardly ever looked at the books in detail. In fact, the previous manager had hired him especially because he didn't care for books. I guess he figured that a tall, lanky, shaved caveman would be much less likely to open a rare book than a trained academic with an interest in original manuscripts. Maybe he was right, too. Alex never touched the books; he followed orders like a soldier. Actually, maybe a soldier is pushing it…He followed orders as if he worked at Burger World—loosely, but he always wore his hairnet.

"I think it means 'a subtle art' or maybe 'the most delicate art' actually."

"These letters?"

"Yeah, just look at them. They are beautiful, don't you think?" The new spread scanned onto the computer screen: four more letters with a date *m.d.xl.viii* at the bottom. He read out the letters as they scanned. "Y…Z…uh, something…D." Marci looked over at the screen.

"What the hell is the last one?" He looked honestly confused. "Seven?"

"Not seven. They used Roman numbers in the 1500s."

"Well, can *you* figure it out, Ms. Marcus Antonius?" Marci was staring at the screen intensely. It wasn't like any letterform she had ever seen. Totally alien to her.

"Hmm…I dunno. Maybe a small N?"

"Nah, I think we already scanned that one with baby H, M, and P." It bothered him a little that he couldn't read the old script and he was sure it bothered Marci even more, but within seconds he was revisiting a moment he had with the delicious Italian girl he met two nights ago. They left the club full of the 'animal desire' he mentioned to Marci and stumbled next to a quiet main road. His arm was around her body, wrapped onto her right breast. He could feel the nipple, a little pea under the fabric. Her hand was in his back pocket. The pheromones were pumping and they stopped next to a car, making out against the side of it. The street was quiet and Alex fumbled with the backdoor's lever. To his surprise, it opened and they got inside to get to business. Because he was too tall for the small car, intercourse was out of the question. So he just fingered her on the backseat. Now, the moment he is struggling to get out of his head is when she came. The sensation itself, like a daytime hallucination was on repeat: all over his hand, she sprayed juices everywhere in the back. So to complete the set, she jerked him off and they got out of the car to continue their trek.

"Arrr!" Marci screamed.

"Eh?"

"No, I think it's definitely R, not A."

"Oh, that!" he was suddenly back in reality. Eyes (and attention) refocused on the screen. It really might have been an R. But then it looked more like a 7.

"Yeah, could be," he admitted, slightly indifferent now. "You just might be right. But it could be a seven, a wacky small I, or a Q even," he took a deep breath, "but for your sake," (and then in a Martin Luther King Jr. voice), "let's record this day in the history of typography as the day Marci Antonius Wood discovered the miniscule 'r' in '*Arte Sublissimus*'!" She smiled a little reluctantly. "There," he returned the smile, "you feel better now?"

"A little. But it's 'sub*tilis*si*ma*'."

"You little sourpuss! Why don't you just admit you are interested in a wee drinkie-poo tonight and get it over with?"

"Ok, ok ok, but only because you are virtually forcing me!"

"You know you want to come." Actually, he was pretty sure she had been interested in going out with him for a while now, and Alex also had his own motives for asking her out.

You see, Marci is kind of a secretive person, and although they had gotten close, she still hadn't shared much. At least not the most important things.

After work, Alex changed, as he always did, in the storage room. Today he wore European-style briefs, you know, the kind without the front flap that looks like a speedo in disguise. He also wore navy blue pants, a tight red t-shirt with navy rims, all covered with a heavy sheep-skin jacket. He thought it went well with the hefty sideburns he was nursing. He was ready to go out.

When he came out, he saw that Marci was waiting in her grey suit in front of the elevator.

"You're not gonna change?"

"I didn't know there was going to be a party, so I left my jumpsuit at home, unfortunately."

"Well, it doesn't matter. Just don't act all work on me when we get to the bar."

"Yeah, that reminds me," the door opened and they both stepped in, "where exactly are we going?"

"Now *that's* the spirit! You're gettin' excited, aren't you?" He smiled a broad smile and checked his hair in the reflection of the silver panel above the buttons.

"Hmmm…Just wanna know what to expect, I guess." At that, the door opened and they both exited onto the street.

"Let's walk," he said and lit a smoke. They walked for about 10 minutes, crossing the city seemingly on old Indian trails, using backstreets, transversing parks, and zig-zagging diagonally between major intersections. Alex knew his way around. See, he was a born walker. The city has been his home ever since he was old enough to go out alone. What childhood he had in Greece, had long since became foggy memories and photographs under the basement stairs. So he felt comfortable in the alleys and parks and the tiny, little streets where Chinese people grow vegetables in their yards and high school dropouts turn houses into fashion boutiques. This, to him, was the real city.

This and 'The Dishonest Preacher' pub.

The building itself was a mish-mash of colonial and hyper-modern. The bottom floor was all glass—enormous, industrial-sized sheets, with dollar-signs and frilly crosses etched into it. The top floors were lushly decorated Victorian-style Romanesque pilasters and brick arches. The building itself glowed from the warm lighting and laughing faces inside.

"This is it," he said and held open the door for Marci. "See, I can be a gentleman."

"You're very kind," she smiled at him, still in awe of the place. Inside, the lighting tinted everything a peach colour, but

Marci's suit remained stubbornly grey. Her white shirt, however, came to match her skin tone remarkably well, creating the effect that she was wearing no shirt at all, just a grey skirt and jacket with a very low cut front.

The atmosphere inside was friendly and many people greeted Alex.

"Inside this place, you're a bit of a Greek god, eh?" She sat down at a small round table on a high chair. He joined her after winking a hello at some women at a nearby booth.

"What can I say?" He still seemed distracted, looking around. Then he made eye contact with a busty brunette and waved her over. She hopped along and waved spastically. When she arrived, they greeted each other familiarly and she was introduced to Marci as Franscesca. Then he ordered two gin-and-tonics from her.

"Gin-and-tonic, huh?" Marci's mouth was scrunched a bit.

"Yeah, girls like that, right? You won't be disappointed they make them killer here." Then he sat back and suddenly focused on her. "Now, Marci tell me: why do you never go out?"

"No, I *do* go out. I do, but just not so often anymore."

"You should have more fun, Mars," he said and pulled a pack of cigarettes from his pocket. "I'm not trying to accuse you, but I see that deep inside, you are sad or depressed or something not good. I just wanna help you, little one."

"Well, I..." she sighed deeply and suddenly a squeaky voice handed over two gin-and-tonics, glowing unnaturally blue. While the waitress chatted with Alex, Marci knocked back the drink as if it was water. It did taste really good, so she ordered another one.

"Wowzahs!" he said and downed his too. "Make that a duo, Fran." He shook his head as she walked away in a gesture of disbelief. "Anyway, you were about to say something momentous, I think," he said.

"Well, I was just gonna say that I feel a little disappointed with the job."

"The job? Marci, this job is made for you. You can be honest with me, man. I'm not going to judge you. Just look at me! Who am I to judge?" She was suddenly confused, what was he trying to do. *Why the interrogation?* But without a moment in between, he changed the subject to the table of women sitting in the booth. "You see those chicas over thar yonder?"

"Yeah?"

"The one with the red dress is actually a man. He trannied it up in order to get into the country. He got married with a Green Peace guy to fool the government. The year after he got in, they changed the law to make same-sex marriage a legal option. Anyways, he started dressing like a girl as a means to an end, but liked it so much it he eventually changed his sex. Didn't want his wanger back after the dust settled, I s'pose."

"How do you know that? And why are you telling me this?"

"Well…I, how shall I put this," he took an extra long drag off the smoke, "discovered it first hand one night. We were gettin' it on and I asked if I needed to put on a condom. She told me that she couldn't have kids." He had been staring at the woman-once-man in the red dress and she sent a small smile his way.

"So, what did you do? I mean…" She didn't really want to know, but without thinking, the words were said.

"So, I came inside her. I didn't even think about it. I mean, a woman says something like that to a man after two hours of dry-humping…"

"Jesus! Stop already!" She made a grimacing face and stuck out her tongue. "So you didn't know it was a man?"

"No idea," he said, "it only occurred to me to ask why she couldn't have children the next morning. And let me tell you… After that I have technically done *absolutely* everything."

"Well, she's pretty hot for a man, I must admit."

"Yeah, anyway, how about you, Marci Wood?"

"Well, for a woman, I'm not too shabby, if I do say so myself." She held up her glass for a cheers. He laughed an explosive one, a mock chortle of sorts, then *klinked* his glass with

51

hers.

"True, but that's not what I meant. I mean what's the strangest thing you've ever done?"

"Well, certainly not changed my sex." She stared at the woman in the red and felt the alcohol slip down her throat, and momentarily realized how it was affecting her brain, her co-ordination, and eyesight. "How about sleeping with another woman?"

"What?!" He looked deep into her eyes, trying to detect any trace of lies. Then he asked, "Seriously?"

"Maybe?" Smiling widely, she gave no hint either way.

"Come on, Mars," he said, "You can't do this to me. Tell me."

"I'll just leave it to your imagination. Ask me later when I'm more drunk. I'm going to talk to Ms. Tranny over there." And she got up and left him burning on the stool at the table.

The majority of the night she spent avoiding serious conversation with him, instead talking to hipsters, wannabe movie stars, flirting with the transgendered, and drinking a wide array of coloured beverages. He found her in the final moments before closing time in the women's washroom, sitting on the counter, bathed in blue light. She was talking to a tall, black woman with long dreads. It was utter nonsense, but Alex was happy she was enjoying herself. He grabbed her by the arm and made her say goodbye to her new friend. Then they left the establishment.

The night was a bit cool. Marci had a little trouble walking by herself, so Alex supported her, but found it very awkward because of their size differences. He thought about hailing a cab, one of many flowing down the street in a yellowy procession, but she was soon crouched in the flowerbed.

"You OK, toots?" There was no sound of vomiting, so he checked on her. It looked like she was sleeping. He touched her head, the hair was out of control. She looked up and they made drunken eye contact. She hiccupped and said to him in earnest: "Do you want to sleep with me?"

"Now? Here?" he laughed. "Come on, girl. I'll take you home safely."

"Can we go to a coffee shop, Alex?" He agreed and after 10 minutes of convincing her that she can walk by herself, off they went.

The nearest coffee shop was one of the typical 24-hour places where homeless people go on cold nights, and the ugly side of nightlife rears its head. The store was empty except for the college student mopping the floor. Alex sat her down at a corner table near the toilet and ordered two coffees and a bunch of soft cookies. He also got a giant bucket of water, the biggest cup they had.

"Drink," he said, "You need this. The cookies are great too." She sat up and sipped the water. It seemed that the smell of coffee was sobering her up.

"Did you really sleep with a woman?"

"Nah, but I almo*sh*t did. I almost had a threesome once wi*ss* anotha' girl at my friend's cottage."

"Respect!" he shouted and the staff, looked over at him. "Yeah, man! Threesome chick over here! D'you hear that?" She stuck her tongue out and punched him in the arm.

"Dammit, Alexander," she became instantly drunk and wobbly again. "Why you gotta tell everyone? That'*sssh* why I never tell you the im*por*tant things."

"OK, I'm sorry. But I really want to know something and I promise not to tell anyone."

"What?"

"Why are you so sad recently?"

"You *really* wanna know?"

"Yeah."

"Even if it is kinda a buzzkill?"

"If it's sad it's gotta be a buzzkill, don't it?"

"Last Monday was the anniversary of my mom's death."

"Shit." He made her drink another gulp of water, and scarfed down a cookie. "Well," he said, "I knew something was wrong. How did she die?"

53

"A sign from a building fell on her. She died instantly."

"Oh my god." He really didn't know what to say. "Well, at least it wasn't cancer." She frowned and tried the coffee, but it was still too hot.

"She was the only one I had, you know. My mom was a waitre*sssshh* and had a one-night stand with some shmuck. Nine month*sh* later, little Marci was born."

"That sucks. Well, I'm not going to sleep with you, Marsipan, but you should know that you can talk to me anytime."

"You don't have to feel sorry for me, ya know!"

"No, no. I know. I am just sayin' what I heard friends say in these kinds of situations. Take it easy, alright."

"So you don't wanna kiss me?"

"Well…" He looked her in the eye and kissed her on the mouth. A little kiss. An *osculum* with a plump, pursed mouth.

"How's that?"

"OK. Let's go home," she said and finished off the last cookie.

THE FLOOD

That morning Marci realized that the grey had claimed her closet. It seemed, when she was getting dressed, that her regular clothes had disappeared. There remained hanging in her closet only a fraction of the colourful, eccentric wardrobe she had collected over the years. In its place was a hand-painted, monochrome photograph.

She pulled a grey suit off the hanger into the vivid world of her bedroom. It seemed to become instantly 3-dimensional when it was surrounded by the rainbow spectrum of books on her shelf and was displayed against the backdrop of Klimt, Rothko and yellow daffodils. She put it on and got ready for work. At the door, she glanced into her apartment, and without knowing it smiled goodbye at her sanctuary for the last time.

Outside, it was a crisp autumn day. The neighbourhood was covered in brightly coloured maple leaves. She kicked them as she walked, creating storms of Pantone™ colours: red 32, (Halloween) orange 143, and brilliant yellow, all stirred about with sienna, and the slew of ochers. Overhead, the sky was deep and dark, almost a purple. The clocks had not yet been set ahead for Daylight Savings Time so the morning seemed particularly dark to her. In the distance, ominous clouds hung low, blocking the morning sun.

The morning was completely routine. She could have lipsynch'd Alex's lines. Although he could easily be confused with a chaotic presence, his form of behaviour was, in fact, tightly controlled. They had gotten to know each other well over the last year, and formed a mutual respect. Alex mostly did the scanning; Marci mostly used the software and made sure that the colours were pure. The room inside also seemed dark when she arrived and remained that way until around 2:20pm, when the intercom crackled to life. It actually startled Alex so that the scan of a griffon and a greyhound wrinkled onto the screen behind him.

"Jangly-jehosephat!" he said and the intercom sprung to life. It was the manager: "Archival staff, there is a severe weather warning. A violent rainstorm is incapacitating our city right now. You have the chance to go home early; however, I recommend you finish your work according to schedule and join the rest of the library staff in the auditorium. Those who remain will stay there until the storm subsides. Thank you." They looked at each other. Alex raised his eyebrows and announced: "Well, I'm outta here!"

They both finished up the last scan and proceeded to pack up the book. Because there were no windows in the Archival Office, they didn't have a chance to check the weather until they walked out to the staff lounge. Marci was complaining that the manager recommended they stay, but when they stepped out of the office into the hallway, the sound of the rain could be heard everywhere, like a heavy thrumming beating the windows of the building.

Marci immediately walked through the nearest stacks to look out the windows. Seen from behind, she was a shape in front of a waterfall. The sky was dark and some lights were on, and except for the thrumming of the rain, everything was silent.

There's no way I can go home in this, she thought. When she turned around, she expected Alex to be there, but he was gone. She wondered if he really would go home.

Going back to work was an inconceivable option at that point, so she decided to take a walk around the public part of the library. The library is one of the most beautiful ones in North America. It had been renovated during the city's latest renaissance, in which we saw hundreds of new, well-designed buildings go up. The original building was the university-Gothic style you see on any campus worth its salt. Attached to the 250-year old building, was a large, minimalist concrete structure built in the 70s—the kind of Brutalist fad, now long out of style, that would have forced people to commit suicide had it been a housing complex. For years the concrete fortress served as the public stacks, but after the last addition—an innovative glass shell covering one side of the Gothic building—the majority of the stacks had been returned to the original building. The overflow had been relocated inside the glass superstructure, around the 200-year old stone walls. All in all, the redesign of the library gave it an inviting air and, ultimately, allowed it to become a shared public space once again.

Today, the library was especially packed. Full of people from the Children's to the Reference section, the Mystery to the Religion section, the microfilmed Newspapers to the coffee shop. Walking between the outer glass wall and the stacks, Marci was struggling to find a spot to sit. Those not sitting or sleeping on the chairs, were staring out the liquid windows, watching the storm. It seems as if people had come to the library from the streets as soon as it started to rain. Some seemed to be sleeping for a few hours, others were reading intensely. The whole outer wall had become a waterfall and some children were marveling at it. "I see a whale!" one proclaimed.

Marci walked for a while, watching the people until she found herself in central aisle of the renovated Gothic building. She stood still in the current of humans swirling around her and looked up. Above the 2nd, 3rd, and 4th floor galleries the glass ceiling could be seen: a dancing river, illuminating the library with the turquoise fleck marks of light shining through the water of a swimming pool. The 4th floor seemed like an aquarium, students studying with little lamps completely under water. In that moment, life seems so surreal to her: the solipsism of maintaining scholarly focus in the midst of a gargantuan storm, as absurd as Odysseus thwarting desire with waxed ears. Something seemed out of place. Then, suddenly, she realized she was staring into the crying eye of the heavens in the main thoroughfare of the library, while people flowed around her like boats around a buoy in the harbour.

She headed straight for the auditorium, back into the concrete fortress (a suitable place to weather a storm) where she remained, chatting with colleagues and helping with menial tasks. As night fell, the rain petered out to a moderate downpour and three hours after the library's official closing time employees and citizens alike started to go home. Marci never did find Alex. She wondered what happened, but was unable to get through to his cell phone. So she ushered the last few straggling people out; she woke a man soundly sleeping, and warned a teenager reading an Ursula Le Guin book with a red dragon on the paperback cover that the library staff were going home.

Outside, the street looked like an urban creek, water flowing endlessly down the gutters. It was impossible not to get wet. All the trains had already stopped and after about 10 minutes of trying, she finally managed to get a cab. As soon as she apologized for being soaked, she noticed that the backseat of the taxi was already wet. The cabby told her not to worry, that everything was wet today. "No one was spared by that rain!" he said.

The ride was quick, because the city looked almost abandoned. *Had people evacuated?* she thought. Getting out of the car was tougher than expected because she had to hop over the water flowing down the side of the street into the garden without landing in Mr. Killarney's rose bush. Finally, she was home. It had been exactly 12 hours earlier that she left, kicking leaves across the sidewalk. Once she was standing (in a shallow puddle of water), there were two things she noticed. Firstly, the leaves had disappeared; they were all washed away down storm drains into water management facilities, where they would become beautiful red-yellow-and-brown mulch. Secondly, there were no lights on in her building. The latter realization made her bite her bottom lip, as she fumbled for her keys in her purse.

The rain had become a soft drizzle.

As she unlocked the door, she wondered what had happened to Mr. Killarney, who surely couldn't be asleep yet, but also had nowhere else to be. She promised to check on him once she got inside and took off the 98% grey suit. The lock turned and her door swung open. The lights wouldn't go on. She swore under her breath, and took off her shoes at the door, so as not to trudge mud and water into the apartment. But when she stepped down the first step towards her home, she splashed ankle-high into water. She froze in place and as her eyes adjusted, the white reflections of streetlamps could be seen on the rippling water covering the entrance like the infinite, blackness of a subterranean lake. At that moment, one ankle in, one out, something inside her broke. She felt the acute loss of her own life. She sat herself down on the top step, both feet now in the water and wept. She cried for herself, for her house, for Mr. Killarney (wherever he may be), for love lost, and for her mother and for any other reason that popped into her head. Then she cursed fate, because she had no one to call, nowhere to go.

She took her shoes in her hand and left without locking the door. She thought about faking an illness to sleep at a hospital, about calling the police, her ex-boss, her alienated childhood friend, and then finally settled on Alex. She pulled her phone out of her purse, now also soaking, and dialed the number. Amazingly, she got through on the second ring.

"Yo."

"Alex?" she said.

"Yeah, Mars, what's up?"

"I," she paused to swallow, "My house is flooded. I'm fucked."

"No way!" he said. "Well, what are you gonna do?" He realized almost immediately what she wanted and added, "You can stay at my place, man." There was no response.

"Marci? You OK?"

"Yeah…I guess," she said. "How do I get to your house?

THE CONSEQUENCES

Alex lived in a cheap loft on the border of the gay village. It had peeling hardwood floors, but little else to offer in the sense of luxury. The building was commercially zoned, so his buzzer was labeled as Prime Alex Ltd. And once inside, she realized that he was living in what could easily be mistaken as a crack den. There was a small sink, which served as the kitchen, a bathroom with a leaky shower. In fact, there was no handle to turn on the water; however, a pair of rusty pliers was left conveniently on the soap tray. The majority of the space was his living room, decorated with band posters. Aside from one couch, there were some books and CDs next to a toaster in the bookshelf, and in one corner a mini fridge with a microwave on top. The only window looked out onto a brick wall.

As for the bedroom, there was no door. And it must have served as an office in the past, because, as if defying the laws of physics and geometry, his queen-sized bed fit in the room from wall-to-wall. The only other thing inside was a lamp next to what should have been the door.

"Where can I sleep?" she asked, eyeballing the couch.

"Well, my unfortunate one, I suppose you can have the bed, and I will sleep on the couch. Tomorrow we can sort out the futon and I will set up *ye olde shoppe* in the walk-in closet."

"There's a walk-in?"

"Oh yeah," he said, pointing to a small gap between the kitchen and the front door, "over there."

"Do you have a dryer?"

"A hair dryer?"

"No. For my clothes. This is all I got now."

"What?! You going to work tomorrow?" He scrunched up his face.

"What else can I do?" she sighed heavily. He offered her a

smoke and she took it, coughing heavily with the first drag.

Now, there are some obvious reasons why the shared accommodation would not work out between the two of them, but there are also other reasons much less obvious. Their lifestyles were completely different: Marci liked to relax and read or paint, Alex liked to listen to loud music and smoke weed. Moreover, there was absolutely no sound-proofing in the building, much less room doors, and Alex loved outrageously dirty sex. Marci had nothing of her own except her grey suit; and the room she used to live in, had over the years become the tangible representation of her personality. It was her, and she was it. Living anywhere else seemed like betrayal.

In fact, the shared accommodation lasted exactly three days before she decided something had to be done.

The third day, after work, Marci Wood went to the Kensington neighbourhood, tucked between the Chinese and the Italian areas of the city. Historically, it had been the Jewish settlement area, but today the area was filled with people from all corners of the globe. It was also the area where Baxter lived. Baxter was a blond, super-slim guy, who had once been a whistle-blower at Pfizer Pharmaceuticals. He was a wild man, not particularly good-looking, unpredictable, and given to all the vices of the world. The word 'heroin-chique' springs to mind. He lived in the attic of an old synagogue, which now served as a Chinese community centre. The neighbourhood is filled with evening hipsters, and tattooed 20-somethings, shopping at used clothing stores and doing clandestine deals on the street corners. Marci showed up unannounced at his place, since (despite knowing him since childhood) she had lost his phone number a few months ago. The door opened a crack and above the safety bolt, peered a set of crystalline blue eyes, set deep in an ivory white face.

"Marci Wood!" he said surprised, and opened the door. "Come in. Come in." The house was a mess. There was very little furniture, and books were stacked in pyramids everywhere.

"I'm sorry, I haven't had time to clean these days.

I apologize for the disaster that is my house."

"Don't worry, Baxter." She sat down on an old, creaky armchair. "It's only me. I don't care." He was only wearing pants and his ribs could be seen protruding beneath the pale skin. It was cold inside the house—too cold to be wearing just pants! He didn't look well. "Did I wake you up?"

"Nah, I was just…uh, lying around." He moved into the kitchen, which seemed to be the only light source in the building and was immediately illuminated by the light from the setting sun. "Want some tea?" he asked and fiddled around with dirty dishes in the sink.

Baxter used to be a brilliant man. He was talented in the arts as well as in science. The only thing that kept him from becoming great was his inability to say 'no' to any temptation. He was her oldest friend.

The last few years had not been so good for him. He got involved in a major case against one of the biggest pharmaceutical companies and ever since, he has been unable to find a job. Marci knew well, but they never spoke about his methods for making money. She allowed him his secrets, and he supported her in many other ways. They were a pair of silent accomplices.

"So, little one, what brings you here on such a dank and depressing day?" She took a sip of tea and breathed out a cloud of vapour.

"Baxter…" It was desperation. Her eyes teared up, but she struggled to maintain herself. "I lost everything."

"Marci, you OK?" He came closer, grabbed a blanket sitting nearby and wrapped it around them both. "Did you get fired?"

"No…"

"What happened then?" She explained how her house had flooded, became unsafe for living and that most of her effects had been destroyed. She talked about the storm and the library, and how she wasn't allowed to touch the books. She described her house, the colours and the feeling of unconditional safety, and the how the 98% grey had invaded her closet and then her life. She talked of Alex and how he had tried to help, but always made things worse. Then weeping, she explained how she missed her mom, but every last picture and memento was stored in her basement apartment in the house.

During this catharsis, Baxter listened. He was shivering with her under the blanket. He wondered what he could do. How he could help her, but his thoughts found it difficult to settle on anything. In fact, he was more powerless than she was. Reduced to their most basic parts, they were just two bodies, consoling each other, sharing heat.

After a long silence, he thought she had fallen asleep. "Marci?"

"Baxter," she said with a calm voice, "I need your help."

"Anything you need, my dear Marci. Anything at all."

"I have decided that there is nothing left for me in this world."

"What do you mean?" he sat up straight and looked at her. She had calmed down and seemed completely rational. She was unemotional and serious.

"Listen, I know what you do. How you make money. I want you to help me make some...uh, medicine."

"What do you mean?" he said again.

"I know about your lab. I want you to make me a poison."

"Marci, I will not help you kill yourself!" he stood up and walked over to a pile of clothes on the floor. He found a hooded sweater and put it on. "Why would you want to do something like that? We all go through bad times. Things will get well again, Marci. I promise."

"Baxter, you can say that if you want, but I just can't do this anymore. What's the point of living? I got my dream job and I am so frustrated. I have to work in a grey room and now my only possession in this world is this grey suit. You know better than anyone that things don't just work out"

"Ok. Ok. Ok, listen. There's no poison that kills you instantly, they are all painful. Even if I wanted to help you, it's a cruel way to go."

"Well, if you don't help me, I will throw myself in front of a subway train. And besides, I did my research. Suicide is a serious thing. There's nothing worse that screwing up. I could end up brain-dead, or paraplegic, and you could end up taking care of me. Imagine that? Trust me," she said, "I have thought about this, planned it well."

Baxter was staring at the bookshelf next to the chair she was sitting on. Inside his head, all kinds of cogs were turning. A domino reaction of cause and effect had been set off and he was visualizing their awful consequences. He said nothing.

"Can you make these?" She handed him a piece of paper with two chemical formulae on them.

"Yes. But these are both devastatingly lethal toxins. And they are not nice. The neurotoxin at the top paralyzes you before unravelling your liver's DNA. The bottom will stop your heart in a matter of minutes, but I imagine it is very painful."

"I want both."

"What?! Why?"

"I want to be *very* sure. And I figure I will die painlessly if I take the neurotoxin first. I will be paralyzed and unable to feel my heart stop. If I wait 10 minutes before taking the potassium chloride, the timing will work in my favour. Will you help me?"

"This is serious stuff, Marci. I can't just..." he sighed and looked at the bookshelf again. "I'll think about it. Just don't throw yourself into the tunnel when you go home. Don't do anything stupid, OK? I will see what I can do."

"Thanks, Baxter." She hugged his frail body in the fading light streaming in from the kitchen.

"Come back in five days." Marci nodded and handed him three hundred-dollar bills.

"This is for supplies." She said, knowingly giving him more money than necessary.

*   *   *

The truth is Marci really did consider it from every angle. She listed the possible death scenarios in her head.

i.) Jumping from the Bloor St. Viaduct. It is one of the most popular suicide spots in North America. Number 3, to be precise, after the Golden Gate Bridge and the Aurora Bridge in Seattle. However, a few years back the local government erected 'the Luminous Veil', a wonderfully poetic suicide prevention barrier. This would have been her first option since there hasn't been a single unsuccessful attempt and the fall, exactly 4.7 seconds would have taken her sailing past the rail lines and into the beautiful Don Valley.

ii.) Cutting her wrists. Too dramatic. Plus she didn't have a bathtub of her own anymore. Although, the painting, 'The Death of Marat' by Jacque-Louis David did linger romantically for a while even after she rejected the idea.

iii.) The cliché sleeping pills and whiskey combination. This one was dispelled in conversation with a librarian during lunch. Apparently, before you overdose on sleeping pills, you vomit. Most people fail on this one. You wake up covered in vomit with a head full of broken glass and an abused liver.

iv.) Hanging. Not something she preferred. It also seemed impossible due to not having a good place to hang from.

v.) Gun shot to the head. Effective, but difficult because of the bureaucracy involved with getting a firearm. Also, she felt that this method was not her style. The end was somehow too sudden. At least with jumping from the Viaduct there would be the surreal flying sensation before the impact.

vi.) The subway. This one was not originally on the list, but waiting on the platform, the idea came naturally. She toyed with it, but it was rather dramatic as well. Too public. And then there was the chance of surviving with missing appendages.

vii.) Finally, there was poison. On this planet of ours, nature has devised some of the most lethal toxins, killing organisms in a wide variety of ways from the brutally visceral to the sublime. On top of this list, there are the poisonous gasses and lethal chemicals humans have invented. She finally settled on taking two poisons. One would be a neurotoxin which would paralyze and kill over a medium time frame (in other words, immediate paralysis but certain death after about 6 hours), the other one would be the fast acting chemical used in lethal injection executions in some states in America. The combination of these two toxins would ensure her mortal body come to an end without paralysis or other disfigurements. And most importantly, both of them could be created in a well-equipped lab.

She never talked about her planned suicide attempt to Alex, but she relished in her secret. It became her only solace after a few days. She would rent a hotel room, an expensive one, overlooking the lake and she would have her last meal the night before: a fine reisling-braised pork shank, with wild mushroom risotto, and braised leeks smothered in black currant sauce. She would drink champagne (the expensive stuff), and order a dessert special left to the chef to decide. "Spare no expense!" she would say.

What about the note, you ask? Well, the thought had obviously occurred to her. But everytime she thought about what to write, no words came. In fact, she didn't even know to whom to address the letter. The hotel staff, or likely some detective would find it, and what could she say that would matter to them? She would postpone it, she thought. Perhaps she would write it under the influence of a $200 bottle of champagne.

Until she returned to Baxter's temple-*cum*-home, her moods fluctuated like a manic-depressive's. She was happy (usually momentarily) when she saw the scans of each new page, delicately engraved, in the Archives. But when she was alone, she felt such a deep emptiness inside her; she felt truly alone in the universe, and far from everything that mattered. She fantasized about her death, and wondered if Heaven existed. She never considered Hell, because it was a foreign concept to her, one that she couldn't accept because her paranoid nature would obsess about it until suicide was out of the question. She imagined angels and her mom, frozen in time as the beautiful, long-haired hippy with the 'BAN THE BOMB' placard in the pictures floating in the subterranean water of her house.

On the fifth day, a day so dreadfully cloudy that it seemed almost no sunlight entered the city, she returned to Baxter. It was dark by the time she arrived and the temperature had dropped to winter levels. She tucked her coat tightly around her body, the wind biting the exposed skin between her glove and sleeve. The synagogue looked ominous under the opaque sky. Everything was tinted in a Pantone™ 435, a warm grey. And by 'warm', I mean mixed with an almost insignificant amount of red. In reality, the 'warm grey' actually made the whole world seem colder than it actually was, covering everything in a film of nimbostratus pregnant with snow.

Again Baxter peered through the safety-lock crack in the door before cooing and letting her in. She walked into the building, this time alive with heat and electricity, and sat herself down on the same creaky armchair. Again he offered her tea and she accepted. Hardly a word was exchanged until he brought the tea and sat down on an overturned milk crate.

"So, I was doing some thinking," he said, "I know I can't talk you out of it, so I won't even try." She nodded. "But," he said, "the chemicals you asked me to make are difficult without testing. I have tried my best, but had to change the formula."

"How so?"

"Well," he sighed, considering whether he should go into the technical jargon or not, "The problem was with the potassium chloride. It was easy enough to make," he took a jar of white powder from under the coffee table, "but it's no good."

"Why?" Her face wore a look a child wears when he knows he is being deceived by an adult for his own good.

"Before you get your panties in a knot, lemme explain." She relaxed a bit and nodded. "You see," he said, "according you your body weight, you are gonna need a dumpster's worth of this stuff. There's no way you can take it all orally. We'd need to hook it up intravenously, but it would defeat the purpose time-wise. Here, taste it." He unscrewed the jar and handed it to her.

She dipped her pinky into the mix and placed it on her bottom lip. *Salty*, she thought and tickled the end of her finger with the tip of her tongue. The taste was identical to salt. Then she picked up the jar and inspected the crystals.

"It's not salt, I swear." She looked directly at him, doubtful. "Ok, you don't believe me, huh?" he said. "Take a few crystals on your finger and try to look through them. He pulled a naked lamp over—long divorced from its lampshade. She did as he said and peered through the tiny crystals on her fingertip. The light streaming through them seemed like a van Gogh. Shards of rainbow were trapped in those colourless shapes, each reflecting the lamplight a thousand-fold. The deeper she looked the more colours she saw. It seemed to somehow bend the invisible spectrum into the visible. *A tiny view of Heaven*, she thought. The warm colours were particularly vivid, but whether this was from the yellow nature of the incandescent bulb, or because of the transmission of infrared rays, she could not tell. She only knew it was like looking deep into a universe of radiating paint chips. *Salt*, she thought, *does not do this.*

"It burns purple too," he said. When he saw he had her attention again, he straightened his spine and continued, "Also, in executions, they add a barbiturate to the mix so that the condemned are virtually asleep before they die. All of this would be way too obvious for the first sleuth through the door of your place…er, your, uh, hotel room."

"You are the brain, Baxter, what do you suggest?"

"Funny thing how you can rely on me to pluck your mortal coil."

"So you have something then?"

"Well, yeah. I think this should do the trick." He said and pulled a vial from his pocket. "Warmed to body temperature."

"What is it?"

"I'll give you a hint: it is tasteless, less than 50 micrograms can kill you, and it smells like almonds."

"No, it can't be!" she said.

"The Queen of Poisons. The poisoner of queens. The death of Napoleon Bonaparte." He smiled, secretly proud of his substitution.

"Arsenic?" she asked, head tilted to the side.

"BINGO!" He handed the vial to her. "The irony of the matter is that the metal I made this from was the same colour of your suit. Ninety-eight percent metallic grey."

"Yeah, I know about this mineral." She said. "Why didn't I think of this?! I mean, it was originally made into two pigments both of which had toxic effects and were ultimately banned."

"What colours?"

"Actually one was called "Paris Green", used by the impressionists to get a colour of pure emerald. But you could call the colour 'Impressionists Bane' more accurately, because, along with leaded paint and turpentine, it caused Monet's blindness, van Gogh's mental disorders, and Cezanne's severe diabetes—a symptom of arsenic poisoning, right?"

"Yeah, I guess if you take a weak dose."

"It was Cezanne's favourite colour."

"What is the second pigment?" he asked curiously.

"The other one is lesser known. It is a yellow made from an arsenic byproduct. Actually made from crystals found around hot springs, the mineral is called 'orpiment', but is better known as 'King's Yellow' or 'Chinese Yellow'. It is extremely toxic and hardly ever used these days."

"Well then, it is the perfect poison for you, isn't is? Two of the most vivid colours of death."

"Yeah, I read somewhere that the Queen of Portugal, who was suffering a severe and drawn out death, asked for a tonic to ease her pain. Her most trusted maid brought her a mixture of pot and arsenic. History records her death as the most sublime ending to a journey through the pits of hell."

"That's a cool story," he said. "Actually, you know, arsenic is said to have psychedelic properties if used in small amounts."

"Really?" She pulled her eyebrows in tight. "I don't know that much about the effects. Why don't you enlighten me?"

"Well, thank you for asking. You see, it fits perfectly into your terrible blueprint because, like the potassium chloride, it will kill fairly fast. After 30 minutes you will taste the heavy metal on your tongue. You might feel pins and needles and difficulty swallowing. After the effects come into full, you will go into shock and die of heart or circulatory failure. Oh, and contrary to popular belief, they say your breath will smell like garlic, not almonds."

"Will it be painful?" He hesitated for a brief second, blinking rapidly. Clearly Baxter was considering his words, choosing to tell the truth, rather than equivocate any more than he already had.

"Marci, I imagine there is no poison that kills painlessly. However, the combination you have selected will minimize the outright pain, since your nervous system will be paralyzed. Basically, you should be detached from it all. Physically, that is. If you *truly* want to be detached 100%, I suggest taking some morphine with the neurotoxin."

"Ok."

"Is that a yes," he cocked one eyebrow and looked in her

direction, "because if it is, I can arrange for some morphine as well."

"Good idea," she said. "I only have one more question."

"Shoot."

"Will it kill me for sure?"

"Oh, don't worry about that! There is enough poison here to kill a woolly mammoth! And if you don't die from severe seizure, you will go into a coma and die from kidney failure a few days later. That is, if your liver somehow survives the untangling of its DNA."

"I trust you."

DOOMED

It was a Thursday, a typical Thursday filled with the minutia of daily life. Work was work. And the weather was still delaying the snow, holding it in a filthy grey cloud over the city. Marci had just finished the last scan of the day, a 9th Century transcription of a Byzantine Hagiography book. The letters were Roman, but the words Greek. The last page came with an image of a Slavic king surrounded by two saints (probably Cyril and Methodius), who are holding a scroll with the 41-character *galgolitic* alphabet. Marci stared for 20 minutes at the single line in the margin—a note written in red ink in a language she had never seen. She hit the 'SAVE' button and her workday ended.

Head and hands, she floated through the greyness out of the room and transformed at the door into a 3-dimensional person. Crisp lines once again. One last look back at the Archive Office. *Yup, it's grey alright!* she thought. She shut off the lights. As she walked down the hall, she didn't look back. In fact, she had seen enough already and was rehearsing the artificial death scene she had constructed in her mind over and over and over. In her pocket were two vials, filled with the chemicals needed to end the mechanisms of her physical body. The metaphorical wrench she would toss into her works. The image of the body-clock with its cogs and wheels, springs, levers and pulleys, screws, and pendula jumped to mind as she *klik-klacked* her way down the marble towards the elevator.

"B'bye, Ms. Wood," the receptionist greeted her as she stepped into the elevator. The journey down, towards her fate seemed to take longer than usual. While waiting tensely, she suddenly had a revelation. *Gorgonzola!* That tormentingly familiar smell in the elevator everyone guessed at but no one could place; it was Gorgonzola! *Mystery solved,* she thought. Too bad she would never be able to share that piece of information with anybody ever. She would take it too her grave.

Oh my God! Would I have a grave? Shit! I never even thought about that. Oh well...I'd rather be burnt anyways. Graves are stupid. I'll make that my suicide note. "Graves are stupid. I'd rather be burnt." Real estate for bones is a silly concept. A waste. But I suppose I can't donate my body to science if my kidneys have turned to stone and my liver to meat-juice. Do they even take poisoned bodies for med school anatomy classes? Besides, who knows what kind of weirdness my hair will look like on my cold, naked corpse? Nah, let's avoid all that, shall we? I want to be dead in peace. An urn-full of carbon molecules, indistinguishable from the—Holy shit...I am going to become that awful grey. In death, my ashes will become the same 98% grey as the Archives Office.

Well, what'dya know!

The elevator door opened.

Marci proceeded to the most expensive hotel just as planned and checked into a suite room. She then went to a La Maquette, a fine French restaurant and ordered the Chef's special.

"Spare no expense!" she told the server. The waiter, a diminutive man with a beautiful mouth (lips like chiseled marble from a Roman bust), delivered the appetizer, a wild mushroom strudel with leek and spinach cream sauce and balsamic drizzle along with a regal bottle of champagne. A woody aroma filled the area around Marci's table and she noticed she was salivating. While she was savouring the mushroom pastry, she filled the vacuum of romantic conversation by stealing peeks out the window onto St. James Cathedral and the sculpture garden, where groups of teenagers did their mating dance.

Next came a sampling of golden brown chicken and Québec foie gras, served with Island Pumpkin, Bosch Pear and wild berries compote. *The taste of the season*, she thought. As she was scraping the last morsels of flavour off the plate, the next dish came: thinly sliced roasted fillet of venison, juicy and served with wild berries, apple and aged port reduction. Although Marci rarely ate meat, she made certain concessions because it would be the last meal of her life. When she bit into it, she had a momentary pang of regret that she hadn't come to the restaurant during a happy time of her life. She imagined a feast complete with a roast wild boar—you know, the kind with the apple in its mouth. All the people she had known and loved could sit around and gorge themselves on the multitude of flavours and the rainbow of scents, while subtly expressing their love through the warmth of their conversation. Then she imagined meeting Baxter for lunch while he still had furniture and a good job. They would talk and laugh, Baxter explaining the mechanics behind the tastes in her mouth. She even digressed further to when she was young, a semi-maladjusted high school girl and she would have dinner with her mom on their special occasions, like when Marci won 2nd prize in the national art contest.

All this fantasy was interrupted by the next course, a seared yellow fin tuna, flavoured with scotch bonnets and served with pickled ginger, avocado and Yukon chips. The tastes in her mouth—sour/spicy ginger, then salty tuna, then smooth avocado—complimented the bubbly of the champagne beautifully. The bubbles were starting to go to her head and when the waiter returned, she noticed tears wear silently rolling down her cheeks. A little embarrassed, she hiccupped and said: "I'm ready for dessert now." The waiter overcompensated with his niceness, but Marci could tell by the quiver of his lips that he was uncertain how to proceed.

The dessert came. It was poached pear and almond tart served with caramel ice cream and chocolate sauce. Before she picked up her dessert fork, she quickly downed the flute of champagne, filled it up again and necked a second one. Then she steadied herself for the sweetness. Although she was small, Marci could eat her share, and when it came to dessert, there was no holding her back! I have often wondered what such a little woman does with so much food. They say that some people have a higher body temperature, that some bodies are like furnaces, burning calories at a ridiculous rate. But Marci far surpassed all these people. On her good days, she could pack away food like a frozen storage locker.

The dessert was exquisite and the waiter brought a coffee. He asked her if everything was OK. It was an ambiguous question and Marci just nodded. The moment to confess had passed and she realized what she had to do next. *So far everything was going perfectly to plan*, she thought.

Sublime lighting greeted her in her room when she returned in step with the sunset. The plain white walls were bathed in a kaleidoscope of pinks and oranges, and outside the city lights had already sprung to life, shining like earthbound stars. The skyline was shadow puppet buildings on a flowing watercolour canvas of colour. The room itself was seductively decorated in a faux-European style resembling a bedroom in Versailles. There were frills and carved furniture everywhere, silk and velour in abundance, immaculate antiques defending their honour against a giant flat-screen TV in one corner.

She plopped down on the bed, sinking deep into the sheets, and spread herself into a snow-angel position. Although she closed her eyes, the marvellous colours of dusk remained and her thoughts turned to darker matters. *I want to be found during sunrise or sunset*, she thought. *I want a beautiful death, painted in warm light—nothing white, no daylight 6500K.* She imagined the expression on her face. Would it be peaceful? Or perhaps an awful grimace? In the battle of chemicals in her blood, which would control her face? Would she wear the zen-like bliss of morphine, the bitterness of arsenic, or the contortion of a painful mortality?

These questions fluttered through her mind as she reached into her pocket, where she found the small bottle of arsenic. She pulled it out and held it to the light. The lamplight glowed in the clear liquid inside the brown bottle.

The next few minutes happened in silence, slow and purposeful. It seemed ritualized, as if every action has its place and purpose in a gracefully choreographed dance of death. Marci stood up in front of the giant window overlooking the city and removed, one by one, the grey layers of her suit: the jacket, which she folded in half and placed over the back of an armchair; next the skirt, which, when it fell to the ground, revealed her black, boyish underwear; then she unbuttoned her blouse, which she neatly placed on top of the folded skirt in the lap of the chair; and finally, she removed her underwear, all the while looking out of the room onto the city. She had become a silhouette of a silent Venus against the backdrop of a metropolis. No one could see her through the window, but had a curious bellhop decided to peep through the keyhole, he would have seen the contours of her naked back in monotone. The image might have had him waiting for her to turn. But Marci stood still. Naked and still, her back to the door. She removed the pins holding up her hair and it too fell over her shoulders into its natural place. She became a siren. Her beauty was in the lack of hope outlined in the arpeggio of curves (the neck, waist, and hips) of the female form.

The fear of death is strong even in someone who has already given up on life. So she thought about everyone who knew her. She thought about how they would feel about her death. It was as much about validating herself as it was about them. Time has slowed to a snail's pace and eventually, after she had emptied her mind, she turned.

The hypothetical bellhop would now be overjoyed. He would see her breasts and pubis, covered with curly hair, as well as her bottom reflected in the window, bouncing mechanically as she walked away, out of his line of sight, towards her doom.

In the bathroom (just as lavish as the rest of the suite), she took the chemicals. The morphine pills were time-released so she crushed them to a powder and washed the bitter whiteness down with a glass of water. Next, came the neurotoxin. *Such a tiny amount*, she thought, *yet so lethal*. The poison was in an empty 35mm film canister and she dipped an ordinary sewing needle into the liquid and pricked her fingertip. A small drop of blood rolled into the sink. She did it twice, just to make sure. Then, she set the timer. Eight minutes started rolling by on the digital clock. As she flushed the remaining toxin and needle down the toilet, the morphine kicked in. At first, it was a slight warping of perspective, a drunkenness of body, and her loins felt like they were getting hotter and hotter. She felt completely detached from her actions. The canister dropped onto the floor and rolled in big echoing sound waves across the tiles and into her ears. Her mind clung to reality as best it could; it was trying to remember something. She left the bathroom, and walking felt like swimming through the air. Her step was Jello-y. She suddenly realized she was naked. Then, she touched the skin on her stomach. *No feeling. Just pressure.* She ran her hand over her body, upwards over her breasts and onto her neck. It needed stabilizing, she thought. Still her mind was clinging to the procedure. Nervousness was flowing out of her, away from her body, out of her ears, upwards from her crown, seeping from vagina, and dispersing in the air. The limits of her body had become diffuse, blending her physical form into the molecules of air surrounding it.

She noticed that her hands were shaking unsurely. And then she couldn't remember where the arsenic was. She stood up abruptly and the earth felt like it was sitting on a giant trampoline. She scanned the room and noticed that everything blurred together in speedlines if she moved her head too fast. *I am the bullet train*, she thought. Her hands felt cold, but when she touched them to her body, there was no feeling of temperature—only pressure. Maybe it was the air around them that felt hot.

She was searching the room aimlessly. Up was down and down was up. She flowed with the spiralling swirl of consciousness and the airflow around her contracted time and gravity. She was trying to retrace her steps in her mind, but dancing images of Cyril and Methodius, like Twiddle-dum and Twiddle-dee, with their failed alphabet kept appearing. Then, the cityscape. Then, she was staring at her fingernails. *Hands or eyes are shaking*, she thought, trying to take a scientific survey of her state. *I will die empirically. Slowed down by time like a bogman, or icewoman.* She was now sitting naked on the bed staring into space. Then a flickering tongue of consciousness licked her cerebellum. *The key!* she thought. She looked down and saw the tiny bottle of arsenic in her hands.

"Where did you come from?" She opened it and drank the tasteless liquid. Her sensations were all muted. And it felt as if she had spilled it all over herself. She felt a dripping sensation down her neck, like liquid running down her chest onto her stomach. She tried to wipe it, but her hands either didn't move, or didn't feel anything, so she looked down. There was no liquid on her skin. The image she saw, somehow entranced her: it was simply her hips, how they were bent, how her legs folded and formed a triangle of fur. *An up-arrow.* The colour of her skin was rosy. She was blushing. *I'm leaking colour,* she thought and in the background, the sound of a recording of a recording of a gramophone played the ringing of a digital alarm. She slipped to the ground, pulling the velour bedcover on top of her. Her vision became black and it seemed like she was drooling, a waterfall of saliva, pooling near her face. She felt the heavy metal in her bones, particularly her jaw. It felt solid and unmovable.

Garlic-like tetanus.

sophisticated finale…

…metrication.…salivating

worms fail.   *broken.bronchi–actics…breath…*
Breathe!

I'm soffi–cue–late–ting…

She lost her ability to swallow completely, and even with her mind unhinged she felt compelled to record the symptoms of her death empirically. As her eyes adjusted to the darkness under the blanket, her consciousness, or rather a *second consciousness* emerged. Individual particles of light, shining dimly through the fibers of the cloth became illuminated like stars in the night sky. The internal monologue turned off completely, but there was an understanding. It was a part of her self that persisted below every other conscious part. You might argue it was her purest subconscious flashing images at her suffocating brain. But she wasn't suffocating; she was going into a paralytic shock. She saw the universe, the stars and nebulae. There was a calmness that balanced the chaos happening inside her body. Then, like a silent movie, she watched herself as a child playing in the backyard. She was 6 years old and an enormous dog jumped skywards in the background. The dog froze in time and his shape became the letter D in gothic letterform, composing with the sky behind him, an illuminated capital, over which exotic vines grew constricting time and space itself. It was *horror vaccui* of the mind. Once the vine completely covered everything, she found herself looking at an apple. She was eating it, but it tasted like metal and smelled of garlic. In her mind, the crunch of the fruit interrupted the utter silence.

Kkkkka-tcghuuuurrgh

Only the crunching, juicy, breaking, bursting sound could be heard. It echoed inside her head. It rolled back (*Kkkkka*) and forth (*tcghuuuurrgh*) and she looked deep into the apple, past the bitten flesh, into the core, where two seeds lay exposed. The seeds remained, while gradually everything else faded away. *tcghuuuuuuuuuuuurrgh*.... The tiny seeds stretched vertically into long, dark elipses. The two apple seeds, like snake eyes, whispered into her ear: 'we are arsenic'. Then everything ended. There was no pain. She knew her experiment had succeeded, but could not think it into words. She would like to have thought: *'There was no pain. No ghastly conniptions, diarrhea or cramps, my body was still. I died silently, draped in velour.'* But she could not think. Her brain, along with every other part of her body, had stopped.

ODDS

It was actually several days until Avram found out. You see, she had no next of kin and the only piece of identification she brought with her was her swipe card from the Library. Fingerprints told them her name and address, but I imagine there must have been a plethora of proceedings, you know, behind-the-scenes CSI stuff. Perhaps they were looking for suspects immediately after. A jealous boyfriend? A psychotic neighbour? A mysterious lone-wolf killer? A pimp perhaps? A maladjusted bellhop in the wrong place at the wrong time? Or it could have been some secret service stuff…CIA or the KGB!

Whatever they were doing behind the scenes, their investigation eventually lead to her tenants. Fortunately for the police, Marci's world was remarkably small. She didn't leave a suicide note, so they really had very little to go on. I imagine they first told the Library, who also had no further contact information. In reality, it was part of the deal between Marci and Baxter to keep their relationship secret—mostly from a legal standpoint. So, one cold Tuesday morning on the day he was to light the first candle of his menorah, Avram opened the door (his coat thrown on over his pajamas) to find two well-dressed detectives on his doorstep.

"Mr. Israel, do you mind if we ask you some questions?" There was an awful wind whipping upwards, through the fire escape and directly into his room. He was freezing and really wanted to cut to the chase.

"I'm sorry, vhat is this about?"

"When was the last time you saw Ms. Marci Wood?" Without knowing the truth about the situation, he could only expect that Marci had done something terrible. I suppose that when he determined the investigation was not about him, he decided to let those two men into his house. After all, they were just as cold as he was.

"Please come in."

His house was hot. Unfortunately, they had to walk through his bedroom, then through the kitchen to get to the living area. They told him it probably wouldn't take long, but he put on some coffee anyway.

The next few minutes were simple questions, a bit of snooping while he was in the kitchen, and then they asked him if he knew her family. Avram Israel told them that Marci's mother had died when she was young and that he wasn't sure, but she never talked about her father. When he handed them their coffees, he realized this was far more serious than he had thought.

"Is Marci alright?" he asked. The officers exchanged a look that said: *You want to tell him?* There was a small pause that answered his question before the older man started talking.

"Well, I'm sorry to say this," he took a breath, "but Marci Wood is in the hospital. She's in a pretty bad state."

"Vhat happened?" Avram showed genuine sympathy— more like how a parent would feel for his child, than a tenant would for his landlord.

"That's what we are trying to figure out." When they realized he knew nothing and that he was truly worried. They gave him the details of the hospital and left. They both said they were sorry for the bad news and the awkward interruption. Then the younger man, the one who was last to leave down the fire escape, yelled back: "Oh! Thanks for the coffee!"

*   *   *

The detectives didn't give him much to go by. He had no idea how serious the issue was. He figured it was pretty bad if it was bad enough to send out detectives. Avram hated hospitals, but he had to go. There were too many unanswered questions. Since flowers were out of the question for him because it was winter (normally, if he needed flowers he would just ask to pick them from Mr. Killarney's garden), he decided to bake some cookies.

When Avram got to the hospital, he told the nurse who he was looking for and, after a series of questions, she pointed him in the right direction. When he walked away from the counter, she stopped him and asked about the cookies. She was kind of cute and very gentle, so he beamed a great smile and told her that he had baked them himself.

Marci's room was in the west wing on the top floor, right at the back. It was basically one of the farthest ones from general pedestrian traffic, tucked into the proverbial corner of the intensive care unit. It was sterile and quiet up there. The only sounds were those of his footsteps and the rhythmical chorus of beeping machines. While walking down the long, long hallway, he suddenly assessed the gravity of the situation. I suppose the clue to him was that the wing was completely abandoned and lacked the one thing that redeemed hospitals: the hopeful chitchat of relatives bearing goodwill.

It was a sharp left turn into her room. She was lying there in the room with three other people; all of them hooked up with a multitude of wires and tubes violating what seemed like every orifice and opening in their bodies—more mechanics than human.

"Oi vey." The words simply escaped entirely without volition.

Avram Israel sat down on a small chair next to her. He didn't know what to do or say, so he just waited. He sat and remembered his youth. For a year while he was in college, he had the job of watching corpses. You see, in Jewish culture, a funeral must be held withing 48 hours of the death of an indivudual. The Torah also states that a body must be watched constantly and that to leave a dead body alone would be tantamount to condemning it to the sinister realm of demons. Of course, the highest paying job for Jewish students was to sit *shivva* with the deceased. Avram was 21 years old and, although he didn't believe in the sinister world of demons, he sat with corpses. He justified

82

it by saying to himself "If I weren't here, some rodents might come to eat the flesh of the body." There were often candles lit around the corpse covered in the white *tachrichim* sheet.

This is what he remembered sitting there with Marci in her transient state.

Eventually, a doctor came in. Avram could hear him coming down the hall towards the room. Perhaps he became mesmerized by the footsteps, because even when the man entered the room, Avram remained frozen.

"Well, hello," the man said, "It seems Ms. Wood finally got a visitor." The doctor's soft voice broke the spell and the old Jew stood up and turned to him. He was an older black man, tall with silver hair and beard.

"Good afternoon," the doctor said and shook his hand. "Are you a relative?" Avram told him he was not, that he was merely her tenant.

"You know, it really is a shame that such a beautiful girl has no friends or family. I just don't understand it myself."

"Doctor, vhat happened?" He found himself saying and added, despite knowing the cliché value of it, "Vill she be OK?"

"Well, to be honest, I am not supposed to go into details about her situation with anyone except for her family. However, since it has been more than a week and you are the first visitor, I will tell you in hopes that you can pass the information on to someone who cares about this poor girl." Avram nodded.

"You see, we are not sure exactly what happened. The police are involved because it is suspected that there might have been some foul play. Ms. Wood seems to have suffered toxic shock from a bizarre cocktail of...uh, elements."

"Drugs?" Avram Israel was very surprised. He didn't think Marci was the type for designer drugs, much less one to *overdose* on anything.

"Well, we suspect she might have been poisoned. The amount of toxins in her blood should have killed her outright. To be honest, it's sort of a personal mystery for me why she did not die. Lucky for *her*, the two stronger chemicals seemed to have cancelled each other on a cellular level."

"Yes, but will she be OK?" The doctor tightened his lips and 'hmmm'ed a bit. He seemed to be choosing his words. Or perhaps he thought he should wait until they find a true next of kin.

"Actually, I'm not sure if she will. Currently, she is in a coma. The procedure is to wait a week or so, before we reassess her situation. After the reassessment, if it is determined that she has stabilized, we will schedule a MRI to check the condition of her brain. In cases of toxic shock, brain death has been documented."

"So she might be dead?"

"I'm truly sorry…it is a doctor's most loathed job to give bad news. You must know, however, we are doing *everything* we can. And as of now, there is no way of knowing whether she will wake up tomorrow, or be in a permanent state." He shook his head. "Once again, I am very sorry, sir."

Avram's own chemicals felt like they were blended inside his head. He felt a little bit of everything at the same time; somehow he was still detached, yet involved as well, taking on his role as the first visitor, a surrogate father. He thanked the doctor and left. When he got back to the counter in the lobby of the hospital, he gave the cute nurse his cookies.

"They didn't tell you before you came, eh?"

"No."

"I'm very sorry for you." She said, dropping her head every so slightly. She obviously didn't have as much experience with bad news as the doctor had. Then she asked, "Was she your daughter?"

"No, I am her tenant."

"Oh, well, maybe she'll wake up sooner than you think." He smiled and bit his bottom lip.

It was on the subway ride home that he fully realized the responsibility he had been given purely by being the first visitor in the hospital. To be honest though, Avram worried a lot about himself as well. He worried about the house. Although his room was untouched by the storm, the basement was flooded and Marci, his trusted landlady, was unable to breathe by herself, much less deal with building damage. He thought he would have to move. I mean, he could spend his time going to the hospital to sit next to her, he could start a search for her closest living relative, or he could simply move on. He could give up on her, a person who he hardly knew yet felt some fatherly affinity for, and move to a new, unflooded house in some distant part of the city. It wouldn't bother him that much.

However, the goodness in him won out in the end and he called the city. He told them the situation with his landlady and how part of the house was still submerged. His explanation was mostly to get advice. He had no idea of what he should be doing, but the city said they would come assess the damage.

In the meantime, life went on. The first snow of the year fell, coating the world in white. Avram continued to visit the hospital every few days. It was within walking distance of his work, you see. The doctor told him that a man from the library had come to visit her, and that the MRI had been put off until after Christmas. The timing was horribly bad, because the city deemed that the house is unfit to live in and that the remaining two occupants (meaning him and Mr. Killarney) would have to move out.

He tried to tell this to old man Killarney downstairs, but it seems that no one had been able to contact him since the flood. My guess is that his apartment must have seen some flooding, too. He probably moved in with a relative in the city until they sorted out his living area. And I'm guessing that he found it impossible to get in contact with Marci, so he was probably waiting for her call.

During the holidays, the hospital was very quiet—almost abandoned. The lights had been turned off intermittently and the lobby was empty. Marci had been moved to the neurology department, which was staffed by two nurses. You had to call them on an intercom before they would let you in. They only let family into that ward, but Marci was an exception. The doctors had ordered the nurses to open the door to anyone who said Marci's name, in the event that somehow some relative would find their way there. The nurses had gotten to know Mr. Israel, since he spent most of his time talking to them. I mean, he ran out of things to say to Marci pretty quickly. At first they talked about the house, the problems in the community (you know, landlordy things), the weather. It was only the third time he was there that the doctor told him she couldn't hear. His words were so shocking that Avram would never forget them: "She can't even feel pain, much less hear anything." *How can she be unresponsive to pain? And how do they test that?* he thought. The doctor told him that in the early stages of a coma, the patient is usually completely unresponsive. "Deep unconsciousness," he said, "means they even lose involuntary muscle control of the muscles in their face and throat which helps with breathing." That explained the tube running out of her nose, attached to a bubbling canister.

Avram did take notice, however, on the day that yellow drip hanging from the ceiling disappeared. One less tube, that is. The view out the window was of a rooftop courtyard, covered in Astroturf, where people with different problems in a different part of the hospital could go to walk around outside. He often saw an old man smoking out there. *Cheating the system,* he thought.

It was on that day that he met Baxter. He noticed some commotion amidst the beeps outside the room, but he ignored it, staring at the old guy in the cold courtyard. He walked out, wearing far less than any normal person would in the winter weather. When Baxter saw Avram, he hesitated and was about to walk away, but Avram had already noticed him.

"Hello," he said, glad to be able to talk to someone, "do you know her?" He didn't say anything. So Avram introduced himself. He told the younger man that he was her tenant and that he would probably have to move as the house is all but

86

condemned. He asked jokingly if perhaps the stranger was her lawyer, willing to work out the details of the house, the insurance, etc.

After Avram Israel finished his spiel, the man remained quiet for another second then finally, slowly started talking.

"I suppose I am the closest thing, dear Marci here has to kin." When Avram saw his teeth, the image of a vampire flashed in his head. A vampire drug addict. *Is this the demon world which I sat protecting corpses from so many years ago,* he wondered.

"You can call me Baxter," he said. They talked briefly about the house, because although Avram was joking about the lawyer, Marci was in serious need of a legal representative. Baxter told him that he knew a good lawyer and that Avram shouldn't worry. He told the older man he would take over from there. I think he saw that Avram was there by her side simply by proxy. Avram assumed something was funny, but the more they talked, the more relieved he became. Baxter seemed to know a lot about medicine and hospitals, so Avram also felt as if he could pass on the torch. So he said goodbye to Marci Wood. It was unemotional, perfunctory, but clean—not that she could hear him anyway. On the way out, he said goodbye to the two nurses and left the hospital.

EPILOGUE

Lucky for you, Marci's story doesn't end there. Although Avram Israel and his wrestling angel were officially out of her life, and although she was permanently unconscious, things were happening. Some behind the scenes, some in the dreams of a chemically induced sleep.

For one, Baxter became her minder. It was a long vigil, watching for any sign of activity. He became an expert at reading the peaks and valleys of her *beep-beeping* heartbeat and the long plateaus of her breathing. He became acquainted with the doctors and nurses, just as Avram had, but he was able to understand from a biological point of view. Baxter learned everything he could about her state. After all, he felt responsible and I think he was trying to find a way out of the terrible limbo.

Through conversations with the doctors, he had come to understand that most comas don't last past the 5-week mark. Marci had been in a coma for about three weeks now and her brain scan proved that she was not brain dead at all, nor did she have any brain hemorrhages—instead, she was progressing in the usual stages for a coma patient. She was moved back to the Intensive Care Unit, where she hung suspended from a web of IVs, hanging from a metallic frame attached to the roof. Baxter also learned that after the 5-week mark, some patients gradually come out of the coma, others go into a vegetative state, and others simply die.

There was hope, because she showed a normal brain scan under the circumstances; however, the doctors warned that even if she did come out of it, she might have severe psychological or neurological disorders. When reduced to mathematical basics, the odds of her emerging from the coma dropped after the 5-week mark. The next marker was the 4-month period. After 4 months, if she hasn't woken up, there is less than 2% chance of partial recovery and a full recovery would require something short of miracle. Most patients emerge from a coma gradually, as if plants sprouting from seed into the light; day by day becoming strong enough to breach the soil with a single, thin, fragile stem.

Baxter had set his lawyer to the task and got the house cleaned and boarded up. Afraid of being directly associated with her affairs, his lawyer became his public face, dealing with the city, the insurance companies, as well as her work and bank accounts. He spent most of his time in the hospital and with the fullest onset of winter, Baxter even quit selling drugs.

Mind is the umbilical cord of consciousness. It's amazing to think that our essence—what medieval philosophers would have called the 'soul'—is walking around tethered to the world, by such a simple thread of mind. The mind is an anchor to reality. It is the only thing guaranteeing the laws of nature—and more importantly, chance!

Your belief in the order around you guarantees it. You may be waiting at an intersection, watching a procession of cars glide by you, but it is simply faith that stops any one of those cars from hopping the curb and slamming into you.

Of course, mind and body are the same, but it is mind that maintains luck and probability through belief. It is as if your mind is pre-programmed to trust the laws of nature, but what if for one second you stopped believing? Would cars fly off the road? Would gravity suddenly stop? Or maybe if the connection of mind is interrupted, an uncanny, swift death is unavoidable. Perhaps a meteorite would strike you down as soon as your mind rebelled against probability. The abandonned connection between mind and reality would leave a crater on a sidewalk somewhere.

And here, Marci was lying on a guerney, mindless. She had completely lost the connection; her mind was void and her body a vapid container. All the advanced evolutionary technology of 2.5 billion years lay there useless. She was a digital clock in perfect working condition, but her mind was unplugged.

Fortunately, Baxter was there to keep her parts in working order. He would move her joints and massage her muscles. He talked to her in hopes that her mind wasn't actually unplugged, but simply disconnected. He though of her as a Swiss watch, fallen to the ground, where the teeth on two cogs were shaken apart. He believed that inside her head the wheels were turning, but the arms couldn't move. This is what he hoped, because the alternative was by far worse. To me, however, this was the worse case senario. It meant that Marci could think, hear, and dream, but was unable to control her body.

What actually was happening we will never know. I will tell you though, that Marci had, in fact, turned off the laws of probability inside her head. With loss of mind comes loss of time. While she was frozen inside her body, time outside passed by. Snow had settled on her windowsill and her body grew frail in tune with the trees. She was expressing the eternal frost of her soul.

That year, the winter was particularly warm,
it had *snowed* and melted,
snowed and *melted*,
snowed and *melted*. In 2 week cycles of snow and sun, time passed. Gradually, the daylight became longer and soon birds appeared. At first, they flew high and far away, but one morning Baxter noticed a chickadee perched on the windowsill from which the snow had completely melted. Squirrels were playing tag on the lawn in the courtyard of the hospital and a gentle breeze carried the fragrance of lillac through the 2 inch crack in the window.

Marci, however was still in her timeless, spaceless place, while her body lay prone in the Wing of Lost Hopes. Perhaps in some primeordial way, the beam of sunlight cast onto her from the heavens was warming that seed of consciousness inside her brain. It had been 2 months and with each passing day the odds of her recovery were evapourating into thing air.

With spring, Baxter became busy with legal matters and he stopped visiting as often. He did show up punctually for her 3-month check up, though.

"No change, I'm sorry." Baxter just stared out a window.

A small unfamilliar bird was sitting, singing a song on a budding branch outside her window. Russian miniarettes of young green speckled the branch and behind it was a cloudless sky.

"Perhaps it is time to rethink her recovery," the doctor said. Baxter kissed her on the forehead and walked out. Marci's hair grew and her palor was slowly disappearing thanks to the beautiful spring weather. The nurses had started to open the windows periodically during the day. Meanwhile, Baxter was dealing with a massive insurance settlement of Marci's house. He was also in the final throes of his own case. Weeks passed and he didn't go to the hospital. *Maybe it is a lost cause,* he started thinking.

Near the end of spring, about 5 months after she went into the coma, he returned to the hospital. His case was resolved and he once again had freetime. Outside, the sun was shining and the entire world was in bloom. The great tree in the courtyard was filled with flowers and greenery, surrounded by a carpet of purple petals, the brightness of which seemed untenable by the humble branches. The air itself was abuzz with the action of life awakening. All along the walls of the coutyard, tulips shone like rubies and other precious stones; others bore feathers from exotic, yet-undiscovered birds of paradise.

Inside, however, the hospital was sterile, trapped in the seasonless smell of anti-septic and fermaldahyde. Marci was a time traveller. Time had become inconsequential. Five months, 6 months, 9 moons, 3 seasons, 1 year, 12,365,021 heat beats, uncountable circadian cycles, and suddenly she opened her eyes: beaching herself onto reality like a disoriented whale.

Imagine rising, breaking the surface of the water for air at night. Her eyes were fuzzy with the miniscule solar systems we see just before we wake up. Billions of stars refracting light, dust particle comets and invisible, electric eels swimming in her vision. Her consciousness returned from the spiralling arm of the Milky Way to find the geography of her body emerging from an ice age. The balance in her system had been thrown off. Her voice was a silent echo in the desert that was her throat—dust mucking up the mechanics of her esophagus. She was a ruined garden, burnt by frost and whithering from drought. She was an ecosystem emerging, awakened by some cosmic accident.

When her vision cleared, she could see Baxter standing with his back to her, looking out the window. He was almost skeletal, emaciated and fascinated by a child playing in the courtyard. To Marci it was all a very strange scene. She breathed spring air undeniably and the sound track was that of the coy giggles of a youth. These first bits of data fired through her nervous system and overlayed with the image of Baxter in his long coat with his unkempt hair. It didn't make sense. The lighting was warm. *Am I dead?* she wondered and licked her lips. They were cracked and dry and the movement of her tongue was like the volcanic eruption of some prehistoric geyser that once held the key to primeordial life.

She cleared the dust from her throat. As if all her senses finally stepped into sync, Baxter turned to her.

"Marci?"

"B?" Her voice was the wind of a sandstorm: hoarse, arid, barely audible. There was a sudden dark flash in her warm spring vision and she closed her eyes, just to make sure. Inside her head were beautiful spirals of consciousness sewing together a rhapsody of unfinished dreams. All beaming in technicolour of spring sunbeams penetrating the thin layer of skin of her eyelids.

When she opened her eyes, Baxter's guant face greeted her, smiling just enough to show off his pointed teeth.

"All the gospels don't have the words…" Marci cleared her throat again and tried to sit up.

"No, Marci. Wait." He said and fetched a cup of water from the shelf nearby. "Drink, drink. You'll feel beter." And with the touch of liquid slipping down her troat, she immediately understood the life-giving and sustaining power of water. She could feel it coating her insides, greasing the mechanics.

"Don't tell me you've gone to religion, Baxter," she managed to say.

"Welcome back, my dear Marci."

A NEW BEGINNING

Now, emerging from a coma is no easy thing—no matter how long you've been frozen in time. In Marci's case, there was muscular rehabilitation issues, systemic re-adjustment to things like eating, drinking and sleeping, as well as legal issues.

The doctors, I have to say, were the most surprised of everyone. Baxter held on to some flimsy ribbon of hope that Marci would one day wake up, but the nurses and doctors had clearly given up hope once the 4 month date had passed on the Wing's calendar.

Perhaps because of her athletic physique, Marci retained a significant amount of muscle. She started moving almost immediately, and perhaps because of a newfound reverence for water, demanded a bath. The nurses offered a sponge bath, but she was ardent. She wanted her body submerged in water. She needed the weightlessness, the viscosity wrapped around her limbs.

After a few days (and a lot of negotiations), she was wheeled to a tub and undressed by a nurse. Her body, it seemed, had shrunk. It could easily have been confused with that of an elderly woman or a teenager on the way to anorexia. You could see ribs striated beneath her pale skin, joints overrexaggerated agains the thin limbs, and her pelvis seemed to stand out in scale as if it was the only reminder of her former self. Her hair was long and lifeless, compared to when Marci herself was in charge of taming it. There was a rarefied layer of gold hair covering her shins and the tufft on her pubis stoof mildly aflame, boxed in by the boney iliac crests of her over-emphasized pelvic girdle.

I am the frame of a human, she thought.

She was light enough that the nurse had no trouble lifting her, and when submerged, she closed her eyes. It was as if she absorbed the water directly into herself through the tiny pores in her skin.

The water was paradise. Beneath the surface, she could easily move her body, bending her arms and legs, splaying herself out. While her hair floated Ophelia-esque on the surface, she imagined lillies in a Monet style, splashed out onto the tickling miniscus of the reflecting water.

The nurse bathed her and they talked about current events and the little things she had missed while she was having her spectacular voyages.

Upon return to her bed that night, she fell asleep staring at the lines on the ceiling tiles. She was afraid to lose consciousness again, but moments before she closed her eyes for the night, she found the smiling face of a reclining buddha with its narrow eyes among the lines on the ceiling. Somehow reassured, she passed into dreamland.

A few days later, Alex came to visit her. With his trademark bravado he entered carrying a bouquet of red and yellow tulips and a newspaper under his arm. His afro was gone, replaced by short, spikey hair and he was wearing rectangular, black-framed glasses.

"Well, well, well, well, well," he said, "if it isn't our local celebrity invalid." She smiled when she heard his voice.

"Nice haircut."

"I thought a little Alex action would cheer you up." He put the tulips on the windowsill and sat down on the bed. "How's your brain? Can you still think straight?" She frowned and pursed her lips.

"I'm fine," she said. "Exi-perfecksie."

"Not much of a talker though, huh?" He unbuttoned his pilot jacket, showing off his untamed, mediterranean chest hair. "That's alright," he said. "Otherwise you'd be just another Jane McPlain, no wits and all talk. And you know, Marsikins, I like you better just. like. *this*." He punctuated the last three words by tapping the beat against her shoulder with his index finger. She smiled.

"What?! No snappy remark?" he acted surprised. "And no

'thank you' either! What happened to Ms. Goody-Goody Two Shoes?"

"Still wearing the Superman briefs?"

"*Whoa! HooOOOooold* onto your panties, toots! They're boxers, not briefs…and yes!"

"Thanks for the flowers."

"You know, I thought you'd have been more surprised to see me," he said slimming his eyes at her.

"It feels like I saw you a week ago." She noticed the paper he put on the counter near the bed.

"Are you serious, Ms. Wood? Don't you remember all those times I came here and recited those French fairytales to you? You mean you didn't hear anything?"

"You did?" Now she sat up a bit wide-eyed.

"Yeah, are you saying you don't remember? I was sure that's what woke you up!"

"Really? You came?"

"No way, man! You know me!" He laughed out loud, but Marci only mustered a forced photograph smile.

"Yeah, I didn't expect anyone to come." She pressed the incline button on the bed until she was sitting up fully.

"You know, I've gotta stop calling you 'toots'," he said, "You feel like one of those twiggy, Italian catwalk models. I thought you had more boob than that, kid." He made a cartoony disappointing face.

"Well, I've been dieting," she replied, "and don't call me 'kid'."

"Why? You like 'toots' better?"

"Yea, I guess." Then her attention turned back to the newspaper almost within reach. "Alex," she asked, "what did you mean by 'celebrity invalid'?" He grabbed the newspaper, flipped a few paged and folded it into a square. Then he tossed it lightly (yet dramatically) onto her lap.

The headline read: TORONTO WOMAN AWAKES FROM A 6 MONTH COMA

"Has it really been that long?"

"You can bet your booties it has." Alex stood up, towering over her. "You can call this your pad for now, but what are you going to do when they kick you out? You coming to live with me again? Cause if so, you gotta start eating right!"

"I'll think about it," she said, still reading the article.

Then suddenly she remembered her house. "Any word about my house?"

Blue

*I am Nun, the Sole One, who has no equal, and I came into being
yonder on the great occasion of my flood, when it came into being.
I am the one who came into being in my form, 'Circlet who is his
Egg'. I am the one who originated there, in the primeval waters.
Look, the flood is subtracted from me; look, I am the remainder.
It was by means of my power that I created my body, and made
myself as I wished, according to my heart.*
~Spell 714 of the Coffin text of the
Egyptian Book of the Dead

Reflecting back at her were her own blue eyes. They were
still exactly the same cerulean blue, but what was different was
her cheeks. Somehow they remained rosy—a Pantone™ 162, a
perfect peach. A maquillage side effect of the arsenic, perhaps.

She laid down the mirror gently, which took more
strength than she expected. After a month of physiotherapy, she
was slowly recovering, learning how to walk, how to balance, and
lift a handheld mirror all over again. It was a draining process.
Luckily, there was Baxter. He was her ever-vigilant guardian.

On the counter lay about 16 envelopes—unopened
backdated mail, which she was catching up on a handful a day.

Her eyes looked up from the mail and addressed the room. Once again she found herself in a hotel room. A nice hotel room. The walls were a pale avocado green, a faux-Victorian type wallpaper. Everything matched from the counters, to the kitchenette, to the perfectly puffed and fluffed and satisfactorily beige cushions placed on nearly every conceivable surface lower than hip height. The last time she was inside a hotel, of course, was when she tried to trim a branch of her own family tree.

Looking back at the mail, she found a letter with Baxter's arabesque handwriting on it. "*Keep Important!*" it read. *Let's start with this,* she thought.

It was a pleasant, thick envelope to touch and bore the elegant, embossed letterhead of *Tiesma, McArthur and Valleymede Barristers at Law.*

A few of Marci's remaining possessions had been dropped off at the reception by Alex the day before; they included: a French-English dictionary, her pencil case, expired coupons for a bento box at a Japanese restaurant near the library, a few grey suits, her letter opener, a discarded medical sculpture of a human heart, and a journal she kept, chronicling every book they archived.

She picked up the letter opener, a sleek silver blade with a handle in the shape of a hippo carved out of turquoise. It was a gift from an acquaintance who went to Egypt. Marci loved the letter opener. She believed, incorrectly perhaps, that the hippo was an Egyptian god that fit ever so ergonomically into the palm of her hand. It cut through the thick envelope easily, despite her frail muscles and miscoordination, making a crisp leafy sound.

Inside, she found a cheque from her insurance company for just over a million dollars.

"Baxter," she gasped.

THE MUSEUM

Although she could walk short distances now, Baxter still forced her to sit in the wheelchair when they went out. His skin was regaining some of the colour it had lost during the drawn out legal procedures and he had found a job at a small pharmacy in town.

They had promised to go to the Egyptian exhibition at the museum. The mummies, Baxter explained, would show Marci how everything could have turned out if she hadn't woken up. The entrance of the Museum of Natural History had been renovated since she had been there last. Her memories of a whale skeleton floating in the vaults above the atrium had been betrayed by a thousand birds of varying sizes looking down at the museum-goers in an awe-inspiring flock of colours. They passed by some posters with pictures of Egyptian pharaohs hanging from the walls as they entered the main hall.

"Baxter, I have to thank you for taking care of the insurance for me."

"Oh, it was nothing. I was already seeing my lawyer more than my own mother, so I figured, why not help dear Marci while at it and fix the mess I made." As they talked, they passed by a variety of small artifacts used in the day-to-day life of someone in the New Kingdom somewhere in Lower Egypt.

"I really appreciate everything you've done for me. And I know you feel responsible, but none of this was your fault." Baxter pushed her at a steady pace and the voice of a museum guide briefly interrupted their conversation.

"The Egyptian creation myth centres around *Nun*, a chaos deity, upon whose waters the world floats…" There was a throng of people surrounding the guide, who continued to tell some key Egyptian myths. "The hieroglyph for *Nun*, was an inverted sky glyph…" Baxter stopped the wheelchair and

99

Marci stood up, grasping onto his arm for support. The guide continued, explaining Osiris and Isis, and the cycles of the sun Ra. He explained in graphic detail how Set chopped up Osiris' body in an attempt to usurp him, scattering the pieces across the land and into the Nile. Then in a tone of melancholy, how Isis collected the pieces to put her husband back together again.

"Of course, she couldn't find one crucial piece," he said. "Does anyone here know which piece was missing?" He now turned the attention back towards the audience.

Through the silence Baxter whispered into Marci's ear: "His penis." The silence continued for a few seconds and Marci raised her eyebrows.

"Yes, ladies and gentlemen, she was unable to find his loins, the progenerative piece that would make Osiris a man, a father, and complete him. How*ever*," he stretched the word a bit for suspense, "he *does* return to life to become King of the deities after all."

"Let's go," Baxter said and helped Marci back into her chair.

They continued past mummified cats and hawks and crocodiles. Baxter briefly guided her into a rebuilt Egyptian tomb. It had a small entrance and he had to duck as he entered— she, however, just rolled in. Inside was dark.

"What are you going to do with the money?"

"Hmmm…Not sure yet," she said. "Maybe take a vacation once I can walk around by myself."

"Well, it shouldn't be too long now. You're looking much better already."

"Thanks, you don't look so shabby yourself," she said, "once you clean up, that is." Baxter smiled.

Soon they saw the mummies, the main attraction. The tour was already inside the room and the guide was explaining the mysterious death of Tutankhamen at a young age. He was at maximum, 19 years of age at his death, which may have resulted from a chariot accident, a malignant infection, or a murder. We will never know."

A member of the tour raised his hand and asked about the drawings on the sarcophagus.

"The pictures on the sides are instructions for the soul once it gets to the afterlife," he explained. "They were usually prominent excerpts from the Book of the Dead."

Baxter and Marci, while half listening, were examining strips of papyrus found in the burial chamber. On them were pictures of the gods, the pharaoh, and perhaps representations of *Nun* and his waters. Marci was enthralled by one picture of a man rising out of the waters and holding aloft a boat, on which others much smaller walked and on which the sun-disk was balanced on top of a scarab.

"Excuse me," she said with a firm voice and Baxter flipped her chair around to face the guide.

"Yes?" he responded, dropping his story of supposed curses.

"What do the pictures on the papyrus on this wall represent?"

"Well, the papyruses along the outside wall are pieces of the Book of the Dead. They are the best evidence we have for the Egyptian spiritual beliefs. They enlighten us about their conception of the soul, the afterlife as well as their world view."

"What does this one in particular mean?" she asked then added, "the last one here with the waves in the sky?"

"Actually, good question, Miss." He took a breath. "As you might remember from before, I mentioned Nun, the god of chaos and water. Well, the Egyptians believed that the waters of Nun will one day inundate the world once again washing clean any trace of existence. It is the Egyptian apocalypse." The crowd shifted their attention from the mummies and their sarcophagi to the brown strips which covered the far wall. "*Nun*, however, was a protective and beneficent deity and many scholars argue that his spontaneous coming into and out of existence is, in fact, a metaphor for the soul. If you like, I could explain more at the end of the tour, but I'm afraid we must move on. If you would please follow me…" And with that the crowd started petering out of the room, leaving Marci and Baxter alone once again.

"Interesting."

"Yeah," Baxter was now studying the preserved skin of the mummy in the centre under the glass. "You know," he said, "if I ever die before you, will you make me a promise?"

"Sure. Anything."

"I want you to take my body—as is!—and throw it into a bog somewhere. And be sure to leave my cell phone in my pocket, ok?" They both laughed a small, sublime laugh.

TIME AWAY FROM THE CITY

The thing is, Marci was serious about her vacation. She saw this as her goal and worked harder each day to get to the point where she would no longer need the nurse coming in to help her flex and stretch and lift her limbs. She envisioned a perfect place somewhere far away with a tropical sea where she might find peace once again and reflect upon her life and its direction.

The critical moment came when, for rehabilitation, she sauntered by a travel agency in her grey suit. The board was full of discount flights and old 'bait-and-switch' deals, but what caught her attention was a picture of a floating marketplace. In a terribly gaudy, red typeface the word '*Malaysia*' was scrawled child-like. There was a token palm tree in the foreground, a small fisherman's boat balanced on the bluest blue, set against the wooden houses on stilts in the background. The word '*Malaysia*' seemed to rise (or set) like the sun in the tropical sky. All of this she seemed to breath in, filling her body and mind with the warmth of the azure sea.

This is where I will recover, she thought.

(As a side note, Marci was still unemployed and not looking. She rotated between three 98% grey suits and lived in the Athabasca Hotel. The large, lump sum of money she received allowed her a significant amount of freedom.)

When she left the travel agency, the word 'Semporna' echoed back and forth in her mind like an old steam train pulling out of a station. It was her destination: a small coastal town on the easternmost point of the island of Borneo, extending in the slow, lazy trail of an archipelago towards the Philippines. "The perfect peace" the agent had told her.

Since she really had no affairs to finalize and hardly anything to pack, she decided to leave immediately. In her mind she made a list of things she would need to buy: sunscreen, flip-flops, a towel, etc, etc, etc.

The plane left at 6:20pm the same day.

SEMPORNA

A 16-hour flight. One layover. A hot night in Kuala Lampur. A 3-hour flight over unspoilt jungle in a single propeller plane.

Inside the 1978 Cessna plane, Marci watched the scenery blur by beneath her. It was green—a tropical, intense green unlike the North American boreal forest she was used to. The main difference was the palm trees dotting the shore and others standing soldier-like in platoons along the dirt roads. Inside, the cockpit was noisy and every once in a while, the pilot would shout something back at her, but between the noise and the accent, she couldn't hear him. She simply nodded. Below her, on a river, she noticed a small wooden boat ferrying jungle-people around. The sun reflected off the brown, snaking waters and Marci had to squint her blue eyes. She closed them momentarily and considered the beauty of life. Bright, golden rays passing through the thin skin of her eyelids tinted her imagination in a womb-like pink. A feeling, more than a colour. A warm Pantone™ 170. When the sun twirled above the plane in a wide arc and gravity pulled her leftward, the imaginary space returned to a neutral tone in which Marci could sense—for a fleeting second—the goodwill of the human race. She opened her eyes and thought about the beauty surrounding her, the jungle-people down on the river on their carved canoes, and the inaudible pilot smiling back at her every so often, Baxter finally unthawing at home. She felt like she understood the marvellous intricacy of creation. She felt her very molecules vibrating in the wave pattern of life itself.

They landed on the ocean in a vast natural cove, which looked like a shallow crystal bowl—a pure pool, reflecting the few clouds in the sky. About 50 meters from the shore stood a collection of wooden houses akin to the ones she saw in the poster at the travel agency. There were a number of people standing on the boardwalks, watching the metallic Cessna Titan make its water landing.

They exited onto a long dock and walked towards the *Aoh-Aoh Water Hotel*, where Marci fell into a dense, 10-hour long, dreamless sleep.

*   *   *

Around sunset, she slipped out and rented a water taxi. The owner wore a red Indonesian fez, proclaiming his faith. Since he spoke no English, they negotiated using a map. She pointed up the river to where a marketplace stood. They cruised along accompanied by exotic birdsong. It was quiet so early in the morning and passersby exchanged friendly salutes. The closer they came to the market, the more canoes they passed. Some carrying bananas, others fish, others yet undetermined vegetative matter. There were a few glorious ones, enveloped in sublime perfume, carrying baskets of nutmeg and spices. Along the side of the river, boats were tied together, forming makeshift stores and restaurants, and they accumulated the farther they rowed, gradually forming a grander, connected structure.

This is the market, she thought, surrounded by merchants in straw hats and women with covered hair. People were bartering, eating, buying, trying, chatting, rowing, and jumping from boardwalk to boardwalk over the muddy water.

A lively merchant, a darkly tanned, shirtless man, joined his canoe with theirs. Suddenly, Marci's left side had become a buffet of tropical fruit. The man theatrically offered her some to inspect and as soon as she took them, he would babble elaborate explanations in Malay. He smiled and cut a dragon fruit, offering a soft, sweet bite to her. She felt so overcome by his authenticity that she couldn't resist handing him some money, for which he loaded a few fruit into her canoe.

The driver then steered towards a building on stilts nearby and motioned for Marci to wait. He spoke his reason as he tied up the canoe. Marci also got off the canoe and sat on the dock, her feet dangling off the high edge. There, sitting amongst

105

these foreign people, she felt some peace come over her. She felt somehow attached to nature. The blue sky, the green leaves, dotted with multi-coloured birds, the hot sun, and the delightful purple shadows all washed over her, soaking into her like a wonderful energy. She smiled, unable to resist the vibrance of the place. Behind her, some children played, giggling and staring at her. She spotted them and held out a fruit. The little one stepped closer and took it. He probably said 'thank you' and then touched her grey jacket. When she looked down, she noticed that she was still wearing a 98% grey suit, which was now stained with sweaty patches. Still smiling, she stripped off her grey and felt the warm, tropical air caress her glistening skin. She wore a white tank top underneath, now spotted with the camo-pattern of shadows and yellow blotches of sun. Except for her ruddy cheeks, she looked very white to the kids and they scattered away chasing the fruit Marci had given them.

When the driver returned a while later, Marci had planned their route back. She had also planned her next few days: for the most part, going to the beach and swimming in the beautiful cove.

THE ISLAND

For three days she relaxed and swam, eating fruit for breakfast and *nasi goreng* for dinner. Her body gained muscle and colour in the waters. She bought a bathing suit and spent most of her time in it. She felt she was now ready for more adventure, so she rented a boat to ferry her to the nearest island, somewhere between Borneo and the Philippians. It was supposed to be the most peaceful, spectacular place within boating distance.

The water taxi dropped her off on a tiny, long boardwalk in front of a cabin. He told her she could rent it from him for a small price. He said he comes back everyday, so she could come with him whenever she wanted to go back to the *Aoh-Aoh Water Hotel*. She nodded and he unlocked the shack and gave her the key.

After exploring the small island, she found her ideal beach, hidden by a small trail, leading down a cliff to an isolated, tree-canopy, under which was a shaded, white beach. It was perfect. Beautiful and peaceful; uninhabited except for a troop of small monkeys. She watched the sunset there and cried. Why she cried, she didn't know. Perhaps she was overcome with the beauty. Maybe she noticed the value in her life for the first time. It could be that her body just had to release the tears to cope with being in a coma for so long. Personally, I believe it was simply the realization that Marci Wood might not have seen such a prelapsarian sight had she suceeded in commiting suicide. She had never been abroad and had always wanted to lie on a tropical beach ever since those trips on which she would accompany her mother to the saltwater mouth of the St. Lawrence. All Marci knew was that life was good.

That night she fell asleep under the mosquito netting, feeling like an exotic princess in a faraway land.

The next day was equally beautiful. The dome of the sky

was a clear blue, and not a cloud to be seen anywhere. She fell asleep in her grey skirt and white tank top, on a chair sitting on the long deck of her cabin. What should have been an afternoon nap, turned into a solid, dreamless sleep. There was a drink sitting on the deck beside her chair and she was wearing sunglasses, even though she was in the shade. In fact, if she had been sitting in the sun, she might have noticed the upside-down reflection disappearing against her cabin wall. If her sleep were not so heavy, she might have become aware of the frantic, suction of the waves beneath her. Birds flying overhead must have seen the azure waters receding suddenly, leaving a barren stretch of sand on top of which a needless boardwalk ran. It was like a baubling ripple, pulling back past the little shack, withdrawing to a distant point near the horizon. They must have seen surprised fish, flapping on the empty beach, where minutes ago water had been. The ripple, a kind of backwards wave, picked up momentum and tore away the stilts holding Marci's cottage. She plunged into the rapidly retreating waters, drinking a mouthful of salt water. Suddenly she was awake, struggling to swim against the incredible pull of the current. Around her was a deep blue, pieces of wood from the dock, and the white spray of bubbles, going in every which direction. She rolled around, losing any sensation of gravity. Spun and assaulted by forces her body could not comprehend, she became a helpless part of the liquid film contracting *en mass* towards a central point somewhere under the ocean. Her mind was empty. No, it was blue. The same colour blue that surrounded her. And she remembered the Egyptian letter opener that got her into this mess in the first place. She pictured *Nun*, the god of water and chaos, laughing. His immense diaphragm contracting and releasing rippling waves of laughter—and she was stuck in it! Over top of the image of the god, pictures of the Malay children appeared. Then upside-down in the powerful wave, she wondered if this was how it would feel to wrestle an angel.

    I am not ready to die, she thought. And she prayed. To whichever god wanted to hear—to all of them together, maybe.

Please, Nun, god of waters, creator, God of Jacob Israel, and all the prophets and buddhas. I need more time on this planet. I cannot die yet. I know I might have used all my second chances, but I just realized how important life is. Please, please help me now.

Now, picture this: Marci, a grey blur under the tropical blue waters, now up, now down, brings her hands together in a prayer position. Then, inexplicably, she feels a second force, stronger than the wave, shooting her up. Gravity yields to her, and there is a sudden acceleration away from the centre of the Earth. Underwater, Marci becomes a torpedo, salty bubbles trailing behind her until she breaches the surface in a misty explosion of water droplets shimmering like crystal jewels in the sunlight. Yet she keeps flying up, up, up.

Her speed is paranormal, gaining altitude fast: 2 stories, 6 stories, 12 stories. She slows down exponentially as the laws of physics take hold again, and she tops off at about one hundred meters and comes to a stop as upward momentum and gravity equalize.

In that pause at the top of her ascent, she surveys the hiccup of water beneath her. The most luminous lapis lazuli blue overtop of a deeper, darker hue, rolls over the remains of the long dock, erasing it from the landscape. The wave moves at an enormous speed and paints the island blue as it covers it. Near Marci, a surprised bird squawks and she feels gravity tugging at her, bringing her back down towards the sea. But in that moment just before she falls, she sees the sea and the sky become one. The blue water covers the island, submerging any trace of it in the awesome power of the sea. Marci looks at the horizon, but fails to find it, because there isn't one. Around Marci, beneath, and above her there is only blue—the cerulean blue of primordial life.

She falls faster and faster. And as she enters the water again, it feels as if her body is cradled by an invisible watery hand. The wave has pulled back just enough to catch her and place her down gently on the beach.

THE AFTERMATH

The island was wiped clean. Any trace of humanity could only be found in the rubble and plastics draped over broken bushes and bent palm trees. There were a few voices screaming in the background, but her immediate surroundings were void of all life. A bit further on, the soft sand was littered with dead fish. Marci dragged herself up the beach to higher ground, and perhaps from shock, she passed out.

There was a voice talking to her when she woke up again—a touch of warm skin on her arm. She opened her eyes, squinting, and saw blood on her hand. Her vision (along with her notion of reality) faded to black, but she could feel someone carrying her.

Hours passed and her mind seemed turned off, or muted at least. As she came to, she heard many voices talking in foreign languages and, in the universal language, weeping not so far away. She felt cold and shivered, but found that she was surrounded by blankets in a dark room.

"Hello," a male voice welcomed her. As she looked for the source, he continued: "Over here." Judging from the accent he was American, and when her eyes adjusted, she saw his bandaged head sticking out of the bunk next to her.

"We're the only Americans here," he said. "You been sleeping a lot. They thought you were in a coma."

"How long have I been out?" She was suddenly panicked and sat up. It was then that she noticed the bandage on her right arm.

"Not that long. A day or two." From the white bandage around his head, several strands of blond hair could be seen sticking out. He didn't move much, but there was life in his eyes. "I've been kinda out of it too, you know. Can't be sure," he added.

She touched her arm and felt a slight sting.

"I wouldn't worry about that," he said watching her.

110

"Least of yer problems. They reckon you bashed your head hard. But what I can't figure out is why I got this bandage and your pretty face is totally unwrapped." He smiled at her. "You can call me Russ" He paused, waiting for her to introduce herself, then added, "I'm a US marine." Her head was pounding. *Did I hit it,* she wondered, but could not remember.

"My name is Marci Wood," she said. "Where am I?"

"This is a refuge for the injured and orphaned. No one else speaks English."

"I thought I died," she said. "Thought I was dead." Then she laid back in the cot and pulled the blankets over her head.

"They found you on a nearby island. You survived." He paused. "That tsunami… It was massive. It wrecked my ship. Hundreds of thousands are dead or missing." Two Malaysians came in and checked on Marci. They were happy to see her alive. The woman rolled up the window and along with bright light, hot air rushed into the canvas room. They were in a tent, she realized.

One of the attendants grabbed the bedpan from under the sailor's bed. It was filled with blueness. The other one switched the soldier's IV bag. After some hustle-bustle, they were alone again.

"What happened to you?" Marci finally asked.

THE SAILOR'S STORY

My name is Russell Andrew Ivy, third son of Chester and Monica Ivy. I was born in Newport, Rhode Island on a naval base. But, to tell you the truth, I grew up all over the States. I come from a long line of navy officers. My grandfather was Arturus Echo Ivy, a Captain for the old Merchant army sailing out of Florida and Bermuda. My dad, on the other hand, joined the army, much to the chagrin of my grandfather. So, we moved a lot. I saw deserts, the Appalachians, New England winters, flat plains with endless corn fields, more desert, the everglades with their gators—snippets of American landscapes like route 66 postcards. My older brothers both joined the service and I was left over on the base. After a series of unfulfilling jobs in landscaping and construction around the bases, I joined the navy.

I clearly remember the moment I decided to join the navy. I was eight years old and I was standing in Grampa Art's study, behind his enormous wooden desk, looking up at the ensign flag which hung from the ceiling. I loved his study—the deep, brown wood everywhere. He had maps passed down through generations of the Ivy line hanging on the walls; rough and leafy, hempen ropes tied in the most intricate knots adorned the wooden shelves; and placed in his umbrella stand was an officer's saber, which we often (and most secretly) played with. I spent my summers listening to one of the greatest sailors tell me about his adventures and when he explained about rigging and tacking and how the Nor'Easterly would make the topsail dance, I pictured the flag in his office undulating ever so slightly. I imagined it blowing high off the mast while Captain Arturus Ivy fought off pirates and outran competing ships.

He taught me how to use an astrolabe. And with stories, I learned the names of the constellations. Looking back, I now realize he was passing down that which gave meaning to the Ivy men. He was training me and I loved every minute of it.

In that moment in his study, I was drifting through my imagination. I saw the pastel blue of ancient maps in my mind's eye and I was carving out the contours of an undiscovered land. I saw myself birds-eye view on an old whaling schooner, charting a wiggly line around rocky coasts amidst the pale blue. And all the while, I was wearing Grampa Art's white cap.

Atop the mast, the Ivy ensign beat a rhythm in the wind. It was then that I felt the blue of the sea in my blood.

When I signed up, my dad was posted in Georgia, and it was as if the waters called me. When I announced my decision, my grandfather was very pleased. He put a fat cigar in my pop's mouth and cackled that he just assumed I would sign up when the time was right. I moved to Florida and eventually became a seaman on the USS Gettysburg about 2 years ago. Again grampa was pleased because that's where he sailed from as well.

The Gettysburg is a cruiser, usually assigned to the Indian Ocean. During the time I spent on the Gettysburg training in the Caribbean, I learned a lot and worked hard, harder than in construction. And then we saw the world: Caribbean islands, European ports, Egypt, Dubai, Zanzibar, Kuwait, Qatar, even Iraq. The life on the sea gave me a reason to live.

I was a good sailor, an even better *soldier* and my superiors liked me. But things really got interesting on the Gettysburg. That is where we fought for the first time against real enemies. We rescued a ship from Somali pirates, and supported teams in the Middle East. I became an officer.

It's not like I believe in war or anything either. Don't get me wrong, here. The navy is a tradition in my family. How would I feel to be the only sibling without a saber to spear my champagnes one day?

The Gettysburg was a nice place to make home. It was a Ticonderoga-class, guided-missile cruiser. What this means is that it is one *badass* ship. Whenever we docked in a foreign port, we became the target, you see. Now, the Navy has procedures in place to counter sabotage and terrorism while in port, but when

113

we docked in Basra there was a major festival going on.

We were just resupplying, but the sailors got jittery because we were all overdue shore leave, so we persuaded the Captain to let us go and we happily took to the party. Finding alcohol was no problem even in Muslim countries because the culture of 'port' is the same anywhere in the world. No matter where you are, there will be people catering to the perverse needs of sailors. It must be one of the most rewarding careers to own a watering hole in a major port.

Anyway, the men spilled out of the ship and joined the throngs of drunken men and women around the harbour. We never questioned the celebration, just started our own drinking groups.

Some men held out, saving their shore leave until they got to tropical Indian Ocean islands, but I couldn't resist. It had just been too long. I slipped out with a few other officers, finally sitting down at a wannabe Irish pub. The barkeep was a Sunni Arab, who spoke English with a British accent. He was very friendly and even joked around with the boys.

Let me tell you, that night was a serious bender! Martin Jessup, the physical combat trainer was with us and he snuck a pair of boxing gloves out. They were passed between the guys periodically until eventually a right hook would come out of nowhere and sock you in the face. I still only have these blurry memories of sucker-punching my subordinates. That and a single other memory stands out.

I remember leaving the bar. A sombre, moonless darkness had settled on the ancient city. The party had moved well beyond the port, where singing, yelling, and gunshots could be heard. There were a few limbless beggars haunting the empty streets, and navy personnel dribbling back to the ship upon hitting just the right level of inebriation. My group stumbled down the streets, discreetly donning a left- or right-handed boxing glove. Then we saw a few other officers pulling a giant cart with a box on it. Clearly, something was up. They were trashed too, one of them shoeless.

"Let's ambush them," somebody said and the two of us with the boxing gloves (myself and Midshipman Evora) stepped into the shadows. We would have been a dead giveaway in a real ambush situation—both smelling of pure tobacco smoke, and both too drunk to walk straight. Luckily, our targets were preoccupied and equally drunk.

As they pulled the cart past the narrow alley we were hiding in, I jumped out and roundhoused the closest guy. Evora, wearing a left glove, boxed the other guy. We tackled them and showed them who's boss. Then things settled down and we helped them up. Everyone became very gregarious once they realized we were friendlies and we did our drunken salutes—mine complete with boxing glove.

"What's in the box?" someone asked. There were attempts made to keep it a secret, but we quickly learned that there was a giant customized cake in the box.

"Who's it for?"

"The Captain, dumbass!" *Thwack!* The glove landed heavily on his jaw. Everyone laughed overtop the throttled guy's complaints.

"Yo, it's the Cap's B-day on Thursday, so we got him a little thank you gift."

"That's very kind of you, Mills."

"Yeah, aren't you good little boys?" I said.

"Shut up, Ivy." Good thing I had the glove, I thought. It was hard to see who was talking in the darkness of the street.

"You guys gonna help us, or what?"

"Where you gonna put it?"

"Dobbs has access to the cold storage. We ran into him after the resupplying." What we couldn't see then was that Dobbs was practically completely passed out. One of the other men had to hold him up to walk. I reckon he had to play catch up and went overboard...metaphorically speaking, that is.

Naturally, we helped them sneak the cake on board. Jessup distracted the sentries, and we pushed that trolley up the ramps. From a military point of view, we were great—avoiding

115

detection by employing stealth. Drunk as hell, but great! We loaded the cake into cold storage using Dobbs' access card and passed out in our bunks.

The next morning, we all woke up with massive headaches and bruised jaws, but everything else was business as usual.

The ship was sent south towards Sri Lanka, and we motored, because winds and surf were in our favour. About a week later, in the middle of the Indian Ocean, the cake came out. The crew had prepared a little impromptu party for the Captain.

See, we all liked and respected him a lot and wanted to show him our appreciation. The men had stupid hats on and threw streamers and blew whistles. The same few officers brought the cake out of cold storage and in daylight we could see how big it actually was.

The enormous form rolled out on the same trolley we snuck onto the ship that night. It looked like a wedding cake, except there were no bride and groom at the top. Also, it was brightly coloured—baby blue, yellow and pink. Basically, it looked like the most stereotypical, large cake you could imagine. I half expected a cold, murdering suicide bomber to jump out, but the Captain cut the cake and served a few of them to the closest officers. Then we helped ourselves to pastel slices of the giant cake.

And let me just say that it was truly delicious. The cake was massive and everyone on the ship could have a piece. We played music and followed the cake with a ration of booze. Just one, mind you, but it was a blissful few hours on the blue waters.

Later that day, some sailors had stomach cramps and retired to quarters early. I got them at night and couldn't sleep. The next morning, sickbay was full. Several seamen had serious complaints and even the Captain had stayed in his quarters. We kept throttle, though and forged towards our destination. By mid-afternoon, we realized that there was a serious problem. The ship's medical staff was overstretched and they themselves feeling ill. There was a rumour flying around that several men had started to lose their hair. Like, it was falling out by the handful.

I heard about the details through the grapevine. People started speculating that the cake was poisoned. There were investigations going on and Dobbs, Evora, Mills and I were questioned. I told them all I knew, just like I told you before. The thing is, no one could remember buying the cake. Eventually, it came out that Mills bought it from a bakery on impulse. He was drunk and forgot the whole scene and no one else was there to confirm it.

It became serious when two of the sailors became bedridden with serious marks all over their skin. They looked like cancer victims. More and more people became bedridden and the doctor was freaking out, trying to determine the next course of action. We headed for the nearest port, but I reckon the docs figured it out before we made landfall.

Apparently, the cake contained thallium, the Soviet and Iraqi political poison of choice. The effects are brutal and take a few days to kill.

As I explained, most of us already experienced stomach cramps, and more and more men were losing their hair. Some were starting to see blotches and marks on their skin. And most frightening of all was the sensation of burning on the bottom of your feet and the palms of your hands. Midshipman Evora, who despite keeping most of his hair, had the most intolerable nerve pain. He screamed and stayed in bed because to him it felt like the deck was a superheated frying pan. He held his feet in his hands and blew on them as if they were on fire. His torturous screams acted like a sinister warning to the rest of us. The ship's operations fell apart. We realized that we had to keep the radio going and the more able of us formed a rotation.

I was there when the ship's doctor contacted Singapore. He talked about the possible courses of action and they weighed the options. Was there time to return to port, or would they be airvac'ed out? And then where would they go?

"We're gonna need about 3 kilos of Prussian Blue," the doctor said.

117

MARCI'S INTERJECTION

"For your info, thallium's most effective treatment is Prussian Blue," Marci interrupted. "It was one of the first synthesized pigments. Johan Frisch and an unnamed chemist synthesized it in 1706. They were trying to create a red lake pigment for commercial reasons. The unnamed chemist, who was most likely a Prussian named Diesbach, worked with insects. He extracted carminic acid from the chittinous shell and eggs of the *Dactylopius Coccus* insect, a freaky-looking flying beatle. He knew carmine red was produced from the defensive acid of the insect and experimented with it, trying to refine it. Cochineal, as the red was also called, originated in Mexico and spread to Europe with the Spanish Conquistadors. In the 17th Century, fabrics dyed with cochineal could be found as Far East as China, Mediterranean food was using it as a colorant, and women brushed their cheeks with carmine red powder.

"Diesbach, however, serendipitously discovered a lightfast blue pigment when he used contaminated potash. See, he borrowed some potash from a colleague, Johann Konrad Dippel, who was an alchemist and physician born in Castle Frankenstein. He supposedly created an equivalent to the achemist's 'elixir of life' in his animal oil. It was this animal oil that contaminated the potash, Diesbach used.

"So, through an uncanny turn of events, Diesbach, the uncredited Prussian, created a lightfast blue. Dippel called it 'Preussisch blau' and they set up factories to produce it.

"It has been a mystery to chemists until the invention of the X-ray, because when mixed, the solution would magically thicken and the colour deepen to get the characteristic Prussian blue. This phenomenon, along with the fact that when reduced the chemical became colourless, baffled alchemists and scientists alike.

"Prussian blue also left us the engineer's blue print, in colouring cyanotypes.

"In fact, Prussian blue itself is a complicated inorganic molecule that has the miraculous property of curing heavy metal poisoning like thallium."

And then she added with a smile:

"Lucky you!"

ADRIFT IN THE INDIAN OCEAN

Yes, uh, just what I was going to say...

Anyways, we had to get us some Prussian Blue and when we were passing through the Straits of Melaka, HQ radioed back that there was a factory in the Philippines, so we headed there at flanking speed. The situation on board got worse and worse, with the first few people going into critical condition. If there were deaths, they kept the numbers to the higher ups. The Captain made a few announcements, explaining our route to Cotobato City. We would be poison free in less than 12 hours, he said.

Meanwhile, the Gettysburg had turned to a ghost ship, tormented by screaming of seamen in limbo between this world and the Great Beyond. Somehow, I was not affected as badly, so I was constantly on duty, doing my best to keep things afloat. I stayed awake for 30 hours that night, running from one sick man to the next, checking in on the guys in the radio room, and taking a turn in the bridge.

The radio sounded at 4am. The voice was an older man, an Admiral or General perhaps. He told us that a chopper was flying in with a shipment of Prussian Blue. I woke the Captain, who looked pale and hairless. He stayed in bed and ordered me to bring the doctor immediately.

Outside, on the deck, the helicopter's distant searchlight could be seen like an artificial star heading towards us. All the remaining sailors ran on deck to salute (and await the medicine).

Since the doctor was with the Captain, one of the orderlies, holding his stomach in pain, waited with us. The longer we stood there, the hotter the deck became. We could all feel the discomfort on the soles of our feet. The insoles of my shoes felt like hot coals. But, resolute, we kept standing.

We got the paint out to the Captain and the sickbay as soon as possible. After a few minutes, the ships PA told us to eat about 7 grams of blue. The doctor fed it slowly to some of the critical patients and told them that all the poison would come out in their blue stool. We all ate the blue by the handful. Men were covered, teeth and hands blue. Lips looking like all life had drained from them. There were stains of blue pigment on handrails, doorframes, and on clothes.

The chopper returned with a few bodies, but in general—although blue—the mood on board was good. Here and there groups of people were cheering and we thought everyone was saved!

I was standing on the deck the next afternoon along with the few men who could still report for duty, when the warning came. I felt the ship shake and tilt starboard. Then the air raid siren went, but the sky was empty. A vast blue emptiness, which tilted more and more to the right, until the wave broke onto the deck.

Tsunami, I thought as I was swept off the side and out to sea. In the distance, I saw the ship flip over onto its side. Then I hit my head against something and passed out.

I also have no idea how I got here, but I reckon God saved me somehow.

THE RECOVERY

They both laid there, sweating into their beds. Russell's dressing had to be changed every few days and it seemed that each time more of his hair fell out. Beneath his bed, along with the blue stained bedpan, was a barn floor of golden hair. Marci had probed him a little about the incident and he responded openly. She asked him why he wasn't affected as much as the others and he told her he didn't like cake. Maybe he ate less, or on the other hand, he explained, perhaps it was God's work. The whole image of the cake on the boat stuck in her mind for days. It was a fantastical story.

But then so was hers.

She hadn't told him about the miracle in the sea. With every day that passed, she wondered if he would believe her. And with every passing day it got more and more difficult to tell him. They did get close, though, being the only English speakers. Russ was a charming young man with mollifying blue eyes and a chiseled bottom lip. He asked her if she was on vacation and when she nodded her head, he asked if she had come with anyone. Marci could tell by the expression in his eyes that he thought she had become separated from her friends or family.

"No, actually, I came alone," she said, which started a long conversation about the people in life that meant something. Clearly, Russell Andrew Ivy was experiencing some deep existential phenomenon. Marci told him how she lost everything, and then tried to commit suicide but the chemicals cancelled each other out. She told him about the coma, and how she sometimes can't believe she is awake, and about the grey room and her grey suits. She explained that she came to Malaysia to recover, to find herself and think about what she should do with her life next. "Life," she explained, "was feeling more and more like wrestling with an angel."

Then it was his turn. He talked about his family, how

122

his oldest brother had died in Iraq from friendly-fire. He talked about his grandpa and how much he missed him. His girlfriend, who was always waiting for him. She sent a perfumed letter with (naked) pictures, which he kept in his breast pocket. With great emotion he told her that he had lost this letter when he fell overboard and how she probably thought he was dead. Then he spoke at length about God, which he seemed to have found after surviving these two near fatal disasters. "God must have some plan for me. Some reason to keep me," he said, "or else, why was I the only one to survive?"

Through all of this emotional bonding, Marci never told him about the miracle in the ocean. Perhaps because she didn't immediately pray to the Christian God, but left Him as an afterthought ("and to any god that would hear my prayer"). He had just assumed she was plucked from the land by the wave and that she had somehow survived.

On the third day, an Australian doctor arrived and when he had time, told his two fellow anglophones news from around the world. He made sure they knew the details of the situation, but he also brought with him a local legend that had grown about a girl who survived the tidal wave.

It goes like this: *"Well, this gal—an American, I reckon— wuz tanning hehself on the beach, ya see. She musta had an ace head on heh, 'cuz when she noticed the woteh pullin' away, she took off ta heh hotel. It wuz chaos and she bahnded up stehs laaik a boomeh only to be bailed up by the woteh flowin' up the stehs. So wha' duz she do? She tries ta open heh room do'. Only, it's locked, ya see. Anyhoo, she's scramblin' t'unlock it, when the wave grebs heh. The mo' the woteh poulls at heh, the mo' she holds onta the do'knob, yeah? Until the bloody do' itself comes off! But she still holds taaight. Eventually, she gets flushed out ta sea on the do'. So she's left on heh room do' laaik a shark biscuit, yeah? They told me she was fehnd driftin' off one of the nearby aaislands in her bathers after a full day at sea."*

That night, Russell asked: "Hey, Marci, that story. That wasn't you, was it?" She paused, considering whether to tell him the truth.

"No," she said, "my hotel didn't have doorknobs." Then she added, "Goodnight, Russell."

*   *   *

Soon enough, Marci was on her feet again. The moment when she stepped outside the canvas tent, would forever remain with her. It was morning, about 8am, and a ray of sun had entered the darkness from outside. She imagined bright tropical skies with the blue ocean caressing the horizon. When she opened the flap of the tent and stepped through the blinding yellow light, it was like stepping into an Anselm Kiefer landscape, she thought: earthtones and neutral greys mixed in thick brushstrokes all across the land, rubble strewn on top of cross-hatched fallen trunks. It was like a scene from the apocalypse with the few figures in the distance desperately searching for things under the nothingness. From the look of things, they were in a camp on high ground, in what might have been a palm forest. A few slow seconds passed and tears welled up in Marci's eyes. She turned her back on the destruction and wiped her eyes before re-entering the tent where they slept.

That night, while Russell Ivy slept in the cot next to her, she decided that she would stay and help rebuild. The tsunami was a sign. She would devote her time to help those who can't help themselves.

The next morning, Marci, in her grey skirt and white tank-top, was sifting through planks that were once either boat hull or cottage walls. She found some good wood, planks that her mother would have loved. She dragged one of the larger pieces off the beach, remembering the one time her mother took her to the sea.

She was just 7-years old and it was still dark out and she woke up in her mother's arms, carried to the car, where she slept in the back seat until the sun came out. Her mother drove into the dawning sun to get to the St. Lawrence seaway. Marci remembered stopping near a rocky shore, where people around her spoke only French. The '*Fleuve*', as the locals called it, was a long, large salty river. It wasn't the ocean, but there were giant ships passing and little Marci didn't know the difference.

"Hey," her mom called to her as they descended the rocks to get to the shore. "Look here!" She had found a wide plank, polished smooth and white from the surf. "Did you know that this is the place with the highest tides in the world?" (A fact Marci would be unable to forget for the remainder of her life).

This memory floated back to the top of her consciousness as she pulled the wide panel of wood back towards the camp.

"This might make a strong wall of a shelter," she told the first rescue worker she saw. But deep down she had wanted to tell him about what a beautiful canvas this would have made her mother. How, with a splattering of colour, this simple piece of wood could become a magical painting that would provide a person with a glimps into the abstract mind of her mother, the artist.

Red

Ring around a rosie
A pocketful of posies
ah-tishoo!, ah-tishoo!.
We all fall down.

et us return to the city where all this began, the city with
tall sky-scrapers tinted in the rosé wine of twilight, where old
Victorian buildings house government and public offices. We
find Marci Wood standing in the biggest office of the library. She
is looking out of the window down the streetcar tracks towards
the lake. A man sweeping the floor in an adjacent building spots
her momentarily: a female figure in grey, framed by the pillasters
of the window, like a modern variation of Roman frieze—a
suited Ceres, or Diana perhaps. She steps away from the window
and is lost to him in the reflections of the city.

Inside the library, it was hot. Marci took off her suit
jacket and placed it on the chair. The office was hers now. She
ran her fingers over some deep gouges in the old desk. She had

been very suspicious when they asked her to come in for a job interview. In fact, she hesitated until she ran into Alex on the street and he told her how the old manager of the library had quit.

"Marsikins! You won't believe it. The old soldier of a manager went raving mad one day. She just snapped. We found her locked in her office weeping. She'd been there overnight and didn't reply when we knocked. The security dude saw her on the cameras, so we knew she was in there. Finally, she came out, looking like she spent the night dancing among witches in the forest. Honestly, I could never have imagined her like that: hair all tangled, face dirty from running mascara. She was barely wearing clothes—just an extra-large, white collared shirt. I mean, sexy legs and all, but not kosher. Know what I mean?"

So Marci decided that she would go back. It seemed like the timing was right. She had just returned from Malaysia and was trying to find a job and a place to live. One thing led to the next and then all-of-a-sudden Marci Wood was in charge of the Archives. She once again had to wear a grey suit, but this time her duties included buying rare books, and examining old books for which priority they get in the scanning process—a much *much* more glamorous job, right? And even the grey suits somehow made her feel good. It had become her persona, her public face, afterall.

Marci hadn't thought of it yet, and maybe she never would, but somewhere inside the Security Office of the Library, there exists a recording, a captured video of Dr. Brown (or *Misteress Catherine Deneuve*, as Marci once used to call her) losing her mind. It would definitely be a grainy black and white—or no! A greenish nightvision! You could see her turn on the light and walk into her office, staring out the same window we found Marci at a few minutes ago. In the video, she is holding something in her hand. A letter, perhaps. Then, she sits at her desk and buries her face in her hands. I imagine she sits like that for a long time, so the video fast-forwards: more sitting, some pacing, she uses her computer, then out of nowhere she wipes everything off her desk with one bold arm stroke, shattering paperweights and electronics as if they had equal value. At this point, any seasoned reality TV viewer would grab the remote and press play to go back to realtime, where we can watch her behaviour like some kind of couch-anthropologist. We see her standing up suddenly. In the backround, the city lights have come on. She takes off her grey, fitted suit jacket and throws it out of the camera frame. Then she digs in the immense drawer of her desk to bring out what looks like a sharp knife. There is a blip in the digits of the microchip in the camera and we see a sudden jump from cubism to realism, but now she is standing in front of the desk, stabbing the surface of it with passion. Of course, as in all security videos there is no sound, but in fact, you don't even need volume to realize she is screaming. Again she brandishes the knife right-way-up with obvious intent to throw it. She swings at the window, but doesn't release. Then she spins around and throws it at the wooden wall.

Now, the next part gets really weird. The well dressed, prim and proper woman falls to the floor and rolls around in a conniption fit. We fast-forward again through the rolling and spasming and flailing of limbs to a point where she stands up and starts to undress. It is at this point that the security guard, if he watched this live, would take a slow drag off a cigarette in order to suck every last ounce of enjoyment out of the moment. She undresses, throwing clothes everywhere.

She stumbles around in her designer, lacy underwear— probably black and pink if we could see colour. In low resolution, the image looks voyeuristic and erotic, and momentarilly we forget that it is supposed to be the scene of a nervous breakdown. She steps on some broken junk and, losing her balance, collapses over the desk, ass facing the camera. I bet the security guard was going ape over this! It must have been way better than watching Marci Wood's floating head in the grey room. She gets up on the desk and takes off her panties, kicking them at the main door to her office. It is at this point that I imagine her doing her witches' dance, but most likely, she jumps over the desk and takes a man's shirt out of a drawer. And naturally, she pulls it over her near naked body. I see her curling into a little ball and weeping until they find her the next morning. This is probably all on the recording in the Security Office—if not all over the internet already!

But let's get back to Marci, standing there in her new office. She felt a bit nervous at the new responsibility, but then she thought about how a few weeks before all this, she was building schools and shelters in Borneo. It was as if the sun in the tropical skies had warmed Marci's cheeks to a nice pinkish brown—in reality, however, it was probably still the residual effects of the arsenic. Her permanent glow gave her confidence, you see. *I am more than ready,* she thought. *I am young and smart and beautiful and have seen a tsunami from a hundred meters above.* She then adjusted her hair with a brush of the hand against the ends curling away from the amber hair clips she was using today.

It is hard to believe that the office was the scene of such follie less than a week ago. *I'm gonna have to redecorate,* Marci thought and walked outside, past the embittered secretary and into the elevator.

*   *   *

That day she proved that she was an able manager by running a back-to-business meeting, bossing the secretary around (in an earnest "I'll try my best" kind of way), meeting with the Head Cheese, and still helping Alex out in the Archives for an hour or so. Yes, she was able to do the job, alright. And *more*, because she still had no place to live and so she spent the majority of her afterhours surfing the net at work. And, in this way she found the ad for the Queen Mary Psalter. It was a 15th Century copy of the gothic book, but the photos looked great. In fact, she saw this as a beautiful symbol that fell from the sky into her lap.

The next day she checked the finances of the library and after a discussion with director (who secretly adored Marci), a plan to purchase the rare book was set in motion. Marci would travel to Paris, attend the meeting of antique manuscripts, and bid on behalf of the library for the Queen Mary's Psalter.

Omigod. Omigod. Omigod! Her mind was racing with the implications. She would go to Paris! *I've never taken part in an auction,* she thought. *I'll have to practice.* And so began Marci Wood's stint as a buyer at the Waddington's Auction house.

She attended a show every weekend, bidding on lamps, paintings, and jewelry. She had no place of her own yet, so her hotel room and office were quickly filled up with a myriad of canvases and exotic lamps—some antique marble, others feathered, others yet with the simple elegance of *art deco.* And although Marci's wardrobe consisted solely of 98% grey suits, it excited her to know that beneath it, she was wearing ancient, golden Scythian bracelets; Turkish rubies and saphires, once worn by the sultan's harem; and necklaces of Japanese pearl smuggled out during the isolationist Edo period. During the day, she would imagine the brilliant rainbow of colours under her clothes, like the mother-of-pearl inside the perfect spiral of a Nautilus sea shell.

PARIS

A few months passed (quickly and uneventfully) and we find Mademoiselle Marci Wood in her grey suit, standing on a boullevard in the City of Love. To her left is a sculpted garden; to her right, bronze heads of Rodin's *Burgers of Callais* can be seen peaking out over a tall hedge. There is a crisp wind that makes you want to sit in a coffee shop or walk around a museum.

It was her first time in Paris and despite the occasional man pissing in the gutters (or *pissoir* as the French call them), she found the city beautiful and majestic. She felt tiny under the *Arche de Triomphe's* carved friezes; liberated while standing in the *Museé D'Orsay* among Monet's *Waterlillies*. She felt cold while crossing the many bridges of the Seine, and cliché while eating her *croque monsieur*. But most intensely, she felt alone atop *Montmartre*, looking out over the lights of Paris with the Eiffel Tower and its reflection in the Seine punctuating it like a giant stylized exclamation mark. *This magnificent view*, she thought, *needs to be shared*. But there was no one she could call, no warm body at her side to shield her from the biting wind. She adjusted the scarf she had bought from a vendor near Notre Dame, and fiddled with the strands of loose hair sticking out of her argyle hat. Her hands were getting cold, so she decided to go back to the hotel. She rode the *funiculaire* down the mountain all the while staring at *Sacre Coeur's* white, Romanesque façade.

The next morning, she awoke early. The reason for this was three-quarters excitement, three-sixteenths jetlag, and the rest was just pure chance. Despite waking up in a dark hotel room, she left the curtains closed because she really didn't care what time it was. She simply knew it was early. She stood up and her eyes adjusted to the level of light. She had been sleeping naked recently. She never had before, but for some reason it just felt right. Her golden body was the lightest thing in the room, tiny under the high ceilings. She stretched her arms upwards, arching her back tensely in a beautiful curve. Her athletic form suggested that she had developed some muscle since she regained consciousness in the hospital. Her back looked like a swimmer's. She then stretched her arms horizontally, leveling them to the floor. She stepped into a the perfect form of the Vitruvian man and you could almost see the drawing transposed overtop of her nakedness.

The room was warm.

Next, she pulled up her right leg against her chest and stood flamingo-esque—maintaining her balance depite the darkness. A vertabra in her lower back klicked into place. *Knack!* Then the other leg. Her body was heating up, and her skin flooded to an arsenic pink all over. When her bare foot touched the floor, she fell backwards onto the bed, enjoying the soft coolness of the silk sheets. I imagine there was a subconscious intent in the way she placed her body into the expressive poses of vuluptuous Rodin marbles. She lay on the bed, planning her bid. She knew the rules, had practiced and even got good at knowing the artificial limits placed on certain objects.

She got dressed (another variation of the grey skirt-suit, with a silk blouse) and slid the curtains open, revealing a brightly lit city, bustling with morning hustle.

The security at this auction house was tight. Marci was searched by an unshaven, suited Frenchman. She practiced a bit of her rusty French on him. He smiled and told her in English to hurry inside. The auction house wasn't as full as she imagined, but it was clear who the big players were. They could be spotted from a distance by the aura of extravagant, over-the-top quality they exuded. Some were parading their glittering necklaces, others carrying decorative fans, and there was even one elderly gentleman wearing a monocle *à la* riche douchebag. She walked past each of them, scrutinizing their lips to gain a deep understanding of their character. Fat buying lips, painted in red; tight, dry conservative lips who stop when challenged; loose, puckering lips that go all out for an unnecessary artifact. She made mental notes of the lips and the attire and the perfumes.

Marci had only one object she wanted. She was focused and therefore had an advantage. She wondered if there might be other rare book dealers there. Then she took her seat, near the back of the room. She wanted to scope out the other bidders to learn their bidding styles. Luckily, there weren't too many people there that day.

The first item was a grandfather clock, carved out of a single piece of wood. Fat-lipped diamond necklace *et. al.* got that one. The second item was a set of 31 cameos, which sparked a wild bidding war between two ladies on either side of the room. The items were various, and Marci waited, bidding every once in a while on something just to make herself seen. After all, it was bad for others to know she only had one object she really wanted.

Finally, the book came out. It looked browner in colour than she thought it would be, but she had to go for it. Monocle bid first. Then there was a long wait, Marci always pushed the first bid, but no one else seemed to want to bid, so she lifted her paddle. The bidding went back and forth for a while, getting closer to Marci's limit. She would have to challenge him in a way that intimidated him. So she doubled the bid. There was a long pause and Monocle's female attachée whispered something in his ear. He bid again, his raised paddle waving theatrically.

Marci waited, knowing the next would be her last bid. The auctioneer, spitting in a fury of hyperactive French, was asking if there were any other bids. He questioned the bidders a second time and then raised his wooden hammer. She waited until she saw the hammer fall before standing up and lifting her paddle high. She had never done that before, but the old man looked at her and her skin seemed to glow. He adjusted his monocle and frowned. The bidding stopped and Marci won the book.

She immediately went to the booth to pick it up and ordered a car to drive her to the hotel, where she put it into a vault. She had brought a environmentally-controlled plexiglass case for it from the library.

But before anything else, she thought, *it is time for a celebration!*
So she asked the concierge in polite French whether he knew of a good bar around the area. He gave her directions and drew on a map. It was as if she was in love, so springy was her step when she exited the hotel. She danced down the sidewalks and past *Art Nouveau* metro entrances, until she saw the place. It was on the top floor of a 3-story building with a copper roof.

THE PARTY

The interior of the place was beautifully stylish, with hanging fabric lamps in warmly coloured reds, complete with black leather couches. The bar was where she chose to sit, perched atop a tall stool. She was just getting used to using French again. That rolling, breezy language that warmed her soul to hear it and pursed her lips to speak it. The bartender was a young, muscular man in a tight shirt. He made some small talk, and joked with her. He even talked her into ordering a *steak frites!* I suppose she came in just before the rush, because soon it was busy and trendy people filled the establishment. Next to her, a man in a black, pinstripe suit sat down and asked the waiter for a bottle of red wine. He rolled up his cuffs, exposing first a red shirt and then his hairy forearms.

He sat silently for a while, waiting for the busy barkeep. *He looks a little sad,* thought Marci, *or maybe lonely.* She found herself staring at him.

"Excusez-moi, mademoiselle. Est-ce que vous etês toute seule ici çe soir?" He turned to her, making intense eye contact and curling his top lip into a gentle smile.

"Oui...Uh, Moi, je suis une canadi*enne.* Je suis ici pour le travail."

"Ah, vraiment!" he said. "Well, what kind-uh wor*h*k do you do?" His rough 'r's made his accent melt all over her. She wanted to speak more French, but listening to him in English was equally beautiful.

"I am a rare book buyer." She wasn't even paying attention to her words, they just slipped out while she was focused on his face, studying every feature in detail.

"Is zhat so? Sounds interesting."

Big nose, but nice eyebrows, she thought. He sipped from his wine glass, staring at her from over the rim. She ordered another gin-'n-tonic and turned back to him—intense, direct eye contact. *Such deep green eyes. Gentle eyes.*

"And you?" she asked, cocking her head, "What, may I ask, do you do?"

"Moi? Ahh," he sighed melodramatically, "I prefer not to talk about it tonight. But I wor*h*k in cinema." Then he changed the topic quickly. "Do you know anyone in Paris?"

"Non, je suis venue juste pour le travail, mais çe soir…" She paused, thinking of the word. "Çe soir, je veux avoir une fête." She struggled a bit and he smiled.

"You are 'aving a par*ty*?" He touched her on the arm, "I am also 'aving a par*ty* tonight. Why don't you come? Paris is not for lonely people."

"I am not lonely," she said. "I am celebrating." He ordered another drink in quick, delightful French.

"Well, zhen let's celebrate togezher." He lifted his glass and they clinked them together, sounding a deep ringing tone. They spoke in French a bit, then in English, switching when Marci couldn't find a word. He quickly discovered that even with her dormant French ability, she actually understood a lot more than he thought.

"I like you, mademoiselle. I want you to come wit' me. It is a shame," he said, finishing his wine in a big gulp, pausing perhaps to stimulate her curiosity. "Beauty like your*h*s needs attention on nights like zhis." Due to the arsenic, Marci was unable to blush, but if she could, this would have been the most appropriate moment to betray herself.

"Merci."

"Let us go and celebrate in style," he said. "My flat is ve*ry* close and I am really 'aving a par*ty*." He paid for their bills and took Marci's hand and led her outside. She followed him willingly. Outside, he called a cab and they drove through the neighbouring *arrondisement* to a beautiful building across from a park. There were already people there. Marci spotted them through the giant windows on the second floor—people dancing, chatting, and drinking.

"Zhat is my flat," he said pointing at the window with all

the people.

"You weren't kidding," she said, barely audible then added in a more assertive voice, "Why are there people in your apartment without you there?" He pursed his lips as they approached the door.

"Well, uh, today is my birt'day."

"No way!" she grabbed his arm and stopped him as he opened the door. "Seriously? It's your birthday today?" Her eyebrows jumped up and her eyes widened; she pulled a little closer to him. "Happy Birthday."

"Merci. But zhat is why I needed a drink before coming 'ere." He whispered this into her ear. "Forgive me for not telling you, but when I saw you, I knew you could save me from all dis." He continued up the stairs and paused in front of the door.

"Madmoiselle, could you do me zhe favour of allowing me to call you my date for tonight?" As he said this, he grabbed her hand and gently kissed it in the way a medieval courtier might have done.

Since words seemed to fail her, she just nodded her head. It was as if she had entered another world, accessible only from that stool at the bar.

How did I get here? It was a momentary thought, which there was no time to indulge as he opened the door and they stepped into the dull, warm light seemingly transmitting perfume and a gentle beat of some kind of Euro-pop. There were bodies in stylish clothes around them and birthday wishes in both English and French.

They mostly ignored Marci at first, but once inside there was a moment for awkward introductions.

"Monsieur, zis is, uh…" They both shared a look that said *'I never even got your name!'* He continued, "Zis is ma chère amie, Ivana. Ivana, zis is my producteur Gabriel Ramineux ."

"Enchanté," he said and they shook hands. Then the conversation reverted to French, then turned to business, and Marci (tonight Ivana) walked into the kitchen, where she thought she could find a drink.

There was a dense cloud of marijuana smoke and a few figures occupying it. Two skinny women were sitting on the granite counters and a short man was gesturing wildly as he told a story in broken English. They were passing around a hand-rolled joint and laughing at the terribly funny story he was telling. Marci wasn't paying attention, but after a few unsucessful minutes of looking for a glass, she asked them if they knew where she could get a drink.

"Oh honey, are you new?" The skinnier of the two asked in a recognisable New England accent and then added: "There's a bah downstairs. Jus' ask Frankie down there."

"Thanks." It was all Marci could think of saying, but it was clear that in that moment, she would like to have started a conversation. The other girl, her long legs hanging in a beautiful angle off the dark granite, was startled by the short man passing her the joint and then they laughed and continued chatting.

Marci left the kitchen and headed down, past the mysterious man who had brought her here. As she crossed the crowded living room, she glanced at him to find him winking at her. She smiled.

The deeper she went the louder the music became. On the bottom floor, there were couches and a pool table near a glassed-in Japanese garden. Here and there were warm red lanterns hanging from the walls and people chatting. There were a few extraorinarily beautiful girls dancing, twisting their lithe bodies in silky dresses to electronic tones. *They're almost too beautiful*, she thought, *like models or fantasy mannequins*. That kind of beauty was definitely not common and usually came with a heavy price. Marci brushed past the hot bodies, inadvertantly rubbing against one as she moved towards the bar.

"Quel-que chôse à boire?" the barkeep asked, leaning in to hear her order.

"Une vin rouge," she responded, "s'il vous plait."

"You are English? You must be crew, yes? Tonight is free." *Never turn down a free drink*, she thought, *especially if it is in such a beautiful house*. She took the glass and returned upstairs, where she ran into her mysterious man.

"Madmoiselle Ivana!" he shouted and put his arm around her shoulders. "I was hoping to find you." Somehow she found his ways irresistable, but she had to put up a show.

"Excuse me, sir. But Ivana is not my name. It is Marci."

"Finally!" he said smoothly, "It is a great pleasure to meet you, Miss Marci, but tonight you will be Ivana from Kiev. I am Maurice, by zhe way." Marci extended her hand but he grabbed her shoulders and kissed her on both cheeks. "Zhat is how we do it in France! Don't be shy." He smiled at her.

"You have a beautiful flat," she said. "It's much bigger than I thought."

"Ah, thank you. I would love to show you the rest, if you like." And with that having been said, he led her through the crowd and up a large staircase to the top floor. She followed in tow, clinking her glass with some other happy partygoers.

Although there were people on the top floor as well, it was quieter and they could now easily manage a conversation. The top floor was dimly lit and, aside from the large landing, consisted of a hallway with closed doors.

"I hope you're not taking me to your room this early." The words sort of just slipped out in her state of liminal drunkeness and she felt embarrassed as soon as she said it.

"Non, non, non," he said, "I want to show you something." And then added, "I promise it is not erotique at all." They danced down the hallway to a door near the end. "But don't look so depressed," he smiled, "I 'ave erotique rooms also."

He opened the door and they seemed to step back in time about 200 years to a library preserved, museum-like, in the post-Revolutionary style. The shelves met the high ceilings with elaborate plaster mouldings. There was a *chaise-longue* in an austere alcove, protected by the ever-greening copper of the Mansart roof. There even was one of those sliding ladders you use to get books from up high.

"Wow." It was a mono-syllabic word—more a sound— and not very articulate. But it was the only thing she could say.

As the sound left her mouth, wonderment entered and filled her lungs and her soul.

"You are a book dealer, non? Is it to you*rh* liking?"

She finally got the hang of her whelm. What I mean to say is that the 'overwhelmed' became 'whelmed'. Or rather, she became 'well whelmed' as she gradually returned to reality with leather spines of old books under the surface of her fingertips. It was almost sexual. The rough-smoothness of the rarely-handled leather rubbing against her fingerprint. No, it *was* sexual.

Maurice stood by the door, enjoying the pleasure the room was giving her.

"Zhey are my mother's."

"They are beautiful!" In her hand she held a pocket-sized encyclopædia printed on rice-paper. It was a volume near the middle, perhaps K-L or N-O and on the open page was a map of Europe showing Austria-Hungary. There was a sound of people laughing out in the hall and Maurice stepped into the room, closing the door.

"You make zhem more beautiful in holding zhem. You a*re* like a painting, or the memory of a pretty girl staring at a painting. I want to watch you read." He sighed and raised his right eyebrow a little. "Alas, I must go back to zhe par*ty*. To *my* par*ty*."

"I'll come with you."

"No, no. Stay. I will give you zhe key." And he placed the cool iron key in her hand. She looked up and watched his lips. They were angular and pouty all at once. His top lip seemed to dance a slow dance when he talked.

"Enjoy," he said.

This is a good man, she thought as he walked away closing the door behind her.

With a drink in her hand, she did look around. The quantity and variety of books was immense and in her head, with each book she pulled off the shelf, Marci was building the persona of the owner. There were French classics, books on art and architecture, encyclopedia, various religions' most important manuscripts, a collection on photography and cinematography, anatomical guides, a huge selection of plays, Homer and Herodotus, Sartre and de Beauvoir, and a wonderful edition of l'Étranger by Alexandre Dumas.

It was in this last book that she found the note from mother to son:

Mon fils, je t'adore.	My son, I love you so.
Ce livre sera, sans doûte, te faire rapeller les instants les plus triste dans la vie. Mais, je te le donnes aussi au tant que te faisse souvenir la joie de vivre. Touts les heures heureux que nous sommes passés ensemble.	This book will, without a doubt, make you remember the saddest moments of life. But, I am also giving it to you in order to make you remember the joy in life. All the happy hours we have spent together.
Même si je morts, comme un rayon de soleil, je te regardera. *Ne sois pas seul toute la vie.*	Even if I die, like a ray of sunlight, I will watch you. Don't be alone in life.

Upon reading this, Marci collapsed onto the *chaise-longue*. She came to the sudden deflating realization that everyone is alone in life. And here she was alone herself in a foreign place. Alone even at home in her own country, in her office, and anywhere in the world. She contemplated the absence of a parental figure in her life, and remembered how it feels to have a mother's love. *It is like a ray of sunlight,* she thought. But she felt the absence deeply. She imagined her own mother writing her notes in homemade birthday cards. She would always make them herself and Marci clearly knew what she was doing because it was only during those rare times that the studio door would be closed to her.

"I'm using stuff that has dangerous fumes! Don't come in!" Irene would say, perhaps aware of her own inconsistency since that noxious fact never bothered her under normal circumstances. "I don't want you to get brain damage like me!" She would smile and disappear to create an artwork birthday card crafted out of pigments mixed in a matrix of love. (Of course, all of these precious memorabilia was lost in the flood.)

I'm so lost, Marci Wood, the neurotic spark of energy, reflected on her possible future. And in the city that gave the world existentialism, she wondered about the meaning of life. Was she to be alone forever? Would Baxter be there to the end? And would she herself become a mother one day? She hoped so.

On the other hand, life seemed so unpredictable. What kind of shape would life have if it were so impermanent? *Surely it's a crescent of some kind,* she thought. *Some form that opens up to the void, but that can contract in on itself like a spring-loaded mechanism of a cuckoo clock. Or a wave that rumbles outwards into a beautiful, rolling cylinder and then crashes in on itself.* I ask you, dear reader. Is Marci right? Is the shape of life a wave or a contracting crescent? Is it a mini golf course with its hills and valleys and trimmed green? Or perhaps it is more like the funnel of water draining from a bathtub?

Personally, I think life is complicated like a snowflake and just as temporal. And Marci, finding a vacuum of lonely space inside her heart, became immediately focused on her mysterious man. From somewhere inside the room, the tolling of an ancient clock woke her from her reverie. *I've got to find him,* she thought, returning the book.

*   *   *

The colours of the hallway had changed and when she went downstairs, she entered a pulsating white cloud of techno music. The cloud fogged out of some sort of mist-machine, flashing patterened lights bounced a tango on the mist.

What is this? A movie set? she thought, feeling drunker by the moment—succumbing to some carnal urge—a bacchanalia of sensual whispers.

(There were lasers,
and people wearing costumes
concealed in the fog.)

She stumbled

and touched a laughing women in a
French Revolution, liberty-waistline dress

and tumbled…
onto a dancing bird-man

and bear-hugged
a man in a gorrilla mask.

"You OK?" he asked in an undecernable accent,
laughing as he held her up.

Ohmigod.

She blinked really hard and pinched herself all to no
avail. *Either this is a wild and white night inside a dream, or I have
had too many to drink! Fabulous fumes, eh?* She questioned for a
moment if she was talking to herself aloud…But then continued.
I loved touching the gorrilla guy. Excellent texture! But this

is getting a bit crazy, isn't it? she questioned again. This time succeeding against her own best judgments. She felt like her body was enveloped by the smoke and the only way out was to feel. Her palms became sensitive bumpers, caressing bodies and furniture like an octopus would feel the dark ocean floor. Sometimes she would get caressed back, followed by the purr of an apologetic French accent. She was stretching her eyes wide open in the hopes to see further than she could. See, Marci Wood became a ninja in the mist. Her 98% grey suit made her a shadowy, little figure—able to blend into the cloud itself. The red lights were still there, illuminating the edges of the room.

Completely unreal, she thought. *Ceçi Maurice est 'Super-chique'.*

And just then, he seemed to appear inches from in front of her, holding a glass and smiling pleasantly. They bumped into each other in the way two liquids merge together. Dancing with drinks in hand, smiling at the world. The pink glow of her skin radiating into the fog.

"You are beautiful," he said and downed the last of his merlot.

"Is this a dream?"

"Let's go," he said and then her proceded to pull her through the fog with one hand.

Where are we going? She wondered and contemplated the possiblity she was drugged. Marci being who she is, then probably admonished herself inwardly and embarrasingly. If she had a free hand, she would have adjusted her hair.

They emerged from the cloud a few seconds later into a wine cellar. There were funky lamps standing here and there. *This guy is James Bond,* she thought.

"Je m'excuse," he apologized, "Zhey started using zhe props. Now zhey have transformed *chez-moi* into a carni*val*."

"So that wasn't some insane hallucination?"

"Non, non. It's for zhat I wanted you to come 'ere. To save *me* from all of dis craziness." She felt his warm hands fitting ergonomically onto her petit shoulders.

"Tell me more." She smiled assertively, but he stayed quiet. He leaned in close to her and she closed her eyes, heightening all her other senses. She could feel the cold, clammy air of the cellar. She could feel him kissing her neck. She could feel his warm breath on her skin and goosebumps ran down her arm and leg. He whispered to her in French, but language was inconsequential, it was nothing but rhythm. Anyway, they were both primal—animals in no need of language.

He was orbiting around her, slowly removing her suit jacket to below her neckline, and she inadvertantly leaned forward onto a rack of bottles. There was a resonant *klink-klinking* of glass meeting glass meeting glass. He kissed her scapula gently and precisely. On her breast she could feel the coldness of the glass through the silk of her blouse and the sensation was so pure that she could tell the colour of the bottles simply from touch. His hands felt like a sculptor's: gently contouring her body.

"Not here." He said and lifted her jacket back onto her shoulders.

Marci opened her eyes to the darkness of the cellar. He was behind her and she spun around, staring him in the eyes with an artificial look of suspicion. He was staring at the door, somehow seeing through to the chaos outside. *What a mischievious look in his eye,* she thought, wondering what would happen next.

He winked at her and then walked away from the door towards the corner, where the lamplight didn't reach. There was a creaking of a tiny, old, hardwood doorway, which opened up into a secret passageway. *He's hot, French, has a sweet house, AND uses secret passage ways!* she thought.

PAOLO E FRANCESCA

This is fantasy! The scene unfolding in front of her
seemed so unreal. *I mean, who still uses secret passageways in this
time and age?* But there it was, a miniature door leading up into
a tight, spiral straircase. There was some light shining into the
turret from above. A warm, orange light cast shadows into the
crevasses of the stone stairway and Marci followed her man
towards it. He was holding her hand, leading her up in a counter-
clockwise spiral—up towards a walk-in closet, where suits were
neatly hung and a pile of black socks filled a rectangular basket.
The closet had the rich, sweet, musky scent of a bachelor. It was
the first time Marci became aware of how delicious Maurice
smelled. They exited the closet, where a tiny, oldskool light bulb
burned constantly, and entered a hyper-modern, semi-minimalist
room. It was mostly white, with a grandiose square-shaped low
bed, some red pillows, a few abstract paintings, and an old wood
fireplace smoldering with embers in the corner.

With a flourish, Maurice turned on his heel and bowed
down low in a cavalier fashion.

"Welcome madamme, to my bed chamber. Hopefully, we
'ave passed unnoticed into zhis quiet space, so zhat no one might
disturb us."

"Well, aren't you a romantic?" She draped her arms over
him and they kissed. Marci closed her eyes and time slowed to
a near stop. She smelled the fireplace and Maurice, and then
she felt his hands gliding up on her back towards her neck.
Everywhere, his hands fit so perfectly—on her neck, her back,
her bottom. He lifted her grey suit jacket off her shoulders again,
this time dropping it on the floor behind her, and unbuttoned
the silk blouse. Piece by piece, clothing was removed amidst
well-placed kisses landing on any promising area of skin. Finally,
they both stood only in their underwear, facing each other. They
were arms-length apart, but stood still and parallel without

146

contact. Marci's whole body was a light pink—a blushing peach colour, accentuated by her dark underpants and a selection of auctioned, antique jewelry, which made her seem like a human Valentine. Maurice stood without touching her, perhaps to build the tension. He was bulky (maybe once athletic) and had a hairy chest. The fireplace crackled audibly in the negative space they had created.

"You don't 'ave to be alone tonight." And with this, he picked her up. She was much smaller compared to him and thus easy to move. He carried her to the bed and dropped her into the soft nest of the goose-down duvet. Then, after a short pause, he jumped on as well. Within that moment more lamps came on and there was some music playing: a percussive and agile violin solo from Paganini. The room had become alive with their hot bodies in it.

Marci's whole self was becoming a nerve sensitive to the world, and she let her sensations take over, washing away any feeling of loneliness as she reclined on the bed. He was kissing her calves and thighs, still whispering in rolling '*rrr*'s of French. She imagined stepping into a body-temperature puddle of kisses, splashing onto her exposed leg. The sensation made her warm inside. The texture of the black and pink lace of her underwear made a ruffling sound as his hand slid over the triangle of fabric. She didn't struggle when his fingers slipped around the edges of the panties, and slid through her pubic hair.

As I said, time was slowing to a standstill for Marci Wood. The quicker things moved, the slower they seemed to draw out—her lace underwear seemed to take minutes, hours, a lifetime, to slip from the cradle of her pelvis, past her knees and off her tiny feet. He rested his head below her belly button.

*His stubble...*she thought, leaving her sentence incomplete. His hand covered her pubis, generating heat like a capped volcano. But it was with his lips and tongue that he made her shudder and moan. Her hand was on her right breast and through it she could feel her heartbeat rise and her breath quicken. Time had stopped, and everything was happenening

147

at once. Sensations, smells, temperatures, and muscles all contracting at once like Dante's vortex of sensations. It was as if everything in her was trying to squeeze through this vortex. This would be the most intense orgasm of Marci's life. In fact, she was unsure if she died or lived. All of life was simultaneously flowing in and out of her and she felt her consciousness leave her body and travel through this erotic tornado and appear on the other side.

She was watching herself, pink and supine on the white sheets. Maurice entered her and they became one. She hovered over them, watching her own face, close-eyed and in ecstasy. The two lovers, she noticed, blurred together, exposing a pink breast or topaz bracelet every once in a while. Maurice, she noticed, had a tattoo on his back. It was the spiralling orbit of a comet flying with a trail of flames through the vast emptiness of space towards a planet. The trajectory was formed with words, spelling out Maurice's philosophy of love.

She was simultaneously there, lying on the bed, feeling his weight and warmth on her and she was also floating above like a cherub on the ceiling, witnessing the blazing act *in flagrante delictio.*

And this time they both came together, rhythmically and exhaustingly as the erotic vortex slowed down and returned her to her body as a settling tornado would put down a stolen barn.

She found herself naked and sweaty, more reddish than pink and breathing rapid, shallow breaths. He was next to her, his arm over her body, hand partially covering her breast, fully covering her heart.

"C'était absolutement incroyable," he whispered and kissed her cheek. She closed her eyes and smiled and almost immediately fell into a deep, dreamless sleep.

THE SET

Waking up can sometimes be so fluid, like passing between two worlds. Marci opened her eyes gradually, emerging from the fog of dreamland. *There's some kind of rustling over there,* she thought. And Maurice approached her, sunlight beaming him in the face.

"Bonjour!" he said. "I 'af to go to wo*r*hk. Come visit me."

Marci was just waking up and slightly disoriented from last night's dilerium, so what could she say, but "yes."

"Good," he said, "Zhe address is on zhis ca*r*hd." Then he finished buttoning up his shirt, kissed her on the forehead, and left the bedroom.

Marci found herself naked. The curtains were slightly open and threw a giant trapazoid of golden light into the white room. So she got up and commenced her stretching regime. Arched back, Vitruvian Woman, Flamingo pose-*knack!*-Flamingo pose, backflip onto the bed. (OK, all true except for the backflip onto the bed…)

She collected her belongings, bra, underwear, skirt, silk shirt, hat, and scarf she bought near Notre Dame. And one by one, as she found them, she put them on. Then, she washed her face and tamed her hair—as always, an ardorous process with opposing forces of the universe reacting on it.

And when she emerged, she was bright and beautiful in her 98% grey suit.

*   *   *

The directions on the bedside table led her to the town of Versaille. It looked like filming had only just started at the site, an older preserved part of the palace. There were big vans and trailers parked on the finely trimmed grass. And Gabriel (*I think that's his name*) was directing the equipment into the building.

Men were carrying microphones, trolleys, and cameras in through a large double-door. She didn't want to interrupt them, so she dodged around one of the trailers and inadvertantly entered the building in the flow of traffic.

Here she was inside, blocking the rush of heavy equipment coming into the building. So she kept moving amongst the porters carrying cameras and grips toting sounds equipment, past enormous rooms, each with a different colour— there were baby blues, greens, and rooms with golden trim. She didn't have much time to look around, and quickly got swept up the stairs. She took the left staircase, while most of the people carrying equipment took the right, marching to a rapid rhythm. At the top of the stairs, everyone had to fit through the same door. *At least the doors are big,* she thought, completely mesmerized by the beauty of the place. *Kings and Queens were born here. They lived and played and died here,* she thought, eyeing a 14th Century dresser. The interior was darker than the entrance, but equally astounding. Some rooms were just empty, while others looked completely preserved. There were paintings on almost all the walls and elaborately carved marble fireplaces. Chandaliers that sparkled even in dark rooms.

They were in a long hallway heading towards the far side of the palace, where you could tell there were windows because of how the rooms were lit up by a bright Daylight 6500K. At the end of the corridor, there was an anti-chamber with a small alcove. The men turned left and carted their stuff into a nearby room. *This is my chance! I get off the train here,* she thought, and jumped to freedom. In the sunlight and emptiness of the circular alcove, she waited for Maurice. The alcove was made of a dark wood, with large, semi-transparent windows glowing in the light. In the rectangular anti-chamber there was a door. It was also panelled in dark wood, but above eye-level, the room had square panels with interiors of royal blue, fabric wallpaper. *Pantone™ 282 with golden embroidered fleur-de-lis. This must be a woad indigo dye,* she thought to herself as the flow of men carrying equipment continued by her.

Then it happened. She caught a furtive glimpse into the neighbouring room in a mirror being carried by a man dressed in black. In the reflection, she saw the purest tone of red. It was like a flash of living tissue—light passing through the skin. This colour was an entity in itself. It was a momentary flash, but it had completely entranced Marci.

Then she looked at the narrow door of the anti-chamber.

THE ROOM

As if stepping into a womb, the doorway opened into an incredible 14th century red room. The lighting was beautiful—perfect daylight coming from inside the room.

But before we continue with Marci's story, allow me a minute to describe the room.

Inside those four walls, absolutely everything was red. The furniture (a princely high bed with dyed red draperies, a delicately carved boudoir painted red, and a wooden chair the colour of cabernet-sauvignon) seemed to vanish in the room. The carved panelling had bright white outlines where it reflected the light, all of which appeared to throw a delicate french-curve pattern onto the magical red aura created in the room. There were thick, velvet curtains in front of the only window and lifting it, peeping outward, was a young boy dressed in an invisible robe of red. On top of this, he wore a conical cap, partially covering golden locks rolling off his head. Simultaneously, the room was full and empty, and the boy, about 6 or 7 years of age, looked like the beginning of a portrait painted by a quick hand.

Marci, of course, knew the feeling of being a pair of floating hands dancing in a monochrome room, so she spent a minute admiring the beauty of the scene before she even noticed the camera crew and the lights in the corner. Observing from another dimension (and another time!), they stood to her left. The colour made everything seem to disappear into a pane of Matisse red. In fact, the only indicator of the 3rd dimension was the slight difference in hue where the two walls met. Without that, the French film crew would have been standing in a badly photoshopped advertisement on top of a single layer of colour.

Maurice saw her first, waving her over. They didn't stop filming, so she scooted along the left wall to a space behind the cameras. From there, she felt like the observer from a multi-coloured, 3D universe. Maurice was behind the camera staring at the intense red image.

On the screen, Marci noticed that the boy was wearing elaborate, red leather gloves. It was a close-up of the outline of red hands opening a red curtain. The shot panned upwards to the boy's face. He was extremely pale, with green eyes and pouty, labicured rouge lips. The boy's face had a classic beauty to it and he exuded the presence of royalty.

What are they filming? she wondered, watching the boy steal a sly glance at a more colourful world outside the window. The bold folds of the velvet curtain reached upwards like titanic columns, and only after adjusting to the visual *hummmmm* of red, did Marci start to notice details she had first overlooked. The boy was wearing period clothing with an intricate, lace ruff— also red, of course. There were paintings hanging on the walls, covered by dense cloth, and there was a red bowl (filled with burgundy grapes, wrinkling passion fruits, and the crystalline red of delicious apples) sitting on the chair.

"Cut!" said Maurice. "C'est tout pour le matin. On continue après déjeuner." And with this people scattered, chatting to each other, one attending to the boy in red, others attending to the equipment.

Marci had an incredible urge to go talk to the boy, as if this visitor from another dimension possessed the key to some understanding that she lacked. The Parisienne woman helping the boy out of his corset was wearing a white shirt, which acted like a second light source in the red room. Marci was watching the pair when Maurice stepped up to her.

"Bonjour, bonjour!" He kissed her on both cheeks. "You came."

"Mais oui," she snapped out of her wonderment and smiled back at Maurice.

"Zis is zhe prince's chamber," he said, "but let's go talk in my office." He led the way out, exiting through the main door of the room. It was about 12 feet tall, stood open and had a trail of insulated, black cables running out of it. Once they left the room, they were back in reality. Well, 'reality' in as much as the Versaille

153

palace is reality to Marci Wood, an archive librarian. Maurice led her across the hallway to a grand hall, in which there was a catered lunch. The chandeliers glittered and people were chatting everywhere.

"I am so glad to see you," said Marci, happy to have found some kind of anchor in this strange semi-fictional world she stepped into in Paris.

"Me too."

"You know, actually…" she paused, "…I didn't realize you were a director." They each poured themselves a coffee and Maurice snatched up a chocolate croissant as well.

"Yes, it's true," he said taking a big bite. "But I'm glad it does not change anything."

"So, what film are you making?" Her eyes scanned around for the boy. She could remember his face, but would have no idea about the form of his body.

"We are shooting a documentary about zhe Black Death," he clearly wanted to explain more, but he stopped abruptly with a sigh. "But I'll tell you later tonight." He then asked about her plans, suggested the Champs d'Elyssés, and told her to meet him at *"vignt-heures"* (or 8 o'clock for the North American readers out there). Of course, Marci had to agree, knowing that she'd be in suspense until they met again.

154

THE BLACK DEATH

That night, lying in bed with Maurice, he told this story just before Marci fell asleep.

Picture this: In the year 1349 the plague had reached Paris. Europe had become poor and malnourished. The massive crop failures at the beginning of the century had made the peasants weak, and left France with an unproductive workforce. If you wandered around the countryside then, though, hunger was the least of your concerns. What you would have seen were mass graves dug to bury the thousands of decaying bodies. There was no cemetary big enough—or sacred enough—to take the piles of corpses stacked up on street corners.

At that time the Champs d'Elyssés was just an empty field outside of Paris. It got its name because it acted as a temporary place to hold corpses. See, 'Elyssés' means 'Elysium' in French. The Plague hit Paris in mid winter and, although the ground was hard, peasants buried the families in a mass grave outside the city walls in the field near a Magnolia grove. When the last frosts vanished for the season and the lucky survivors walked into the setting spring sun, the light made the giant Magnolia flowers illuminate like a celestial ceiling of purple stars. The peasants returning from the burial ground, passed under the magnificent trees with their whorls of white, flapping tepals blotting out the sun. They walked under the vault of Magnolias, and gained respite from the nearby smell of rot and death in the sweet, citrusy perfume of *Magnolia Denudata*. The vault of flowering trees touched these poor farmers' senses and their spirits; it brought them closer to nature and to the old Pagan gods.

Because most people thought God had abandonned them (or they themselves had given up on God), they returned to their forefathers' beliefs of Elysium, the Field of Dreams, where souls wandered. They believed it was the heaven on Earth of vivid colours. They later sowed seeds of wild flowers over the dirt mound that contained the remains of their relatives and lovers. Along with a few lone asphodels, the flowers sprung up, waving in the winds, giving hail to the sun. When you exited the open field of wild flowers, backlit with the filtering light of clouds, the bright, and magnificent, white Magnolias shone light gemlike suns. This became the new Elysium—a physical place where the land of the dead and the living could overlap. Peasants would take off their sandals out of respect and cross under the cathedral of trees barefoot, squishing green patches underfoot. They came to the grove often to escape from the hellish conditions of the rotting city and to commune with their ancestors.

Most city-dwellers, if they had the chance, left Paris for the countryside, where they thought they would be immune to the devastation of the plague. Others, who stayed in spite of the "reckonning," locked themselves in their houses, either tending to sick relatives, or enjoying their last apocalyptic moments in the most hedonistic ways.

Walking through any street in Paris, you would see and smell death everywhere. You could hear wails of mourning and the croaking of those waiting to die. But you could also hear the moaning of the orgasmic, who had already abandonned any concern for this world. You would have the sense that pleasure and pain mixed together in the city in the most Satanic way.

See, people saw that the Church's blessings and prayers made no difference and that the plague took young and old, the beautiful and the ugly, pious and sinners alike. God, it seemed, had abandonned humanity. The Pope proclaimed that since they were agents of the devil, cats were to blame and should be killed upon sight. Of course, this only made the problem worse. In fact, everything people tried only made it worse.

On the street, sitting under an archway, a dying man weeps between coughing fits. (He has the most deadly and most contagious form of the disease, *pneumonic* plague). He will be dead within a few hours, but he is already far too weak to make the trip back to his house. What passersby remain, try not to look at him. No one knows the mechanisms of this terrible pestilence; some think it is God's last judgement and whip themselves out of piety, others simply believe it is the end and that we should enjoy these last moments—yet everyone lives in a forced denial, avoiding eye contact with the sick.

This man, leaning against the stone column, dribbles a reddish sputum and curses God. "I am a good man! A *good* man!" he said, "Why me?"

The Pestilence had been ravaging Italy and the south of France for a year now, and tales speak of once great cities laying empty. Passing the man, you would see piles of bodies, rotting with purple and black buboes around their necks and under their armpits. To some it might seem like humanity had angered God, but to the crowd of dancing maids, wearing their most colourful gowns and most brilliant jewels, it gave the excuse to live life for the moment. In every city, you could see priests blessing the sick and dead around the now-still marketplaces, and families carrying their possessions out of the unmanned gates towards the forest.

However, being in the countryside didn't necessarily spare you either. The plague, you see, is remarkably sneaky. The bacteria *Yersinia Pestis,* a thin green tube, has two phases: in the urban phase, the bacteria is transmitted between people, sometimes contracted from fleas living on black rats; in the sylvan phase, the bacteria spreads between forest rodents and affects the rural population.

During the repeated outbreaks of the Plague, only three places were immune and reported almost no deaths. The first was Poland, which had such a small, rural population that the disease had no means of spreading. The second was the low countries of Holland and Belgium, where it was common for the *nouveau riche* to wear a single nutmeg in a tiny grater around their necks as a symbol of wealth. Nutmeg, you see, is a natural anti-parasitic and acted like a chemical talisman to keep the transmitting fleas at bay.

Finally, there was the city of Milan, which had the fantastic foresight to close their gates in a voluntary quarantine to the rest of Europe once they heard stories of the disease, known in Italy as "the Great Mortality." All three of these places survived their own pandemics without any great loss of life.

However, in France, where our film is set, the palace of the King was locked and no one was allowed in or out. From their high balconies and windows the royalty could clearly see the carnage in their city. A princess in a gorgeous dress might look outward and witness an undertaker collecting bodies, discarded like spoilt goods. She might see a father burying his children in the churchyard, himself coughing blood. All around the city, life itself had turned upside down. The dead were dead, but the living were condemned to some kind of hellish world, where human life was becoming more and more meaningless with each pile of bodies thrown into a shallow trench next to the city walls. Some people got violently angry when they saw a relative die and they would become momentarily insane, killing a leper or a Jew, or raping an orphan, who herself showed the *lenticulae*—the purplish rash of the *bubonic plague*. Life (and, as an extension thereof, the consequences to your actions) would become entirely meaningless.

To most people, life and death seemed to have inverted. The dead gained access to their beautiful Elysium outside the city, and the living were trapped in an apocalyptic nightmare. Those few natural places where mortality could be forgotten became so holy that pilgrims travelling to ancient monasteries would re-route their journeys to sleep in silent valleys or under the branches of sacred trees.

Inside the palace, however, King Philip VI had just lost his beloved wife, Joan of Navarre and to top things off, his youngest son and namesake Philip, Duke of Orléans, was also ill. The prince was 12 years-old at the time, and the King couldn't stand to lose him as well. The King knew that he had a matter of days to act. When his wife showed the symptoms of the Black

158

Death, King Philip immediately sent for the best doctor in all of Europe, Doctor Schnabel von Rom. This peculiar man was said to have the only cure for the plague—the Queen was already dead, but fortunately, he was already on his way to the palace and could still save the boy.

*   *   *

The main gate to the palace complex opens slowly and although the streets are empty, having the gates open has an ominous feeling. A black figure rides in on a horse—a blur against the wintery city. He dismounts; the camera on his thick leather boots. He walks with a cane. Up the stairs, we see his trench coat, covered by a layer of wax. Dark, stained leather gloves. He walks right to the enormous door of the palace, a solemn figure in a wide-brimmed, flat hat standing with his back to us. The courtyard is empty and a cold wind masks the screams of people in nearby streets. These days, no one receives a royal welcome, not even the doctor who is to save a prince. Dr. Schnabel knocks with his cane and the door opens. This is the first time we see him as he is: entirely suited in some kind of medieval hazmat suit; he wears a bird mask beneath his wide-brimmed hat.

Doctor Schnabel is something between a shaman and a doctor. And he looks like a demon come from the other world. Despite all this, he is welcomed inside the palace by two guards and the palace chaplain. They escort him to the Great Hall, where the King and his court waits. Everywhere, there are many torches and candles lighting the way through the dreary palace. The firelight, in a spectacular display of shadow-puppetry, casts supernatural silhouettes of Dr. Schnabel onto the coloured walls as they walk.

In the Great Hall, there is light everywhere so that any visitor might see the splendor of France at its Medieval height.

Golden tapestries and colourful frescoes decorate the walls and beautiful sculptures surround the interior of the room. King Philip in his purple robe, sits on a wooden throne, waiting for the guards to make the official welcoming.

Dr. Schnabel walks into the room, but stops about 10 feet from the King. He takes off his hat, revealing long, thinning, grey hair, and bows without removing his mask.

"Schnabel von Rom," the King says, "I am happy to welcome you to my dying city and my unfortunate palace." He stands up, larger than life in his regal robes. "Tell me, what is the cure for the Great Pestilence so that we may save my youngest son." All eyes in the court slide to the bird-man who is standing completely still in the middle of the hall.

"*Dominus,*" he says in slow Latin, a language they have in common, "I have seen people dying in every city and town in Italy and France. Others have tried garlic, or rosewater, or leaching the excess blood, but I know well that this 'black death' has only one weakness."

"Well, pray tell! What is it?" The King replies in French, but then adds in clumsy Latin, "There is no time for long speeches!"

"Red."

There is a moment of silence before he puts his hat back on. "Your Majesty, I must see the prince immediately! And while I examine him, I suggest your men gather all the red cloth and hang it around the walls of his room."

"It shall be done." The King sits down as the priest leads Dr. Schnabel out of the hall.

"Everything must be red!" shouts the bird-man as he leaves.

And so the King built the perfect red room for his son. A room where everything was red. Tailors were ordered to

160

create red clothes, cooks to bake red bread, alchemists to create rosewater, and painters to paint the prince's possessions red. The prince lived in this carmine cell, locked up for over a year, but he *did* survive.

Exactly one year later, Dr. Schnabel returned and unlocked the doors, pronouncing the young boy healed...

zzzzz

zzzzzzz

zzzzzzzzz

And so Marci fell asleep in the warm arms of her French director, Maurice, and she dreamt of walking barefoot in the glowing Magnolia groves of Elysium.

THE GOODBYE

They woke up early. The sun was shining in through the window and Maurice jumped out of the bed at the first ring of the alarm. Marci fell into a space between this world and the dream world, listening to Maurice take a shower in the room next door.

"I am afraid zhat I must go to work today. I want to take you to zhe aeroport, but if I cancel a job it costs a lot of money." He dried himself off with a towel. Marci, eyes still closed, simply replied "That's OK."

"*Ma chère,* will you come wit' me for break*fast*? I 'ave a car to take you to zhe aeroport." He touched her on her cheek and she rolled out of bed, slightly disoriented and hugely haired.

                    *   *   *

With her scarf, a gyspy-ish warm colour combo of pink, red, orange and yellow, the grey suit didn't seem as empty (or cold) as usual. Her hair was curly today and brilliantly golden, and she desperately needed a coffee.

They sat in a booth of a boulangérie, which they arrived at by following the scent of freshly baked croissants. Maurice ordered for them both, and then apologized again for not being able to see her off properly.

"Maurice," she said, "I think I dreamt your movie last night." He laughed.

"Was it a block bus*ter*?"

"Well, it looked beautiful. I love the red room." The coffees came along with two croissants. "But there is one thing I can't figure out."

"Et çe quois?" he said across the rim of his coffee.

"Well, I don't understand. Was the boy really sick? Or did the bird-man trick them?"

"Zhat is a clever question!" You could see the passion in his eyes light up. He swallowed a mouthful of croissant and washed it down with a gulp of coffee. "You see, it is a true story. Petit Philipe was cured, but modern medicine thinks zhat... uh, zhe story was supersti*çion*. Zhey believe zhat Schnabel is a legend. In making zhis project, I spoke to many doctors and every one of zhem told me *red* is an impossible cure for zhe plague."

"I see…" She had barely started her thought when Maurice continued his.

"But zhat was a few years ago. We started zhis film a long time ago and since zhen much has changed.

"Like what?"

"Modern medicine has made a remarkable discovery not so long ago. Some scientists learned that in laboratory tests, infrared light affects the plague bacteria's ability to reproduce."

"So you are saying Dr. Schnabel somehow stumbled upon a true cure to the plague?"

"Hmm, I do not know. But it is possible zhat he had an intuition which was quite accurate, *non*? Some kind of divine inspira*çion*, perhaps."

"Well, God does work in mysterious ways," she said considering things carefully.

"Drink. Drink," he said pulling out his wallet, "I must go. But, *ma chère*, I will come visit you someday." He took a business card out and gave it to her. "Don't forget me, OK?" Then he kissed her and left the shop in a rush.

I won't.

163

Yellow

There's times when you'll think that you mightn't,
There's times when you know that you might;
But the things you will learn from the Yellow and Brown,
They'll 'elp you a lot with the White!
~Rudyard Kipling

Back in Toronto, her first steps in the city felt like baby steps: uncertain, yet empowered.

She felt new, as if she finally opened her eyes and saw the world for the first time. She was a repositioned star, seeing familiar constellations from an angle different from before. *Am I in love?* she thought, smiling.

It was autumn in the city. Trees erupted in brilliant reds and yellows and when the morning light hit the sidewalks it looked as if they were littered with the palette of van Gogh.

Alex had given her a ride to Huntsville, far in the North,

outside the city the day before. It was even more beautiful out there. Narrow roads enclosed by a canopy of flaming yellow, red, (and occasionally neon-life-jacket orange) colour leaves. Alex chortled as he drove. *"Like a maniac."* These are the words Marci would have used if she could have finished that sentence.

Actually, what had been happening was that Alex had been chewing on an incredibly chewy Charleston Chew™ while trying to sing along to a song without any lyrics.

Due to one of his romances going pear-shaped, Alex was exiled from his apartment into his family's summer cottage.

("If you let me just get away from work and do this, I'll lend you the cottage any time you want...But you gotta come see it first")

She was reliving an orbiting memory of this drive through the glowing autumn leaves and rolling hills of the Great Canadian Shield to the upright Toronto skyline seen from the Gardiner Expressway as she walked down the city street towards the transit stop.

The city seen from the Gardiner, she thought, *was like a hundred bars of music frozen in time in the form of the most awesome 3D sound level visualizer.* The image of the illuminated CN Tower hovering above the tall, glass spires made her feel like she was living in the future, despite the fact that it was built in the 70s. *There is so much beauty everywhere I look. I must be in love,* she thought. *Can I be in love with life?*

Walking to work, Marci in her sun-coloured, gypsy scarf and black, felt overcoat, would jump over piles of leaves. She danced her way towards the streetcar stop, nodding and smiling at random people on the street. She was the spirit of happiness and just wanted to pass that feeling on to every other hairless monkey going to work. A streetcar, hanging from its electric cables, passed her in the farthest set of tracks. *DING!DING!* The smell of coffee leaked out of a nearby coffee shop and suits scrambled to cross the street.

The perfect day... A man (*Nice beige leisure suit!*) , who was talking on his cell phone, jumped into her peripheral vision.

He was passionately talking to an invisible entity and multi-tasking like the best Wall St. stock trader you can imagine.

Marci had calmly arrived at her destination—that is to say, the transit stop. Along with a group of other commuters, she waited to board the electric tram. It's usually crowded at the bigger stations, but Torontonians have a particular way of boarding streetcars. There's no line up while you wait for the car, but you just remember the order you arrived. And when the streetcar opens its doors, you naturally and spontaneously find your position to get on it. There's no crowding as in some other countries and cities and no queues either. Marci once told me that she saw this as a metaphor for the 'Canadian experience'. It's so casual and laid back, but with a certain grace in organization.

Anyway, as she was slyly studying a large lady in a jean jacket and an elderly Italian (perhaps Portuguese) man, Leisure Suit on his cellphone passes Marci and stepped into the traffic. He wasn't looking and hadn't seen the tourist bus gunning towards the intersection. In Toronto, all vehicles are supposed to stop behind the open doors of the streetcars, but this mammoth machine was clearly oblivious to this rule.

A violent, nervous spark shot through her brain, down her spine and her body leapt forwards, saving the business man from certain doom. It seemed to happen so fast, as if she had no control over herself. Guided by her unconscious, her heroic move had the dual quality of being both dreamlike and automatic. When time returned to its usual pace, Marci was more disoriented than the unsuspecting man in the beige suit, whom she had just pulled out of the path of the enormous bus.

"Thank you," he said, covering the mouthpiece with his gloved hand. Then he fumbled in his interior breast pocket, pulled out a business card, and gave it to her. He watched the bus go by, cautiously checked for oncoming traffic and crossed the road on the green—all the while talking business to a person on the other end of the cellular waves.

Bizarre. Marci seemed unfazed by the gravity of this peculiar moment. Perhaps it had not set in that she had just saved

166

the life of a stranger. The tram was still waiting at the lights and Marci could see the overweight woman in her jean jacket looking down at her from a side window. The doors had closed behind her, but opened when Marci walked up to the driver.

DING! DING! She boarded and rode the silver tracks eastward towards the tall, crystalline towers at the heart of the city.

*   *   *

That night she had a dream.

THE DREAM

Wavy heat-lines: a mirage up in front of her eyes. She is in the desert, a massive expanse of golden sand. About 20 meters ahead lies an enormous dune, reaching skyward like the rolling wave of a giant's golden quiff. Behind it, the sky is deep and blue. A pantone 288, the blue of twilight seas.

Around her there is nothing. Just a yellow void of infinitesimally small particles.

Marci begins to climb the dune. She is barefoot, wearing a purple sundress. Every once in a while, she will look down, inspecting the curve of the horizon as it grows more and more noticeable.

Before she knows it, she is at the crest of a dune thousands of kilometers high. The top is a plateau and a little bit ahead of her there is a NASA moon lander.

Two astronauts in their suits are ambling about. Marci brings her hand up to shade her eyes from the giant helmet reflecting the sharp, setting, yellow sun. They don't notice her at all in their concentration. One disappears behind the lander, and Marci walks into the reflected rays of the sun towards the other one.

"Excuse me," her words are masked by the heavy silence in the desert and seem hardly audible. "Is there a telephone around here?"

The astronaut points towards the horizon and (after an intercom crackles) his distorted voice announces "There's a village that way."

"Thank you," she says, and starts walking.

Time seems completely inconsequential because the village grows in steps.

1. A dot on the horizon

2. A few barely distinguishable houses

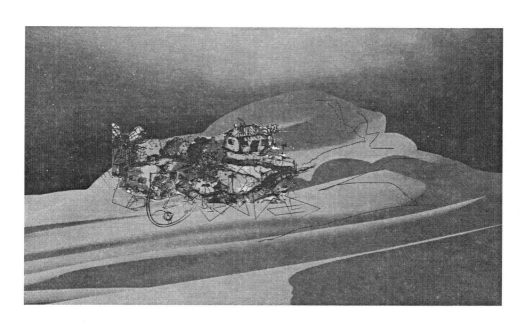

3. Ok. It's a village!

4. Detail: houses with swimming pools and BMWs driving through streets made for ox-carts.

5. She enters the village.

Children are playing, some doing cannon-balls into lush blue water of swimming pools, others are playing ancient games with sticks. The sound of children playing is everywhere. The houses are all multi-story complexes, richly designed with hanging plants erupting from the rooftops. It is an oasis, but the people are all clad in their traditional clothes—that is to say 'peasant' clothes—and their lifestyles are not obviously modern.

As she steps onto the dirt road, a group of children follow her, surrounding her in giggles and awe. They touch her dress and her skin as if they have never seen someone like her before.

Marci just continues walking. Straight ahead is a market, bustling with men and women preoccupied with spices, dried fruit, and wares. There are vendors, lawyers, exotic fabrics, buskers, gamblers who look bored, and women selling nuts.

She stops in front of a fire-eater, swallowing glowing hot metal rods and a man in a fez says to her: "Welcome, outsider! How can I help you?"

"Why is this town so rich?" she asks.

"We are traditional folk, living desert lives," he explains, "but we have a lucky fox."

"A lucky fox?" She is not surprised, but simply asking. Her mind is overwhelmed with the noise, the activity of the marketplace, and asking questions seems to be her default reaction.

"Yes," he says, "anyone who touches the fox will win the lottery. We have all won at least once." A great blast of flame shoots up into the air from the fire-eater behind the man in the fez. "Last year," he continues," the neighbouring village tried to steal our fox, but the fox is so lucky that each of their sneaky plans backfired every time."

"Is that so?"

"Yes, they gave up when they realized they could win the

lottery just by touching a photograph of the fox, which they were using in their ill-fated schemes."

"Lucky fox." She seems to be in a trance, all at once listening to the man and absorbing the life around her.

"Exactly," says the man, adjusting a bag he has slung around his shoulder. "Would you like to meet the fox?" With that he motions for her to follow him. They set off through the market, past some Olympic-sized swimming pools, to what looks like a poorer area of the village. Yet, even in this quarter of small houses and mud roofs, the doors are lined with pure gold. And inside the houses, through glass-less windows beautiful raven-haired women could be seen, clad in golden lingerie and diamond necklaces.

They walk to a wooden shed. It looks like a barn; a remarkably austere building even compared to the mud houses around it, but as they get close, Marci notices the small, yellow flowers blooming all around the edge of the building.

The man opens the door and tells her to wait. Inside, it is dark, and a cool breeze escapes from the open door.

After he disappears into the building, everything is silent again, and the sunlight starts growing whiter and whiter. The purest white she had ever seen, bleaching colours around her and deepening shadows of the grains in the wood in front of her.

The man returns suddenly and ushers her in.

Inside, a faint smell of mushroom—or rather, nature—greets her, and there is nothing but darkness. She can make out the periphery of the house because of the white lines where the sun is infiltrating between the planks of the building. It takes a few seconds for her eyes to adjust, but soon colours fade in from the blackness. It looks like the walls are a deep, deep blue. Profoundly deep. And the floor is the same yellow sand, almost orange in this light. The room is empty except for a chest in front of her at the farthest wall, on which the man's bag is unfurled, moonlighting as a richly woven tapestry. On top of the cloth, an exquisitely beautiful fox is sitting perfectly still, watching her.

177

THE FOX's STORY

"Greetings, Marci Wood," the fox coos. "We are well met here in this dark, unconscious place, hidden away from the sunlight." From where Marci is standing, it is too dimly lit to clearly see, so she steps forward and with a light step, she enters the fox's golden aura.

Ohmigod, it's glowing...literally shedding light.

"I have come here as a voice from far away. Please, come sit beside me." The fox stands up and moves to the corner of the chest. And as Marci Wood closes the gap between her and the creature, she seems to enter a different world—a reality somehow more real that anything she had known. Colour becomes brighter and the curious fox bows his head to her, proud-chested. It's smaller than she imagined, but præternaturally beautiful. *Like a precious gem.*

When she sits down next to it, she notices that even her tactile sense feels more real. She can feel the fabric of the Persian rug under her, and it feels clearly as if someone had placed a hand onto her shoulder. *A man's hand*, she thinks, but there is nothing there when she looks.

And so began the fox's story:

"Dearest Marci Wood; I am here to tell you a story about the man that you saved today.

"His name is Quincy Roth. Until about a month ago Mr. Roth was one of Wall Street's most ruthless traders. He made most of his money on speculation, predicting which companies would succeed and which would fail. He was a beautiful man, perfectly shaped with eyes he claimed could X-ray even mega-corporations and see where their self-destructive spots lay. Spots he could bet on.

"Quincy Roth made a phenomenal rise to power, amassing

178

a fortune along the way and destroying a few precious things every once in a while to make a quick buck. He was young, powerful, and wealthy. People envied him, loved him from nearby and afar—some also often hated him from the sidelines.

"Six weeks ago, he went to the doctor for chronic severe headaches. The doctor—naturally one of the best and most expensive in Manhattan—did a few tests, made a bit of small talk, and sent him off. Quincy, downing a handful of designer painkillers, thought nothing of it and continued life as usual.

"However, the life of Quincy Roth was about to change forever. You see, inside his head (north of his brainstem, nestled between his amygdala and prefrontal cortex) there was a tumor the size of a walnut. He found this out a week later when the doctor called to tell him that he had no more than 3 weeks left to live.

"A variety of different tests had proven conclusively that the tumor was malignant, impossible to treat, and spreading like a power-hungry empire.

("I'm afraid you have 3 weeks left in a best case scenario," the doctor told him.)

"Quincy left the office immediately without telling anyone and went home. After he hung up the phone, he never said a word. He quietly undressed and climbed back into bed. Sitting up, he stared off into space, through the reality of things until the sensation of his mortality became so immanent that he burst into tears.

"He cried and cried, thinking about lovers and family, things left undone or unsaid, and yet other secrets that, luckily, would die with him. As he deconstructed his life, he could not stop crying. He felt so sorry for himself. *It wasn't fair*, he thought.

"Three days passed, all of which he spent crying in bed. Of course, the feelings about his cancerous doom changed during that time. At first, he felt vulnerable, ashamed, and victimized. Then he was sad, depressed, and regretful. Next, he became angry, upset, and bitter; all the while weeping into his pillow.

"On the 3rd day of self-mourning, he became more lucid

179

and resolved with an iron will to beat the cancer.

"*If it's in my mind,* he thought, *then I should be able to consciously think it into oblivion.* And with this he opened his mind and his memories, sliding back to his favourite childhood moment: dancing in the rain with his yellow boots and rain jacket. He could see himself splashing into puddles on the grey sidewalk. White clouds reflecting in the water and then his baby feet in their yellow booties, all of this was so clear in his memory. Frozen moments of bliss and beauty, forever home-movied onto his brain, like bleached polaroids.

"He kept the image of the yellow rain boots and continued to the yellow, tin bulldozer he got for his 7th birthday. Then he added some bananas, straw from his grandma's farm in Indiana, the yellow school bus he took everyday, and the construction helmets in the closet under the stairs. All of these yellow objects transposed from different precious memories until he finally caught up with his 18th year, when he first made love to his high school girlfriend, Kitty Donnavan in a cornfield on a heavy blanket. He rolled off her onto his back and looked directly into the sun. This bright, final memory of semi-innocent, adolescent love and satisfaction blotted out all the previous yellow hapinesses, and tied them all together in some nebulous cosmic harmony inside his brain.

"At first the sun was huge, containing within it all the other things. He could visualize it behind his eyes, tickling his rods and cones with its brightness.

"When he opened his eyes, the room was bathed in a washed-out, yellow light, which faded from the entirety of his vision to a smaller and smaller dot until it eventually shrank to a walnut-sized sphere of a miniature sun just behind his eyes.

"There was an audible popping sound, and the orb of his happiest, brightest memories shrank further until it was a tiny twinkle of a distant star.

"When it was the smallest thing he had ever imagined and completely invisible to him. He got out of bed and took a shower. There was a calmness about his apartment and a silence so thick it could be seen behind your eyelids as a green-grey Pantone™ five-five-six.

"He washed away the dirt, the past, and the tears he shed. He felt better when he was dressed in his best Wall Street suit.

"*No more headache,* he thought as he hailed a cab to go to visit the doctor. '*I feel better now.*'

"At the doctor's office they retested him. The doctor seemed a bit ashamed when he said: 'The immediate test results seem to imply that the first diagnosis was a false positive.' He still took an X-ray, however. The walnut shaped spot was gone.

"'I'm afraid these things happen, Mr. Roth. I am terribly sorry to have misdiagnosed you. I assure you that the diagnosis was based on a lot of evidence.'

"'It was a miracle,' said he. The doctor snorted and laughed through rodent-like front teeth.

"'No miracle, Mr. Roth. Miracles are impossible. Rather let's call it an fortunate failure of science. See, false positives are better to have than false negatives. I do apologize, sir.'

"And thus, Quincy Roth walked back into the city with a purpose. He clearly felt some divine essence at work. It was a powerful force of consciousness surrounding our planet, like a layer of thought. Heidegger called it the 'World Spirit;' Carl Jung, the 'collective unconscious,' and Pierre Teilhard de Chardin, the Catholic mystic, envisioned a thought envelope, which he called the 'noosphere.' From the Greek word '*nous*', meaning mind.

"Mr. Roth felt as if he could merge his thoughts with reality, as if consciousness itself was a kind of matter. He experienced a true form of enlightenment and became a bodhisattva. He wanted to teach other people how to heal themselves, how to heal society, how to tap into the *noosphere*.

"*Thinking is power,* he thought.

"One of the first things he did was to walk to a nearby printing house, ran by some Arabs. He ordered new business cards.

"It was one of these business cards he gave you after you pulled him out of the path of the tourist bus.

"You see, Mr. Roth is an entirely changed man. He has made a business out of teaching seminars to sick people on how to use positive thinking to heal their cancers. His talks have been so successful that he was booked on a pan-American tour. Newspapers called him a guru. He was in Toronto for a conference when you saved him, Marci Wood.

"That is the story of Quincy Roth."

THE FOX's SECRET

Marci has to squint when she looks directly at the fox's little eyes. She feels the invisible hand on her shoulder disappear.

"Why are you telling me this?" she asks.

"You will come to see that your destiny is tied with this man's. You are not well, Marci Wood. The toxins, with which you tried to end your suffering, are still in your body. Quincy Roth is the one who will teach you how to overcome the angel." Marci lifts her hand and looks briefly at the peachy skin tone, then she looks at the golden fur of the fox sitting next to her.   .

She hesitates, then asks: "Can I touch you?"

"It is acceptable," the fox says and closes his eyes in anticipation. Marci puts her hand against his chest and floats it upwards towards his neck.

He's so soft, she thinks, *and warm*. Her forefinger comes into contact with a pendant hanging around his neck. And upon contact with this, she gains the dreamlike superknowledge that it is her own pendant. It is the pendant her mother wore the day she died. The same pendant that the doctor handed her at the morgue.

She closes her eyes in the dream and drifts into the darkness beyond the golden aura of the fox into a deeper, dreamless sleep.

*   *   *

Marci awoke in her hotel room. Personal effects scattered around, especially on the bedside table, which was like a nest of a domesticating animal that scavenged the inside of a lady's carry-on bag. The phone was ringing.

The blinds were still shut, so she had trouble finding the receiver. Papers, coins, and other miscellany fell off the bedside table and onto the floor in her struggle. Finally, she picked it up and held it to her ear.

"Hello?" she said in a hoarse voice.

"This is your wakeup call Ms. Wood. Good morning."
She hung up, and slowly dragged herself out of bed. The room was warm, and she twisted the rod of the blinds, letting in enough sunlight to illuminate herself. Since the flood, she still hadn't bought any new clothes (or pajamas) and so was still sleeping naked. She stretched her body in a few yoga poses. She especially liked the balance poses, because she thought they helped her start the day in the right frame of mind. *Knack!* The sound of her upper vertebrae cracking.

She looked at the mess she made, put on some underwear and sat on the edge of the bed, rearranging the fallen objects. She picked them up one by one, and placed them back onto the bedside table until she came to the business card the man in the beige suit had given her. The name, written in a heavy itallic lettering, read *'Quincy Roth, guide to healthy living.'*

ONE OUT OF THREE

Back in the grey room of the Archives, she was talking to Alex.

"So, what do you think it all means?" she asked.

"Yo *Mars*, there's only one possible answer." His hand flew up and touched his forehead. Except for his hands and face, his body was invisible. He paused dramatically, posing almost. *I wonder what happens to humans when exposed mostly to grey? A black and white world.* She noticed Alex making faces at her. A boisterous, dast-dastery face, charading the meaning "Ok. It's your turn. Speak your lines."

Then she snapped back to reality and said, "Alright, Alex. What do you think is the one possible answer?" She turned her face to look at the clock and, for a moment, to Alex she became 2-Dimensional. A tamed down Picasso, where the world is all monotone behind her—only her face glowing in that radiant peach colour. "If you would be so kind to answer," she finished.

"You gotta get them all under one roof. All those people you met. The universe is telling you something." The wand came out of the book and Alex guided it very precisely. The room lit up with dark shadows as if something in the background shattered. Alex's face was almost entirely whited out. His crisp, black hair forming a kind on spherical helmet. "There's just too many co-incidences, my friend." Behind him a beautiful scan of an alchemical formula came up. It had the picture of the tree of life on it in the most brilliant colours, all outlined in thin, inlaid gold. The author of the text was using a form of writing completely unknown to Marci.

"You know what language that is?" she asked, her hand creating a billboard-like, rosy road sign.

"Never seen it." Marci took the wand from Alex. It was her turn.

"So you're saying that I should invite them all to some

kind of event?" She paused, sticking the wand back into the book and eclipsing the artificial daylight. "Then what will happen?" If there was any mockery in her voice—which there was!—it came out disguised as genuine curiosity.

"Yeah, you know, invite them all out to the woods. Marci Wood's 'Going into the *Woods* party."

"I would slap you if you weren't doing this scan!" She sent him evil vibes with her eyes. "That makes me sound like a tramp."

"Marci, I believe the term you're looking for is 'strumpet'. He said pronouncing the 'p' in strumpet a little more plosive than the rest of the sentence.

"Well, anyway, how am I going to get them all here?"

"No, I was serious, Marci. I'll make the friggin' flyers even! Don't you worry about it. Just call them and ask if they can meet you in Canada. Any date is fine."

She shook her head, smiling at him.

But the truth is, she did make some phone calls that night. First, she called Maurice, the director of the *'Le Plague de Philip Valois'* movie. They chatted, but he said he was still finishing up his movie and had to stay in France because of meetings. He said that he still thought about her, romancing her with all the guiles of the finest Frenchman.

"I'll keep in touch" he said.

Next, she called, Russell Andrew Ivy. And since they last met, he had come back as a hero after the sinking of the Gettysburg. He was the only survivor and—along with Marci— helped rebuild the school and the hospital in Borneo. He apologized and told her that he has a medal ceremony coming up and didn't want to make any promises.

Finally, she picked up the business card labeled *"Quincy Roth, guide to healthy living"* and called the number. It rang five or six times and then suddenly he answered. His voice was soothing: deep and bass with the rough quality of a veteran hypnotist. She continued to tell him that she was the woman who saved him.

He wasn't surprised.

"I'm glad you called," he said. "I owe you a great debt." He inhaled through the mouthpiece. "You saved my life." With that having been said, she just blurted it out.

"I want to meet you. I mean, I need to meet you." *God, that sounds so pathetic.* "I had a dream and you were in it." She was stumbling her introduction. *I should have thought about this before!* "Well, actually, you weren't in it, but a golden fox told me about you."

"What did it say?" he asked in a sandy, warm voice.

"You thought yourself well from a sickness." There was a long pause. So long that she thought time had stopped. "Hello?" she asked.

"Hello," he said. He inhaled again, "It's true. All of it. The tumor, the cure, everything. And I see the universe is giving me a sign as well. Perhaps I was meant to die?" His tone was grave, with an echoing sense of depth in his long pauses. "Yet, I was pulled back from the brink twice already." Marci was silent. "I will come to meet you wherever you say," he said, "especially if a golden fox told you so." A silent beat, then: "A pleasure to meet you, Marci Wood."

"Likewise."

When she hung up, she thought: *One out of three. Not bad.*

White

For our only way to arrive safe at the queendom of Whims
was to trust the whirlwind and be led by the current.
~Rabelais, 'Gargantua and Pantagreul'

Things just couldn't be left like that, though. Marci would then receive two fantastical phone calls over the next few days. Maurice would call her to say that there is an interview for his movie in Montréal, and he could easily fly to Toronto for a few days.

"I 'ould love to see you, *ma chère.*" He promised to meet her at a resort near a ski area. It was Alex's idea, the resort. He managed to hook up a great deal through a friend (*read*: fuck buddy) of his who works for Blue Mountain. He booked three cabins, two for them and one for himself and his lady friend. ("If anyone is gonna come to Canada in the Fall, you gotta show 'em the leaves, right?" This is how he persuaded her.)

Soon after that, the marine, Russell Ivy called.

"Great news!" he said. "I'm coming." Marci was elated. She laughed with happiness and the only thing she could think of saying (other than 'yay!') was "Why?"

"Well," he explained, "I was doing my medal ceremony. The guys planned an awesome ceremony on a historic ship. My gramps was really proud."

"That's great!" Marci felt really happy to hear his voice.

"Yeah, I gotta be honest," he said, "I wasn't going to come to your thing. I know we are friends and all. But amazing things have been happening for me at home. I'm being promoted and I'm giving motivational speeches and everything.

"But you see, during that medal ceremony, something strange happened."

"What happened?" she asked.

"Nothing much. It's just that there were a lot of co-incidences. The Awarding Officer was an Admiral Jonathan Marcy. That and the old ship was actually a wooden yacht. Oldskool wooden vessel," he repeated. "After the ceremony, the Admiral asked me about the girl who helped in Indonesia. He asked where you were and if I kept in touch with you."

"Ok." Marci was keeping up with the story. "What did you say?"

"I told him you invited me to Canada. That you thought we should debrief about the whole experience, otherwise we could have some kind of psychological build-up." Marci laughed. "That's what you said, right, Marci?" he said, kidding her.

"I think I said 'you,' Mr. Sailor, *you* could have some mental problems, yes," she retorted.

"Anyway, he told me that people who go that close to death but come back are tied to each other. He explained to me that soldiers who have near death experiences sometimes gain a link with each other. He went on to say that in dodging death you gain a deep insight into the existence of life. He told he that I, too, was now part of a select few people who could channel the next dimension. Then, he said that terrible things would happen if I didn't go."

"Wow. Smart man," she said.

"Yeah, and to top that off, I told him I was too busy with the speeches and upcoming events to see you. And not five minutes after that, I fell into the water because of a rotting railing that broke. I fell into the harbour with my formal regalia and everything. When I looked up, I noticed that the ship's name was 'USS Manifest Destiny'. The Admiral was right. Terrible things would happen if I didn't go."

"Fascinating." Marci was still contemplating what the Admiral told him. "What do you think the Admiral meant when he said people like us could channel the next dimension?"

"Well, he didn't really go into detail. But I guess we do have a connection, right? How could two people from so far away both survive a massive tsunami and spill up on the same beach? It's gotta be destiny, doesn't it?"

"I wonder if he means that the lining between the dimensions is thinner for us, because we came so close to crossing it?" The idea really appealed to her. "You know, like they wrote in those ancient Greek books. Souls that return from Elysium can never forget the brightness of the colours and long to lay eyes on them again. You know what I mean?"

"Well, ma'am, I was unconscious so I don't remember any of it."

They chatted for a bit more and Marci gave him the name of the resort and direction on how to get take the bus there.

When she hung up, she felt as if an ominous event was unfolding. *What would happen with the guru Quincy Roth there as well?* She sat down on the arm chair in her hotel room and considered for a moment how close she came to death. A myriad of questions crossed the heavenly sphere of her brain in a V-formation.

Questions such as:
- *What do I remember from my coma?*
- *What force, or god, or consciousness saved me from the blue waters of the tsunami?*
- *Am I able to sense the veil between universes? Is there something beyond this reality?*

- *Can it be possible for me to change my physical self through thinking like Quincy Roth did? Is that even possible?*
- *What do all these people I met have in common?*

These unanswerable questions plagued her. She made some tea, tearing open the daily teabag the hotel provides. They only give her one, but she's saved handfuls from days she didn't use in her purse. The water boiled, blowing steam onto the mirror against the wall. She wondered whether dying is just a transformation, like water into steam.

After her phone call, she had nothing to do. No plans at all. So she sat down on the ground and tried—perhaps for the first time in her life—to meditate. Since she had never studied Zen, or any kind of mediation for that matter, she applied what she knew from popular culture: controlled breathing, focussing on a flickering flame in your mind, cross-legged posture with a straight back, attempting to open your third eye and other chakra points.

She started, sitting in a typical yoga meditative pose, then closed her eyes. Those questions were still in her mind, floating through every once in a while, but she tried to ignore them. Instead, she focussed on the flame in her mind. It was harder than she thought, because if it weren't the questions returning, she revisited conversations with Alex she had earlier that day, or she became aware of her body (either her spine slouching, or her clothes touching her skin). It was impossible to block out her ego. Eventually, the flame disappeared and she just listened to the sounds in her room. There was a buzzing of electrical energy coursing through the copper lines to the fixtures. A warm current of air rising up through the vents to heat the room. Then she noticed sounds in the rooms adjacent to hers: a TV playing what sounded like the weather forecast, and a man talking on the phone. In the hallway, a woman pushed a room service cart, ruffling her skirt as she walked.

Marci expanded her awareness to the outside, where the

sounds of cars running through moisture on the road was audible, along with the artificial birdsong of a traffic signal for the blind. She pressed further, stretching her hearing to its limit. Far away and faintly she heard a mechanical *beep-beeping*, her own heartbeat, and voices making indistinguishable conversation in the deep background coming from neither outside nor inside the hotel. Finally, she heard silence. It was a solid tone she had never paid attention to, a deep, greenish-grey that formed the limit of her hearing ability. A Pantone™ 556.

Is there another universe behind the silence? she wondered. Someone once told her that if the human ear were any more fine tuned, you would be able to hear oxygen molecules in the atmosphere crashing together.

THE FATED DAY

Winter came all of a sudden. Earlier than expected and with an unrestrained force. The majority of the snow snuck in during the night, but it was still continuing in the morning. When you live in a cold climate, you gain a natural sense of the amount of snow based on the lighting in your room. Marci herself could tell that it had snowed between the height of a woman's high-heeled ankle and that of a man's knee. She knew because the reflection threw a glare onto the hotel room ceiling.

When she left the building, it was a wonderland outside. Enormous snowflakes were drifting down like Icarus on borrowed wings. The city was transformed. The streets were white, and snow dusted the coniferous trees like the summits of mountaintops. Outside, there was a serenity lacking on ordinary days. Traffic was quiet, and the few people out were bundled up in warm scarves and hats. Marci was wearing a baby blue beret. She had found one in a used clothing store *en route* to work one day. The blue beret, the sunburst scarf, a black felt jacket and her 98% grey pants suit. All tied together with some sienna leather boots, circa 1974.

On snowy days, everyone gets along peacefully. Marci greeted the few people out shovelling snow off their front steps. She waved at them with a red mittened hand, and they tipped their hats (metaphorically...in most cases). There were still some leaves on the trees, surprised by the heavy snow, but clinging on to their supporting branches. Like the last dying flames of a once great consuming fire, those red and yellow leaves continued to deny their inevitable fate.

Overnight it was winter in Canada.

Marci knew the plan was set in stone and, despite the blizzard, everything would still go down just as she had planned: Russell Ivy had already arrived and would go up to the cabin

193

with Marci; Maurice had also arrived early to spend a romantic week with her; Quincy Roth was the loose variable, yet somehow Marci knew he would be there.

And he was.

Quincy Roth was waiting at the resort. He found an incredible joy in the idle time he had between seminars, and interviews, and teaching. He was in the lobby of the resort, a beautiful building meant to look like a *Suisse aubèrge,* constructed out of modern materials at the foot of a mid-sized Canadian mountain from which the immense expanse of Georgian Bay could be seen. He had never been so far to the north. In fact, in his younger more contrary days, he swore never to go further north than where he was born: Bloomington, Indiana.

Marci entered first, followed by Maurice and Russell Andrew Ivy, the sailor. Quincy saw her immediately and rose to shake her hand. They made their introductions ("We've heard so much about you," *"Enchanté,"* "I hope you made it here alright," etc, etc, etc.) They checked in and headed to the lounge, where Russ and Maurice ordered a round of drinks for everyone except for Quincy, who said he doesn't drink.

"No thank you," he said, "I'm trying to keep my head clear these days."

A waitress came by with their drinks just in time for the small talk to come to an end. She was a beautiful blonde girl. Probably a university drop out who wanted to become a ski bum, but started in Northern Ontario, a place whose mountains might be called molehills in other provinces.

"Here are your drinks." She lingered a little too long, looking at Russ, whose conspicuous lack of hair seemed somehow unnatural—it was the thallium, of course. "Drinks're on the house." She smiled an artificial waitress smile. "Boss said all new visitors get a free round because of the Dark Tower."

"The what?" asked Russell.

"Oh, you probably haven't heard," she said, letting the gravity in her voice fill the emptiness. "It's the end of the world."

"So you're giving away free drinks?" Marci piped in, kind

of surprised at her own comment.

"Yup. But next time you gotta pay." She was about to walk away, but Quincy stopped her.

"Excuse me, miss," he said, "Could I have a glass of your finest tap water please?" He smiled, beaming his enlightened face at her.

"Sure."

"Oh, and I gotta know more about this Dark Tower," he added.

"Not much to say, really. Turn on the TV or the radio, you'll hear all about it."

"Give me the details. How about that?" Quincy could be persuasive, it seemed.

"Well…" She hesitated, trying to recall what she heard from other employees. "Um, yesterday a strange tower appeared outside town. Nobody knows what it is for sure. Some think it's, like, a symbol or something. You know, the end of an area."

"I think you mean 'era'." Marci interrupted, crossing her arms over her chest.

"Whatever," the girl licked her lips. Fine, long, puffy lips. "You know what I mean, they say it's the end of the world."

"Why would they say that?" Russell asked, bald head cocked to the side.

"I dunno. It doesn't show up on video. And, like, they can't find it when they look for it, but my little brother saw it. Actually, lots of resort people saw it, too. Scared the sh…" She suddenly became aware of her speech. "…Scared the crap out of them. Everyone's getting outta here, so we're giving away free drinks." She gave another artificial smile, pouted her lips every so slightly, and said: "There, does that answer your question?"

"Thank you." Although he met his entourage less than 10 minutes ago, Quincy seemed to speak with a wisdom and certainty that undemocratically represented them all.

"Zhe Dark Towerrh?" Maurice asked. "It is a joke, non?"

"Yeah, let's not worry about it," Marci said. In truth, she wondered about this dreamlike symbol materializing upon their

195

arrival at the resort. "We have two beautiful chalets with a view of the mountain."

The waitress returned with Quincy's water.

"*Oui, çe n'import pas*. Let's enjoy our time together." Maurice raised his glass, "To new friends and bizarre circum*stance*."

"Cheers!"

THE DARK TOWER

Jimmy Cho was the first person to see it. He and two other kids trekked into the forest outside of town. Jimmy had gotten a BB gun for his birthday and thought he would try it out. The two other boys were dressed in snowsuits and, although initially Jimmy thought they would just shoot squirrels, he wondered whether a snow suit would stop a BB.

It was early on Saturday morning. The sun was not yet up, but they could clearly see because of the long, teasing glow of winter dawn. They hiked the cross-country ski course into the woods and went off-road, following in the hoof-prints of a solitary deer.

Ryan Robinson had brought some left over Halloween candy in a pillowcase, and they chewed on Tootsie rolls and sucked on sugary treats until they were deep in the forest.

These kids spent their summers in the woods building tree forts, so they knew the area well. They also knew they were technically trespassing and had to be in stealth mode until they got out of gunshot range of the ski course.

And it was amidst the lip-smacking and chewing and crunching footsteps in the snow that they heard the sound. At first it sounded mechanical, like the hum of electricity moving a motor, but the farther they went into the woods the clearer the sound became.

"It sounds like an insect," Jimmy said.

"Nah, more like a metal detector or sumn'," Scott Levesque (the third boy and a bit of a nerd) said. Soon they abandoned their plan of shooting birds and squirrels and looked for the source of the noise.

"Let's climb the hill!"

"Good thing I brought my gun!"

"Beat you up there!"

197

Ryan got to the top first, followed by Jimmy then Scott, who arrived in the firm grip of an asthma attack. While he recovered, Ryan lifted Jimmy onto his shoulders.

And when he rose, Jimmy saw it.

The sensation overwhelmed him. Above the forest, at an indiscernible distance, rose a giant black column. It was a long upside-down tetrahedron, the tip of which was obscured by the near-empty branches of the trees.

Upon spotting the shape, Jimmy instantly got goosebumps. He felt something he had never felt before in his young life: reverence.

The subtle muscles around his hair follicles tensed up and he felt as if he extended himself beyond his skin. He was a semi-porous bag of skin, leaking soul into the world.

"What'd ya see?" The other boys were calling to him, but he could only hear the din of the dark tower emitting an oscillating wave, which seemed to be perpetually escallating in pitch. It seemed to hypnotize him once he was able to hear it.

"Dude!" yelled Ryan. "My turn!" He adjusted his footing and slipped on a bit of fresh ice at the top of the partially exposed hill. The pair fell over backwards into the deep snow.

Ryan laughed: "What happened?"

Scott was standing on his tippy-toes on the trunk of a fallen tree, staring off in the direction Jimmy had been looking.

"Hey!" I see it too," he yelled. "There's some *ginormous* tower sticking out of the trees!" Ryan jumped on his back, almost knocking him off the tree.

"Lemme see." He peered into the horizon, scanning right to left.

"Oh my God." His reaction was unexpected. There was a moment when he too got goosebumps and inhaled deeply, but instead of exhaling, he burst into tears. He dismounted from chubby Scott and cried. Jimmy, who was still laying in the soft snowbank, staring at the sky, joined him. Then Scott joined in. None of the boys had any idea why they were crying, but they couldn't stop.

Eventually, they pulled themselves together and hiked back to the town, where Scott immediately went to report the eerie object to the police.

"I think we saw a UFO," he said and naturally no one believed him.

Three hours later, a small aircraft reported radio interference and a haywire compass. He was already concerned, but once he regained radio contact, he couldn't stop ranting about an unidentified building, which he claimed seemed to have appeared overnight. Soon after, it was confirmed by other pilots.

ITALICIZING THE IMPORTANT

"We all have secrets we'll take to the grave. But it doesn't matter, you see. Those secrets make you *you*. I for one, have made peace with those dirty, half-forgotten affairs." Quincy spoke with an elegance reserved for great politicians and reincarnations of Oscar Wilde.

"The best way to go about it," he continued, "is to think about how those buried skeletons add to your soul. We all suffer. It is the plight of humanity to suffer: beatings as a child, lost loves, perpetually reliving a moment of regret, hunger—be it physical, emotional, or metaphysical. Enduring and overcoming those moments is what makes humanity such a marvellous, resilient animal. We suffer to learn. We suffer to become. Perhaps we reflect just enough on that moment of pain and humiliation to change our path, to wander onto that golden road that leads to enlightenment.

"And listen well: by 'enlightenment' I don't mean Buddhist, or any other kind of spirituality for that matter. What I mean is coming to terms with your hidden self, looking your darkest moment square in the eyes and not flinching when the question is asked: 'Who are you and where are you going?' Enlightenment is knowing those secrets and learning from them to commit only actions that benefit the universe and those around you."

And what a beautiful rant it was, thought Marci.

"Easy enough for you to say," said Russell. "My family has always been in the navy. How can I just turn away from that path?"

"I don't think that's what he means, Russ. I think he's saying you have to know who you are." Marci sipped slowly from her drink after her interjection.

"Just imagine for a second where you would be if you

weren't in the navy?"

"Well…" He thought about it for what seemed like a heartbeat stretched into infinity.

"I suppose I would still be cleaning up the base." Then he thought some more. "If my dad never joined up, then I suppose I might have been a surveyor, or a scuba diver. Who knows?"

"*Moi*," said Maurice, "I would be an artist, if not *réaliseur*. Zhere are so many stories out zhere. Death, love, and annihilation. It is the nature of man. And each tale is only at its most beautiful when it is complete." He paused, posing with his wine glass. "*Çe mortalité que fait une ésprite la plus belle.*"

"Woah. I wish I could say it that nicely!"

"Marci, what a motley crew you assembled." Quincy smiled.

"You know," she started, "In the last two years a lot of things happened, and you guys represent something. Something that happened to me." Russell Andrew Ivy leaned back in his seat, becoming more familiar to gripping his draught beer. Maurice clearly wanted a cigarette because between his teeth, spotlighting his ruddy, angular lips, was a cocktail toothpick he had salvaged. She continued: "I have almost died so many times. My secrets are a vast ocean of disbelief." *Quincy is rubbing off on me, I guess.* "Each time, in my darkest low, or happiest moment one of you emerged. Every time when I seem to forget, for a moment, the laws of physics. Life just seems so uncanny. You know? Would you believe that two years ago I lost my house?"

Under the indirect lighting of the geometrical lamps hanging from the ceiling, the water in her eyes sparkled like sidereal constellations. "You know, a year later I woke up from a coma!" This fact—although powerful and gripping—came out with the intonation of a bubblegum wrapper factoid.

"You're kidding!"

"*Vraiment?*"

"I knew something was different with you."

"Boys," said a voice from somewhere beyond the four of

them, "don't let little Marsicans fool you. I think the word you're looking for is 'weird'. You've signed a pact with the devil here, signing up to be friends with Miss Ninety-Eight Percent Grey." Marci jumped up, perhaps glad to be saved from explanations. Or maybe she was overcome with emotions, sublimating them into an exaggerated joy at Alex's arrival.

"Alex!"

"Seems like I came just in time for your vir*gina* monologue." Russ and Marci laughed; they were the closest to ground zero of Alex's joke.

"Someone has to come spice up this party." Marci introduced them in a single sentence and Alex waved over the waitress before he sat down. His body was hopelessly too long for the low lounge chair.

"One of those free Apocalypse cocktails, I hear so much about," he said, shaking an index finger and thumb handgun at her. He puckered a kiss and added, "and get one for yourself too. If the world's gonna end, you might as well be blottered, right?"

The girl smiled, but upon realizing she had no witty retort, she turned and walked away showcasing her trim figure. "Coming up!" she yelled without looking back.

"Girls just find you irresistible, don't they?"

"It's the boyish charm."

"I was *being* sarcastic, man."

And with Alex's arrival, a jovial mood of Dionysian fun began. They laughed and talked and drank themselves silly on Apocalypse cocktails. Outside, a glaring three-quarter moon lit up the fresh snow on the ground. And with nightfall, they were ushered into the dining area, a dimly lit restaurant with large booths and wooden walls and hanging snowshoes. It had the typical Canadian theme of moose, skies, and implements of lumberjacks and coeur-du-bois, found in places tourist go to do typically Canadian activities. They had found their flow in conversation, and jumped from topic to topic, straying from a tone of levity to a profound philosophical depth.

"I have a question for you," Russell yelled. "Would you

rather fly or be invisible?"

"Ha!" Alex said, "Played this game before!" He chewed on his steak a bit, swallowed, then finished his thought. "Flight. All the way. Although I would be able to go in girls' locker rooms and other such fun stuff, I wouldn't need it if I could fly. Just think about all the pussy you'd get, man. There'd be line ups to get into my pants!"

"Me too. When I was in the navy, I often wondered how it'd be to fly. You know, see the world from a different perspective."

"I 'ould like invisibilité. I just want to watch people. Per*r*haps I 'ould discover some secret about humanité, something I could use in my films."

"Yeah, humanity's *dirty* secrets!" Russ almost choked on his Canadian Maple Salmon because he laughed so hard at Alex's comment.

"How about you, Marci?"

"Hmm…Let me think." She sipped a glass of wine. "In the Archives I already feel invisible. I mean, I know how it feels, so I would probably go for flight." She thought some more. "But that would ruin my hair for sure. I mean, that's a *major* deal breaker. You know how hard I have to work to make this mess into something decent every morning?" They laughed.

"Ok, Marci, which one wins? Nostradamus or Revelations?"

"I would have to say Nostradamus, 'cause the Bible's Armageddon sounds like a zombie flick."

"Not if you're Christian! Then you just vanish."

"For me, *monsieur Nostradame* has a better idea. Also, he was from France, washed himself daily, and in part, some of his prédic*tion* have come true."

"You know," said Quincy, "my job was to make predictions. I used to gamble on which companies would go bankrupt. I had a high success rate."

"So, what'd you say on this one?" Alex downed his drink quickly.

"I'm going with the Bible on this one."

"Really?"

"Mr. Guru goes with the Bible? Now *that's* unexpected!"

"Yeah, actually, I thought you'd chose Nostradamus too," Marci chimed.

"Well, it's simple really. We might have already gone through all of Nostradamus' signs and now we are heading to the Biblical *fin du monde*." Quincy glanced at Maurice then continued, "I also believe that if God exists, he could only be merciful—or at least quietly benign—so he would let every one of us disappear in some kind of rapture. If the world ends it will be like solids sublimating into steam. In a moment, reality will vanish and dissipate like vapour into an empty room. It will just blow away on solar winds."

PANTAGREUL

Talk of angels and aliens, architecture and religion, love and destiny finally came to an end amidst a round of answers to the question: Would you rather spend a day in the life of an ants nest, or a century as Mother Earth?

"It's a matter of creation over abuse!" said Marci, who had gotten a bit rowdier over the course of a few drinks.

"Male ve*rrh*sus female," responded Maurice.

"The Earth for sure! Let me tell you, you'd see a lot of trash being trawled out of the ocean, pustules of landfill sites, and nuclear testing just below your skin; however," he said, "You would be able to watch a human lifetime complete its existence from birth to death." Russell was on a roll: "And you'd know the greatest mysteries of all—the creatures in the depths of the oceans, under Antarctica, and you would breathe in the rhythms of the sea."

"You'd take it up the ass from us humans, but—ooOOOoh! The Moon would make a fine lay!" They laughed and Alex started distributing cigarillos as soon as the glass door of the resort lobby slid open. Cool as always, he could sound voodoo charming in that truly bizarre mix of insane genius and sarcastic hedonist.

"The moon would be your gravitational lover." The argument persisted in the background, then shifted to whose car they would take. Maurice was smiling at her slyly, and Marci felt surrounded by love. It was almost tangible, a physical aura coming from everyone around her. He held her hand. The aura *beat.beat* along with the *beat.beat* of her intensifying heartbeat. Laughs were all around her. *Are these strangers my destiny?* she wondered. *Are they the missing pieces of me?* She felt completely connected to each and every of these people around her. *I just wish Baxter was here.*

"Marci, there's one more thing. A little surprise," said

Alex. "I met your buddy, Baxter in the hospital. We hung out there a few times when you were in a coma. I invited him too and he should be waiting for us over there." He pointed to a place she couldn't see through the glowing radiance of her happiness. She hugged Alex around the waist. He towered over her.

She thanked him as Baxter popped out of a car 33 feet away. He looked more stylish than ever before. Purple pinstripe suit, black collared shirt, and the grim, pale demeanor that characterizes him. *He's like a ghost that tethers me to my past. He makes sure I don't forget.* Marci ran to hug him, realizing what an important character he was in her life.

"Let's take two cars guys," he said through the storm of handshakes and formalities.

"I'll drive." Quincy volunteered and took Maurice and Russell. Marci, Baxter and Alex took Baxter's hatchback rent-a-car. Alex refused to go unless he 'savoured' more of his cigar.

"It's a cigarillo, Alex!" Marci joked.

*   *   *

Baxter's car arrived a bit later. They pulled into the snow covered parking lot. There was an autumn lightness to the sky. *Must be a Pantone™ 268 with a serious tint,* thought Marci, a Pantagreul Purple sky. She had just made up the name but it somehow fit.

Then she noticed it.

Maurice and Russell were waving at her wildly from the balcony of the building. Russell looked like someone flagging down a jet on a runway, but neither of them made any noise. They were vigorously signalling to the people in the rental car.

"What in the hell?!" Alex made Baxter stop in the driveway of the parking lot, which along with the chalets, the trees and everything else around them, was covered in snow. The only hint that they were still on planet Earth was the vertical lines made by the shadows of white birch trees and the cabins, which looked rather like a motel building.

206

Marci and Alex got out.

There was a serious tension. No one made a sound, but they were signing to the arriving party to look at the middle of the parking lot.

"*Mars*, do you see that?" Alex whispered in a shadow of speech out of the corner of his mouth. She looked, but saw nothing. Just whiteness. White snow everywhere—no colour except for the red of Quincy's sleek red car, the cabin building, and the three people who were now looking down from the balcony. She looked back to where they were looking but saw nothing. She shook her head.

Alex slowly got back in the car. Then she saw movement amongst the white. It was a human figure. Well, nearly human. It was hard to see because it was so camouflaged in the snow. It had white, polar bear fur—so white it was almost translucent. Like a lanky gorilla, it stood in the middle of the parking lot. Everyone was staring at it.

What in the world is that? Marci was mesmerized by the sudden appearance of what looked like the abominable snowman. *A sasquatch?* she thought. *Impossible.*

At that moment, Maurice ran inside the top floor chalet. While everyone outside was paralyzed by the paranormal, Maurice wanted to prove a point. He thought it was impossible, and that it had to be a man in a suit. You see, years ago he had seen such a suit on the set of low-budget French horror movie. To him, he was certain it was a trick of the light or a prankster in the throngs of Apocalypse mania. And Maurice knew how to prove it was a hoax. If it were a man in a suit, there's no way he would be able to eat an apple, he thought. And so he picked up the bowl filled with Royal Gala apples. He ran out and tossed the red fruit onto the snow covered parking lot.

The sasquatch shouted. It was a noise that sounded remarkably human. The sound a professional wrestler might make to intimidate his foe. It then took a huge step forward, towards the apples and picked one up with a black palmed hand.

The sound it made when he bit into that apple was like a thunder crack in the empty night.

Kkkkka-tcghuuuurrgh!

To Maurice it was indisputable that the furry primate was real. There was no way even the movie industry with its million dollar shots and unrestricted resources could create something so real. Everyone realized that something was afoot.

Panic took over and Baxter gunned the engine. He was trying to turn around. The beast turned and looked right at Marci, whose black coat and 98% grey suit made her seem like a midnight shadow against the whiteness–she was the complete antithesis of this animal. Uncamoflaged and vulnerable in the world of beasts. And it was she that attracted his attention when Baxter tried to flee. Marci turned around and ran after the car. It spewed smoke as it tried to negotiate the snow. Baxter had managed a sharp, 75 degree turn and was about to speed off partially over a giant snowbank. Marci ran with two crunching footsteps into the deep snow. Then she jumped, hoping to hang onto the back of the hatchback.

Somehow the speed and the jump and everything lined up well and Marci was strained, but hanging onto the back windshield wiper. Inside the car, Alex was screaming and Baxter looked like he might have wet himself. Marci breathed in deeply. *Cold fresh air.* When she breathed out, she realized that she too had started screaming. It was an incredibly high pitched scream. A terrible, girly scream which seemed to instantly become a background frequency. *Is it panic? Fear?* she thought, completely calm on the inside. It was as if she was watching herself from over her own shoulder. *What a strange mouth I have when I scream,* thought Marci. She lingered in a moment of self-critique and then zoomed out into unconsciousness.

THE UPSIDE-DOWN TETRAHEDRON

She awoke in the woods on her back. When she opened her eyes, she looked up at the long arm of the Milky Way slinging itself through the dome of the sky. That far north, stars are still stars, brightly reflecting in the almost unbearable white blanket of snow. The moon provided the sky with some light through the upside-down gap between the reaching branches of trees. She stood up.

This isn't going as planned.

The white woods looked beautiful. Scary but beautiful. She knew she was lost and had to find high ground. Fortunately, although it was night, there was plenty of light from the reflective snow. Nature around her seemed like a world of deep contrasts; light and dark were guiding her upwards, past the tall trees to a less densely forested area. The landscape was quiet, except for her crunching footsteps on the snow and a high-pitched humming in the background. *Are there coyotes here? Do they hibernate?* she wondered. She had a stoic calmness that permeated her soul. No worries at all, despite being lost. *Everything will work out,* she thought. She wondered how long she was lying there in the snow as she entered into a coniferous part of the boreal forest closer to the mountain. Evergreen pines and cedars reached towards the sky, forming a hedge maze with their thick walls of needles. Marci heard running water somewhere in the background, but continued forwards and upwards towards a vantage point from which she could survey the land.

Her mind conjured images of French cartographers, travelling with a band of Huron or Algonquins through a foreign, unfamiliar land. Her socks were getting wet from snow that had fallen into her boots.

Near the top of a low hill, the forest thinned and Marci could see a meadow (or perhaps a frozen marsh) with a solitary creek snaking its way through the scene. It was beautiful. The water, which reflected the stars, seemed like a deep, inky brushstroke of Japanese painting, flowing in organic curves across a white canvass dotted here and there with empty trees. The valley might have been a grassland in summer; snow concealed the dried husks of perennials which most likely light up the greenery with colourful, wild flowers in August. *A snow covered field of dreams*, she thought. *But where are the vivid colours?*

The sky was deep and tall. And Marci was a lone figure, clutching the top button of her jacket to protect against a gentle breeze on the exposed rim of the valley. The air felt thick.

The creek was a major obstacle cutting off her path through the meadow in the valley below. She also didn't notice any lights in the direction beyond it, so she decided to follow the edge of the woods for a while. The tree line stopped at the top of the low valley and after walking for a few minutes, she spotted a narrow walking path heading back into the forest. *This has got to take me back to the resort*, she thought.

The snow on the path was compacted—perhaps by a skidoo, or some other kind of machine. Every once in a while there were also orange trail markers tied to branches, which gave her hope. *Where am I going?*

She covered good distance on the path and soon she was back in the deep woods. The moon and stars offering the only light, peeking out above the skeletal branches of the maple trees. *There should still be brightly coloured leaves on these trees.* The sounds of her crunching footsteps carried far in the silent night. The only other sound was a high pitched frequency that lies just beyond your audible range. You know, that buzzing you almost hear in empty rooms. *Fall was very short this year.*

Then as if stepping into the heart of a denser air, the *kkgggru.....kgggru* of her rhythmic gait suddenly stopped being audible. That high pitched sound filled the air, masking all other sounds. *It sounds like the wind.* She stopped in her tracks and noticed a slight tugging force, pulling her off the trail into the blackness of the woods. It felt like her body was affected by some kind of magnetism; she was attracted by some sort of field.

She hesitated. Her heart was beating fast in her chest. The sound wave was so dense. It sounded mechanical. She pulled her hands out of her pockets without the rustling of fabrics rubbing against skin. Then she saw her silver bracelet being pulled in the direction of the sound.

"What is calling me?" she asked in a muted voice.

Without conscious effort, she stepped off the path into the shadows of the trees. She walked noiselessly towards the source of the sound. It never got louder, but it seemed to get denser, as if the closer she got, the slower time seemed to move. There was no other sound, only the oscillating *hummmmmmmm* of some mysterious force. The sound seemed to penetrate her very being, as if the physical body of Marci was mixing and blending with the wave pattern of the universe. A lump formed in her throat, but she resisted a strong urge to weep.

The moonlight seemed a hundred times brighter than it should be. And Marci followed this light towards the tip of a giant, triangular pyramid. It was colourless. A complete void of any colour, but the moonlight outlined it in beam of reflected sun along the edges. Of course, Marci being who she is, had to pursue the scientific truth behind such an odd shape.

As she came closer to it a few things became clear:

1. She couldn't see the height of the shape through the tops of the branches.
2. The vertex hovered about 4 feet off the ground, illuminating the snow encircling it with reflected (*or is it refracted?*) moonlight.
3. It definitely had no colour. Despite this, she decided, it didn't look unfriendly.

But is it real? That is the question. Marci had become boundlessly enthralled by this monstrous, mysterious geometrical form—this tetrahedron.

She stepped forward through the thickness of destiny, it

seemed. Advancing to a literal and symbolic point. This point radiated energy, light, sound. It was magnetic and ominous. Yet, it was mythical and fascinating. Also, moving towards it was intensely pleasurable. She just had to touch it. *To see it if it was sharp,* she convinced herself.

The closer she got, the slower time came to move. There was a certain density at its core. A thickness in which moving a few inches seemed to take hours. Time became inconsequential as Marci's hand moved gracefully towards the conceptual point of this hanging tetrahedron. *Beautiful...*There was so much love in her face. She was lit up in bright white light, which tinted her suit a pale grey. She beamed light. She looked so happy. *What is happening?*

As if she was making it towards some seemingly unattainable goal, she experienced a brief moment of regret. It was perhaps a millisecond, but a perceptible, sober feeling. *My world is coming to an end,* she thought. Her hair was completely out of control, if you must know. A blonde streaming aura of golden lines, blowing away from the vertex of the shape. *I lived a good life...How sad?* she thought calmly, pushing her last moments of consciousness through the density. *How sad but beautiful?*

Perhaps to Marci it took no time at all. The whole ordeal played in slow-motion in her mind.

"Goodbye," she whispered, knowing that she is already in the liminal space between worlds. *I wonder if death is always so sad,* she thought. *What beautiful, fragile, imperfect lives we all lead. I wish I had another chance. A chance to say goodbye.*

"Goodbye, Baxter." *Goodbye link to my past.*

She closed her eyes and time stretched ahead of her infinitely. The universe was unfolding in the white light to reveal all of its secrets. It was pulling her to the vertex of universal consciousness at the tip of the long, upside-down triangle. And in the last moment before the final synapses of her brain fired, she saw the radiant and happy figure of Irene Wood, the artist, her mother. She was standing in her studio in the early morning light. No, she *was* the early morning light.

212

Her mother, the warm rising goddess Aurora, stood there, smiling at her. She extended her hand and reached out to Marci. The divine expression on her face seemed to suggest that Marci was going to a place of serenity, where existence was an artist's canvas splattered with the most intense colours. Marci had no words. Her left hemisphere had shut down, leaving her with the intoxicating feeling of cosmic joy of timelessness. Her mother was wearing the missing pendant, and Marci felt her presence merge with her own. She felt the limit of her physical shape stretch into a million tiny photons, bouncing off the molecules in the air, dancing in the waves of sounds and light, and basking in the eternal love of a parent.

Marci, reaching out to grasp her dead mother's hand, did finally manage to touch the object. It was neither sharp, nor dull. It had the feeling of touching a living body: warm and sensitive. She touched it, and felt a feeling she never had before. She was happy and satisfied, a feeling she had no words to describe.

Her thoughts stopped existing as Marci Wood. And when she exhaled one last time, she was simultaneously everywhere, travelling on the particle-wave form of sunlight and all existence. The feeling she felt was not death or love entirely, but a pleasant sense of completion. An equation played out to a single ending. Or the feeling an artist feels with the last brushstroke of a painting. It was supremely satisfying for Marci to touch the point of the mysterious shape, bringing to an end her universe in the process. In that moment of contact, she was a benign demigod of her own alternate reality unravelling in her dying mind. It was both nostalgic and pleasurable.

ACKNOWLEDGEMENTS

I want to thank Erin Chapman and Cynthia LeRoy for their support and keen eyes. They are great editors and kind friends. I owe a great debt to Mary Dempster, who put the final touches on the text. This project would not have come to fruition without all three of them. I should also thank my family, who stood by and waited patiently for the book to manifest itself, and who believed in the story of Marci. Trish Johnson who showed me my follies in trying to write a female protagonist. Also Kazuyo Kontani, who made sure I survived the year-and-a-half it took to write the book by feeding me during the long, focussed bouts of creativity. And Tamas Demjen, who walked through the plot with me as we circumnavigated the walls of Nijo Palace in Kyoto.

VERACITY OF THE STORY

The historical details are all true. The plague was terrible and Philip Valois was saved by the infrared light bouncing off the red surfaces in his room. And Prussian Blue does indeed cure thalium poisoning.

I did take creative license, however, in the description of Champs d'Elysée in the 1300s. The field was where bodies were buried *en masse*, and perhaps there was a grove of trees that lit the sky like a pagan Heaven. My fallacious addition was the Magnolia trees. *Magnolia Denudata* comes from China, and it was not seen by western eyes until the 1800s, when ginger-haired Robert Fortune snuck into the forbidden lands of The Middle Kingdom, disguised as a Mandarin "from beyond the Wall". Please forgive me this anachronistic addition to the story, but I believe it makes for a beautiful image.

A WORD FROM THE AUTHOR

Please lend this book to a friend. Or leave it on a train someday in hopes of throwing the bottle out to sea so that it may make landfall on the destiny of some lucky stranger. Recommend it to your sister, if you have one. Give a copy as a gift. (They make good gifts!)

Above all, share Marci's story with others.

This is my first book and I created it pretty much from scratch. If I had a bit more moolah, I would have added in colour pictures, embedded the Pantone™ chips, and much more. But I hope you like this manifestation of *98% Grey*. I am currently busy working on my next novel, so keep an eye out.

I would be glad to hear your comments, questions and annoyances. Also, I listen to sad stories with the heart of a bartender and the ears of a desert rabbit.

Feel free to email me at graeme.lottering@gmail.com

Oh, and be sure to check out www.98percent grey.com for your colour chip bookmark.